TELL ME NO LIES (#1)

"Well-drawn characters, a dash of romance, and enough logically constructed red herrings to keep the reader guessing right up to the end distinguish this tightly woven tale."

– Publishers Weekly

"The first in Willis' planned series mixes murder and romance with enough suspects to keep you guessing."

– Kirkus Reviews

"A well-wrought tale of the secrets concealed beneath the surface of small-town Appalachia...Willis is a seasoned professional who gives us just enough red herrings to keep us guessing to the end."

– Margaret Maron,
New York Times Bestselling Author of *Long Upon the Land*

"A page-turning balance of small town life and an unsolvable mystery with characters we wish we knew for real. Tell Me No Lies is a mystery that will not disappoint."

– C. Hope Clark,
Author of *Echoes of Edisto*

"Willis brings to life not only the beauty of the Appalachia, but also the crippling poverty that can and does cause people to resort to terrible things."

– For the Love of Books

TELL ME NO LIES

**The Ava Logan Mystery Series
by Lynn Chandler Willis**

TELL ME NO LIES (#1)

TELL
ME
NO
LIES

AN AVA LOGAN MYSTERY

LYNN
CHANDLER
WILLIS

HENERY PRESS

TELL ME NO LIES
An Ava Logan Mystery
Part of the Henery Press Mystery Collection

First Edition | February 2017

Henery Press, LLC
www.henerypress.com

Trade Paperback ISBN-13: 978-1-63511-145-3
Digital epub ISBN-13: 978-1-63511-146-0
Kindle ISBN-13: 978-1-63511-147-7
Hardcover Paperback ISBN-13: 978-1-63511-148-4

Printed in the United States of America

For my son and daughter, Garey and Nina,
for loving me always.

ACKNOWLEDGMENTS

It's often said it takes a village to raise a child. In the book world, it takes a good critique group to produce a book. I've been fortunate to have very good critique partners. Cindy Bullard, Demetria Gray, Sandra Rathbone, Susie Boles, Sayword Broyles Eller, and Julie Bates—thank you for your input. Thank you for helping me take this story from rough idea to a finished first draft. To first readers Lynette Hampton, Patti Phillips, and Susan Downer—thank you for taking the time to read the manuscript in rough form and for the encouragement you offered. And to my favorite agent, Michelle Johnson with Inklings Literary Agency, thank you for never giving up on this book, or on me.

ACKNOWLEDGMENTS

CHAPTER 1

My husband bled out while a quarreling couple argued over where the boyfriend spent his paycheck. No one held Tommy's hand and lied to him, telling him everything would be alright. No one prayed over him or asked if his heart was right with the Lord. No one told him his wife and two small kids would be taken care of. I've often wondered if he thought of us in those last few breaths.

That day, the one day Tommy left his vest in the patrol car, a bullet severed his aorta and shredded his chest during a domestic disturbance call. Our son, Cole, was five. His little sister, Emma, was two weeks shy of her second birthday.

Tommy's been dead ten years today. The kids and I took flowers to his grave in an outdated gesture of remembrance. Truth is, Emma only knew him through old photos and Cole's most vivid memory of his father was his uniform. So there we were at his grave site, each wondering how long is long enough to stand there pretending to read the headstone we've read a thousand times. *Thomas Coleman Logan, loving husband to Ava, proud father to Cole and Emma, brave officer. Killed in the line of duty.*

He was buried in Jackson Creek Friends Meeting cemetery because it was his mother's church. She insisted. All in all, it was okay because we, as a couple, hadn't thought that far ahead and bought our own plots. We weren't even thirty yet. We were going to live forever.

I sat the basket of scarlet chrysanthemums at the foot of the granite headstone. The collection of autumn-colored flowers placed at the graves brought life to the tiny cemetery. The lemon yellows and blaze orange flora matched the leaves the surrounding Appalachian Mountains displayed, connecting the ever changing to the frozen in time.

Emma quietly shushed Ivy's singing, like she was afraid the dead wouldn't approve. She insisted on carrying Ivy herself and now adjusted the toddler on her hip. "She's getting heavy," she whispered to me.

I took her from Emma, letting her stand beside me, holding tight to her chubby hand.

Ivy wasn't mine. She belonged to my friend Trish, who had asked me to keep the tot overnight. I hadn't asked why. As a single mom myself, I knew why. Just not the who.

"Can we go now?" Cole's impatience grew with each teenage sigh. He'd paid his respects to his dead father and now itched to hit the hiking trail. Truth be told, I did too. It'd been over a month since the three of us had spent time together on a trail.

"Sure." Before I could offer a group hug, they were headed back to the car. I envied the easy way they let go of the mourning, and the guilt. But the guilt was never theirs. It was mine and mine alone.

By the time I got back to the Tahoe, Cole and Emma were buckled in. Emma sang along with Ivy's rendition of "Wheels on the Bus," complete with rolling hand movements.

"What if Trish's not home?" Cole asked. "What are we going to do with Ivy?"

"She'll be home. That was one of the conditions made on babysitting Ivy—that I would drop her off by nine so we could hit the trail early."

That seemed to satisfy his worry that we'd be lugging a two-year-old with us up to Porter's Peak. The trail, winding through Jefferson Mountain, boasted a few steep inclines a toddler's legs couldn't handle. On the other end of the spectrum, at thirty-five, mine barely could.

I pulled away from the church and its dead, heading out of

Jackson Creek. Nestled deep in the northwestern part of North Carolina known as the High Country, most of Jackson Creek sat in a valley surrounded by the Blue Ridge Mountains. It was the second week of October in an election year. Campaign signs were a common distraction.

It was prime time for the newspaper business too. Ad revenue for the month of October tripled. There were members of the Board of County Commissioners, Town Council, school board, district judges, and even the sheriff spending money with me and *The Jackson Creek Chronicle*. As the owner and publisher of the town's only newspaper, they hated me when I divulged their dirty little secrets, but they loved me when they needed me.

A few minutes after leaving the church, I turned onto the unpaved road leading to Trish's rented single-wide mobile home. The tires bit at the sparse gravel, sending chunks of rock and rich dirt into dust-filled plumes.

Trish's older model SUV sat parked at the end of the drive. "See, I told you she'd be home." I treated Cole to a motherly grin.

Ivy clapped her chubby hands while saying, "my housh" over and over again. The toddler defined *cute*. Sandy blonde hair that fell just below her shoulders in upturned waves, eyes the color of emeralds with lashes long enough to sweep the floor, and cheeks full of adorable chubbiness. I had no idea who fathered Ivy so couldn't say what he donated to her gene pool, but I'd swear under oath she got her smile from her mother. Trish's smile was a gift from God, natural, not the kind you saw on magazine covers.

I parked behind Trish's SUV then lifted Ivy from her car seat and propped her on my hip. "Cole, will you put her car seat in Trish's backseat?"

Ivy pointed a chubby finger at her *housh*. "Mommy?"

"Yep, you're going to see Mommy."

I climbed the three concrete steps and knocked on the front door. It partially opened from the knock. Ivy squirmed to get down. Just as I put her down inside the door, I remembered her overnight bag still in the Tahoe. "Cole, can you bring me her bag?"

Stepping inside, the odor smacked me so hard I could taste it. Vile and coppery. I covered my mouth and nose to keep from gagging then fought against it hard and called for Trish. My heart quickened as I called again, this time more urgent.

My eyes followed a trail of blood running from the front door through the kitchen, disappearing around the corner. It marred the cheap carpet and pooled on the kitchen linoleum, glossy and slick.

Ivy toddled through the kitchen, oblivious to her tiny shoes smearing the blood. "Mommy."

My heart beat faster, gaining speed with each rancid breath. Ivy was walking right into whatever lurked around the corner. Adrenaline pummeled my fear. "Ivy! No!" I bolted toward her, skittering in the slick blood on the kitchen floor. Rounding the corner to the hallway, I jerked her up into my arms, shielding her eyes from the ghastly sight.

She squirmed against me, crying for her mommy. I wanted to cry too, but the shock overtook the sorrow. My heart lodged in my throat, stealing my breath.

Trish was on her back in the hallway, her arms and legs splaying in different directions. Her once-beautiful face was now a gorged-out cavity of bone and tissue. Blood pooled around her body.

Ivy fought against the confinement of my chest, babbling for her mommy, not understanding her mommy would never answer. "Shhh, baby. Shhh. It's going to be alright," I lied. My stomach lurched. I rushed outside, my heart ready to explode.

I fled down the front steps, Ivy's confused cries echoing in my ears. In the yard, I shoved Ivy at Cole, screaming for him to take her, then sank to my knees and vomited.

Emma was out of the Tahoe and running toward me. "Mom!" She stared in horror at my bloody shoes, and the tiny bloody shoeprints staining my shirt from where I'd held Ivy against me. "Oh...my...God. Mom, what happened?"

Breathless, I barely managed to speak. "My phone. Bring my phone."

"Mom, where's Trish?" Emma spoke in a low hushed tone, like she had at the graveyard. Maybe she knew the answer to her own question.

Cole hurried over, still clutching Ivy. He passed me my phone. "Are you gonna call 911?" His ragged voice betrayed his age, making him sound much younger.

I looked at the house and wondered if I should go back in. Maybe, despite how bad it looked, Trish was still alive. Maybe she was aware of what was going on around her. Tommy died with no one holding his hand.

"Watch Ivy. And stay here." I leapt up and ran back to the house, not knowing if anything could be done, or what to do if there was.

Back into the trailer, I steeled my nerves for Trish's sake. I moved carefully to avoid slipping in the blood then knelt beside her. Swallowing the sour taste filling my throat, I wrapped my hand around her wrist and concentrated on finding even a hint of a pulse. Her arm was already rigid.

"Holy shit..." Cole said from behind me. "That's not an accident, Mom."

I stood and pushed him down the hall, away from the sight nightmares are made of. My bloody handprints stained his shirt. "I told you to stay put."

Outside, glad for a cell signal, I punched in 911. I sucked in a deep breath, then spoke slowly when the call connected. "This is Ava Logan. We need the sheriff's department."

"Ava? Hey, it's Cheryl. Do you know the address?"

"Um...it's Trish Givens' trailer, off Mountain Laurel Drive. It's the first trailer on the right. There's been a—" I didn't know what to call it. Murder, a foreign word around these parts. "There's been an accident. We need an ambulance. And the sheriff's department."

Cheryl Stafford was good at her job, but she was also involved with a little of everything in Jackson Creek. I used her often as a source for the *Chronicle*. She was also a bit of a gossip, so this story would be all over town before it ever went to print.

"Okay, the EMT is en route and the sheriff's department has been notified," Cheryl said. "Did you try CPR?"

I glanced over my shoulder, wishing beyond hope there was *something* that could be done. All the while knowing the only thing to do now was comfort my children and precious little Ivy. "It's beyond CPR, Cheryl."

After gathering my kids and Ivy, we sat in the yard. Morning dew dampened our jeans. I pulled Ivy into my lap. In the distance, the wail of a siren grew louder.

CHAPTER 2

Two hours had passed since I had found Trish's body. The adrenaline was long gone and had been replaced with exhaustion. My shoulders ached from the weight of the stress. Dr. Bosher Garrett, the Jackson County Medical Examiner, was still in the trailer doing his initial workup. Cole and Emma sat a couple feet apart on the ground nearby with enough distance between them to limit conversation. Ivy played nearby as a bored-looking deputy babysat all three. I leaned against a patrol car and fought off ten-year-old memories of a younger Bosher Garrett pronouncing my husband dead.

Trish's yard had become a parking lot for sheriff's department cars and EMT vehicles. Those that couldn't fit into the yard parked along the gravel road. The front driver's side tire of the transport van that would carry her body to the morgue had bumped her decorative scarecrow, knocking it over the seasonal bale of hay. It lay there on the hay in an awkward pose, its lifeless eyes staring at gray clouds that threatened rain.

At least it still had eyes.

I turned away from the reminder and watched Sheriff Grayson Ridge in the doorway of Trish's trailer. Detective Steve Sullivan appeared to be filling him in on the details. Sullivan would bob his head every now and then in my direction, followed by a nod from Ridge. The sheriff gave a final nod then headed down the steps towards me.

As far as sheriffs go, Ridge was young. He was finishing his first term at thirty-seven. He had been Tommy's patrol partner when Tommy was killed. He was on vacation that day.

He walked toward the deputy babysitting my kids and Ivy, told him something, then squatted in front of Emma. He lightly touched her hair. She smiled.

My kids adored Grayson Ridge. After Tommy's death, he was their rock. His arms, their security blankets. He had coached Cole's Little League baseball team and Emma's soccer. He taught Cole how to shoot and handle a gun. Taught Emma how to fish. With all the interest in my kids, the rumors started flying, and I pushed Ridge away.

He dated the occasional eye candy to combat loneliness or more primal needs but had yet to put a ring on it. He was even named Jackson County's most eligible bachelor two years in a row in a charity auction event.

That was all a long time ago. Memories, both good and bad, had laid dormant under the surface for several years. Now, he stepped over to Cole and knelt. He playfully punched my son's shoulder. After a moment of subdued conversation, Ridge stood then made his way back over to me.

"You okay?" he asked, standing beside me, his hands shoved in the pockets of his jeans.

I shrugged, afraid if I opened my mouth to speak, I'd collapse under the weight of the memories.

"So you want to tell me what happened?"

Although certain Detective Sullivan had already told him everything I'd said to him, I repeated the story, reliving the nightmare. Seeing things again in my mind I'd probably never forget. I told him about the door being partially open, about setting Ivy down inside, about the stench. About the blood trail.

"What were you doing with the baby again?"

"Trish had asked me to babysit. I told her I would."

"When did she ask you?"

I shrugged. "Tuesday maybe?"

The corner of his mouth turned upward in a small grin. "Tuesday maybe or Tuesday for sure?"

I took a moment to think about it. The kids and I had talked Tuesday morning before school about going hiking. Trish called me at the paper that same day because I remembered telling her about our hiking plans. "It was Tuesday."

"So it wasn't a spur-of-the-moment thing?" he asked.

I shook my head. "There were a few days of planning, I suppose."

He gently kicked at a rock then dug the toe of his climbing boot into the soft ground. "And she never told you what she was doing?"

"She didn't say. And I didn't ask."

He nodded, seeming to understand perfectly. "You have any idea who she was seeing?"

"No. She was a private person."

"What about the baby's father? Any idea who he is?"

I slowly shook my head. "We never talked about it."

He laughed a deep unpleasant laugh. "Oh, come on, Ava. You want me to believe you never asked her?"

I let out a breath born of frustration. "It wasn't any of my business. If she wanted me to know, she would have told me."

He stared at me with his Sinatra-blue eyes, doubt perhaps shadowing the corners. But the fact was, I had nothing to hide. I knew how it felt to be buried under a suffocating pile of rumors, so I gave Trish room. Grayson Ridge knew how it felt too. Maybe that's why he finally looked away.

"I'm going to need you to come down to the office for a formal statement. Hopefully we can get you in and out."

My stomach knotted. "Do I need to call Rick?"

His nose twitched. "In what capacity? Your boyfriend or your attorney?"

"Either."

He looked away then turned back to me, his gaze heated. "You probably don't need an attorney, if that was the question."

I slowly nodded. Now was not the time for the games Ridge and I played with one another. "What about Ivy?"

He watched her play with Emma for a moment. Toddling through the grass, high-stepping as much as her chubby legs would allow. "We'll have to notify Trish's parents anyway. I'm sure they'll want the baby with them."

I couldn't take my eyes off of her. "They're four hours away. And they've only seen her once in her life."

He threw me a sideways glance. "She *is* their granddaughter."

I wanted so badly to smile at the way she was playing with Emma, marching around her, stomping through grass that hadn't yet died for the season. But I couldn't. My heart shattered for her instead. "Can we call Doretha and see if she can watch her for a little while? She doesn't need to be waiting at the sheriff's department until her grandparents get here."

Ridge rubbed the morning stubble shadowing his chin, considering the request. Given the circumstances, we had few options. He gazed up at the sky, at the storm clouds rolling in from the west. After a moment, he slowly nodded. "I'll have a deputy call her. It's going to be raining before long. As soon as she gets here, I'll have a deputy take you down to the station."

After talking to the deputy charged with babysitting again, Ridge walked back over to me.

An uncomfortable air settled between us, wrapping us with words unsaid. He resumed digging the toe of his boot into the ground. Finally, after several awkward moments, he took a deep breath and spit out a string of words as if they were molten lava in a volcanic mouth. "Look, Ava...I don't think I have to tell you this is going to be a touchy one. You have every right in the world to print whatever you see fit. Obviously, you're going to know a helluva lot more about this case than information you're normally given. I'm asking you to *please* use good judgment in how you write this, for Trish's sake...and that little baby's sake."

My eyebrows raised involuntarily. "I think you need to put that guilt card back in the deck."

He gnawed on his lower lip and nodded. "You know how investigations work. There are certain things we don't release to the public. But you're right smack damn in the middle of this one."

I glanced down at my hands. Remnants of Trish's blood had caked into the lines of my knuckles. I couldn't stop the tears from welling in my eyes. "Trish was a good friend," I said with a sniffle. "I want to see whoever did this punished for what they did to her."

He reached out and gently touched my arm. Despite wanting nothing more than to give into the grief and fall apart, I pulled back. "Don't tell me what to write, Grayson," I said in a low voice. I didn't want anyone within earshot to know we were even having this conversation.

He blew out a frustrated sigh. "I'm not telling you. I'm asking you. As a professional courtesy."

I got where he was coming from but resented his asking. "A little while ago, I found a good friend's body. Literally—found it, Grayson. I still have her blood on my hands. And I'm not even going to go into what's going to happen to Ivy. The last thing I'm thinking right now is what I'm going to publish." I pushed a clump of stray hair from my face, feeling the crusted blood on my hand, dry and brittle against my forehead.

A minute or two later, Doretha's burgundy passenger van pulled up and parked on the side of the road. The faded white letters on the side read: All Faiths Missionary Church. Reverend Doretha Andrews slid out of the van and hurried over to where I stood. Doretha was pushing sixty, looked forty with smooth chocolate skin, and was my best friend. She had also taken me in to the church foster home when I had nowhere else to go.

The colorful beads in her braids jangled as she walked. "What happened, Baby Doll?" She threw her arms around my neck and wrapped me in a tight embrace.

I collapsed against her, allowing her strength to hold me up. I wanted to spill the horror, to rattle on about not knowing if Ivy saw anything, but didn't. Though my kids were feet away now, they'd never seen me break down. Today wouldn't be the day either.

Burying my head between her neck and shoulder, I sobbed silently, holding back a well of tears. Doretha stroked my hair as she whispered a prayer.

Ridge gave us our time, then softly cleared his throat. "Sure you don't mind taking the baby until we can make other arrangements?" he asked Doretha.

"Not a problem at all. Do you want me to take Cole and Emma too?" She looked at me then back at Ridge.

Nothing would satisfy me more than for my children to bask in the comfort Doretha Andrews offered, but Ridge shook his head. "Maybe after we talk to them."

She nodded, sending her beads into swinging pendulums. She turned back to me. "Don't you worry about anything, Baby Doll. Lord's gonna give you strength." She squeezed my hand then asked about Ivy's schedule.

I filled her in as best I could. The realization of how little anyone knew about this child gnawed at me. "Do you need her car seat?"

Doretha shook her head. "Got one in the van. Don't you worry about her. She'll be fine." She wrapped her arm around my shoulder, giving it a gentle squeeze. She then walked over to Cole and Emma and spoke to each, and with the softness of a cloud, picked Ivy up and held her. Within a minute, the toddler was giggling and batting at Doretha's braids. A deputy followed behind her, carrying Ivy's bag.

Tears stung my eyes as Doretha buckled Ivy into the car seat. Partly for Ivy, and partly for myself. I wanted badly to siphon just an ounce of the comfort those strong arms offered. They'd been wrapped around me my entire life, it seemed.

It was late afternoon when Detective Sullivan cleared me to leave the sheriff's department. Doretha had already picked up Cole and Emma and taken them back with her to the foster home. A steady rain fell as I sprinted to the Tahoe. Just as my hand reached for the door handle, Ridge grabbed it from behind me, jerking the door open. "You sure you're going to be okay?"

I slid in behind the wheel to escape the rain and lied to him. "I'm okay. I'm going to hang out at Doretha's for a while then head home. Looks like a good night to stay in."

The storm had set in with the promise of rain all night. Heavy drops dripped from the brim of Ridge's Braves ball cap. "I'll call you as soon as I hear back from Trish's parents."

I nodded, not knowing what else to say, and closed the door. I barely missed tapping him with the front bumper when backing out. I glanced in the rearview while driving away. He was still standing there, in the pouring rain, watching me pull away. The truth was, I pulled away ten years ago. When the guilt became unbearable and the truth, buried so deep in the lies, threatened to ruin more than just the two of us.

All Faiths Missionary Church was about a mile from the sheriff's department, on a side road, hidden away from money-spending tourists and the trendy arts district. The church was a small white-washed building with stain-glass windows depicting everything from the birth of Christ to his crucifixion in glorious hues of blues and reds.

The foster home was next door in an old multi-level house dating back to the Civil War. I grew up there, in the front bedroom on the left. Two sets of bunk beds, two dressers with enough coats of paint to increase the overall dimensions, and a student's desk in the corner. When there was more than just me in the room, we took turns using the desk.

A campaign sign for Ed Stinger stood proudly in the center of the yard. A black and yellow bumblebee encouraged votes for Ridge's opponent. Doretha stopped liking Grayson Ridge the day Tommy died and would have supported a goat had it run against him. He should have been with Tommy, she'd said. He should have been there.

I parked behind the passenger van in the driveway and hurried into the house. The smell of Doretha's homemade spaghetti ignited hunger pains deep in my belly. A banjo and fiddle blared from the CD player Doretha kept in the kitchen, accompanying the vocalist in a foot-tapping rendition of "Ain't No Grave." The music competed with the cacophony wafting up from the playroom. Doretha's "kids" were doing what kids did and apparently enjoying every minute of it. I wasn't sure how many kids she had now. The numbers changed daily.

"Hello?" I called.

"Mom?" Emma poked her head around the doorjamb and smiled. "Doretha's letting me help make supper."

She seemed okay, given what she'd been through. The night and its surrounding darkness would hold the truth.

In the kitchen, Emma and Doretha danced to the music, hands clasping spoons in the air, hips knocking into one another. Doretha threw me a quick glance and grinned. "Grab a spoon and start stirring."

Ivy toddled over to me, arms outstretched, hopping from one foot to the other as her signal to pick her up. I gladly obliged and hugged her tight, then followed with big wet kisses planted on her chubby cheeks. She cackled and returned the gesture.

Doretha turned the music down a notch then blew out a deep breath. "Whew! Emma's done got me all sweaty." She pulled a paper towel from the holder and blotted her forehead. "Dang menopause."

I grinned. Doretha had been going through menopause the entire time I'd known her, which was most of my life. She blamed her hormonal changes for everything from hangnails to the occasional sinus infection.

"Emma, be a sweetheart and go tell everyone downstairs supper'll be ready in a few minutes." As soon as Emma disappeared down the steps, Doretha turned to me and winked. "You got a good kid there, Baby Doll." She stirred the sauce again then put a tray of buttered bread in the oven.

I sat down at the table and pulled Ivy onto my lap. "Did Emma seem okay this afternoon?"

Doretha joined me at the table. "She was a little quiet at first. I put her in charge of tending to the baby so that kept her mind occupied. She's good with the baby. Reminded me of you taking care of all the little ones always underfoot around here."

I stroked Ivy's hair and let out a slow breath.

Doretha reached out and gently touched my cheek. "Been a tough day, hasn't it?"

My eyes stung with unspilled tears. "We took flowers to Tommy's grave this morning."

She slowly nodded. "Emma told me."

The happy noise that had filled the basement made its way upstairs. A swarm of kids, seven including my two, invaded the tight kitchen. Doretha patted my hand then bounded up from the chair while barking orders. "Trenton, take the silverware tray and plates into the dining room, please. Amber, you and Emma can pour drinks. Cole, help me drain this spaghetti, please."

The little soldiers had the dining room table set and ready for the crowd in record time. Cole carried the institution-sized pot of spaghetti into the dining room while Doretha carried the pot of her prized sauce. "Amber, can you get the bread, please?"

Amber, a fair-skinned black child with a head of springy orange curls, danced her way into the kitchen to help with the bread.

"Highchair's in the corner," Doretha said, bobbing her head to the left.

I put Ivy in it then pulled it to the table, alongside the bench where Emma already sat. She scooted over so I could sit on the end closest to Ivy. The massive oak table sat twelve—two benches on either side and two heavy chairs on the ends. It always reminded me of that television show, *The Waltons*. The show was part of Doretha's forced family fun. She always told me I was most like the character Mary Ellen, strong and independent. I told her she was most like grouchy Grandpa.

With everyone sitting except Doretha, she doled out a large helping of the pasta then topped it with a ladle of sauce, plopped a piece of bread on the plate, then handed it to me. I handed it to Emma. "Pass it down." After all these years, the house rules remained embedded in my memory.

Doretha glanced at me and winked. When everyone had a plate, we joined hands while Doretha blessed the food. I cheated and glanced up, only to meet my son's eyes looking back at me. Ashamed, I squeezed my eyes closed. Every meal in this house began with prayer. It was tradition. Why had I not carried on the tradition in my own home?

After the collective "amen," the only sound emitting from the dining room was lips smacking and forks clattering against plates. Even Ivy lapped it up with her little fork. The kids started telling Doretha about something funny one of the others did or a new joke they had heard. She belly laughed right along with them, believing suppertime was a natural time for good sharing. She used to encourage us to share the best parts of our day. It was her way of helping us, the kids no one else wanted, see our daily blessings.

Right in the middle of a joke Amber was telling, a loud knock on the door brought a hush over the table. Doretha glanced over at Trenton. "Mind getting the door?"

He shook his head then disappeared into the living room. A moment later, he came back into the dining room, with Sheriff Ridge behind him.

Ridge smiled a gentle smile and removed his ball cap. "Doretha, Ava...I hate to bother you during supper but I need to speak with y'all for a moment, if you don't mind."

My heart squeezed in my chest, threatening to shut off my air. "Sure." I slid out of the booth, pushing the highchair to the side, then followed him into the living room. Doretha told the kids to go on with their meal then joined us.

Ridge stuffed his hands in his pockets. "I talked to Trish's parents a little while ago. They're coming to claim Trish's body on Monday."

"Monday? That's two days away." I looked at Doretha then back at Ridge. "Are they out of town or something?"

Ridge held his hand up. "No. They're at home. Apparently, they have plans for tomorrow."

My mouth dropped open. "You told them their daughter was murdered, right?"

Doretha draped her arm around me and patted my shoulder. "Ava. No use getting all worked up about it."

Ridge was slowly nodding. "I told them."

My stomach knotted. "I knew they didn't have a good relationship, but that's just not right. What plans could be more important than claiming your only child's body? What about Ivy?"

Ridge looked at Doretha. "Can you keep her until Monday?"

"Why can't she stay with me?" I asked.

He pushed his hand through his hair, cocking his head to the side. "That's probably not a good idea. She really needs to be in foster care until her next of kin can take her."

I choked back a sudden flood of tears. I had been a foster kid. If it hadn't been for Doretha taking me in when no one else wanted me, no telling where I would have ended up. "Even for just a day?" I asked, my voice breaking.

Ridge reached out and started to touch my face but stopped, catching a strong glare from Doretha. "I'm sorry," he said. "I really am."

CHAPTER 3

I left Ivy, and my heart, at Doretha's and drove home in a steady rain with Cole and Emma. Ivy cried when we left her, reaching for me with her chubby arms. I'd babysat the tot several times so she was comfortable at my house. Comfortable with me and the kids. To my knowledge, Trish had few friends. For whatever reason, I was the one she trusted with her baby's life. And now I was leaving her.

Rain splattered against the windshield then, like magic, disappeared with the hypnotizing swipe of the wipers. I wished life was that simple. Whenever you felt the sting of a broken heart, the crush of a disappointment, or the torment of a bad decision, you could just flip a lever and a giant mechanical arm would wipe it all away. It was a nice thought but, like the rain, there would always be more to come.

"I still don't understand why we had to leave her." Emma's voice was soft, like a whisper.

"I guess there's a lot of legal things involved." At least that's what Ridge had said.

"Are we suspects?" Cole asked. I could feel his gaze on me from the passenger seat.

My concern about the direction his thoughts were going grew. "Of course not. Why would you think that?"

He stared at me for a moment then huffed and turned back to the road. "I don't know. All the questions they asked. It was like we were guilty of something."

"Honey, they had to ask those questions. We were the ones who found her body." The words tasted nasty in my throat.

Cole's cell phone chirped, indicating he had a new text message. The screen of the phone glowed blue in the darkness of the Tahoe. "Brady wants to know if he can spend the night." He threw me a glance, probably anticipating my answer.

"I don't know, Cole. Tonight's not a good night."

Brady O'Reilly was a year older than Cole and came with his driver's license and an arrogant attitude. His father, Brent, was the Athletic Director and head football coach at Jackson Creek High School where Brady played and Cole sat the bench.

Cole's phone buzzed again. He read the latest message. "Him and his dad are fighting again."

I looked at my son, knowing how everything involving teenagers initiated drama. "I really don't want to get in the middle of their family stuff."

"You'd want me to have somewhere to go if *we* couldn't stand to be in the same room, wouldn't you?"

My experience with family units was limited to Doretha and the rotating kids at the foster home. But I understood where he was coming from. "Okay. But we're going to have a quiet night."

Cole's thumbs blazed across the keypad as I turned into the driveway. Our drive was a quarter mile long, canopied by yellow birch trees. In a few weeks the leaves would fall and smother the gravel beneath. My private yellow-leafed road ended at the side porch of the old two-story farmhouse Tommy and I purchased when Cole was a newborn. We renovated much of it ourselves, adding a sunroom across the back overlooking the river, complete with a rock fireplace and furniture softer than cotton. It was my sanctuary. I couldn't wait for it to welcome me home.

The kids helped me unload our backpacks and the cooler from the car. Seemed like forever ago we were on our way to Porter's Peak. Finn, our border collie, greeted us in the kitchen with a tail-thumping welcome.

"How about some hot chocolate?" I asked.

Emma perked up as she patted Finn's head, safe in the familiarity of home. "With marshmallows?"

I grinned. "Let him out and I'll get the cocoa started. With marshmallows."

She and Finn both disappeared onto the porch. Cole passed my cell phone to me as he unpacked our bags. "Wonder if word's got around town yet?"

I hesitated to check the messages, knowing full well with Cheryl Stafford manning the 911 operations center, word about a murder in Jackson Creek had already spread like a gas-fueled fire. It was a rare day I didn't have my phone at my hip, but today was supposed to have been our day. Whatever newsworthy event that would happen could wait until Monday morning. Still, maybe someone had information about the murder?

I keyed in my password and peeked at what was waiting. Nineteen missed calls, fourteen new voicemails, three emails, and twenty-two texts. Four of the missed calls were from Rick, my on-call attorney and sometime boyfriend, as Ridge had pointed out at Trish's.

There were so many, I thought about clearing them all, even the ones from Rick. It was a fleeting thought, but the messages could wait until the kids were in bed. They needed me tonight.

Outside, the motion lights flickered on. Finn barked as Brady O'Reilly pulled up and parked his fresh-from-the-showroom Silverado beside my four-year-old Tahoe. Emma called Finn back and tugged him inside, oblivious to the muddy paw prints spotting my hardwood floor.

A moment later, Brady was in my kitchen shaking the rain off his jacket like Finn after a bath. Finn continued barking, ensuring himself alpha dog position.

Brady laughed and patted Finn's wet head. "Hey Finn—we're both wet as a dog, aren't we?"

Cole playfully punched him in the shoulder. "At least Finn don't smell as bad."

I shook my head, grinning, wondering if *any* teenage boy

smelled good. "I was just getting ready to fix some hot chocolate. Want some?"

"Sure."

"Why don't you get out of those wet clothes first. I'm sure Cole has a shirt you could wear."

"Yes ma'am."

While Cole took Brady upstairs to change, I started the cocoa. Emma wiped up Finn's mud spots then sprayed him down with doggy perfume. I turned my nose up at the mixture of wet dog and Doggy Fresh.

"How long do you think she'll have to stay with Doretha?" Emma asked in a quiet voice.

"I don't know. Could be just for a day or two, or...it could be longer." Although I had the same questions, I didn't want Emma to know my concerns. "If I had to hand pick someone for her to stay with, I'd pick Doretha anyway. You know that." I mussed up her golden red hair then lifted her chin with my finger, forcing her to look at me. I smiled and kissed her forehead. Her perfect lips turned upward in a slight grin.

Emma Rose Logan was my strength. Smarter than most her age, she had a way of keeping me in line. Her body was beginning to show signs of the change that was coming, but the splash of freckles across her nose froze her in time as my little girl.

"Grab a mug and help me carry these in the sunroom."

"Can we play Life?"

A board game was the last way I wanted to spend this evening at home, but if it took her mind off the day, I'd muster through it. We sat the mugs on the coffee table then Emma sat out four floor pillows. She dug the game out from the armoire and set it up in the center of the table.

"Cole and Brady may not want to play." I assumed playing a board game with a kid sister and mother probably wasn't high on two teenage boys' Saturday night plans.

"They'll play. That is if they want their hot chocolate." My kid.

I turned the gas logs on in the fireplace then settled into my spot at the table. Finn stared out the window into the darkness, watching only something he could see. On quiet nights you could hear the sounds of the river. However, tonight wasn't one of those nights. The rain pelted the tin roof and splattered against the glass walls. But I loved this room. It was where we celebrated Christmas and birthdays and shared stories of our joys and our pains.

Cole rolled his eyes when he and Brady joined us. "Life? Really, Emma?" His annoyance didn't stop him from sitting down on a floor pillow. He shifted his butt around until he was comfortable then took a long sip of his hot chocolate.

Brady took the last pillow and did the same. Stuffed into a long sleeve t-shirt, his bulging biceps stretched the fabric. I understood more why my son sat the bench on Friday nights and this kid protected the end zone. A thin mustache even shadowed his upper lip. He was a good-looking kid, with soft eyes and blond hair that fell in waves along his collar. He was sweet and polite too. A little spoiled, but as an only child, it was almost expected. I wouldn't mind if his politeness rubbed off on my own son.

Scratch marks along his jawline made me wonder how bad the argument with his father had been. When he lifted his mug to drink, a noticeable bruise glowed across his knuckles.

The mother in me couldn't ignore it. I reached out and lightly touched his hand. Embarrassed, he quickly jerked away. I let it go, not wanting to embarrass him further.

I didn't know the issues between Brady and his dad, and truthfully, didn't want to. But if he needed a place to stay for the night to cool down, I was okay with providing the sanctuary. I often wondered if Tommy were still living if he and Cole would be fighting the same battles.

For the next hour, we escaped the day's tragedy. It was never far from my mind though. I couldn't stop the stray thoughts of Trish and sweet little Ivy from finding their way into my head. Trish had been a friend, yet I knew so little about her. All I knew was she was a talented artist who sold her work at a gallery in downtown Jackson Creek. Occasionally, we ate lunch together at The Patty

Melt. She liked Reuben sandwiches and craft beer. And mustard on her fries. Go figure.

The outside motion lights flickered on as headlights came up the driveway. Finn barked a bone-jarring alert. I pulled myself up and headed to the front family room with the kids behind me.

"Who is it?" Emma asked, close enough behind me I could feel her presence. I heard the fear in my daughter's voice. And it pissed me off. Whoever had killed Trish had robbed my daughter of her sense of security.

With the blinds still open, the headlights from Ridge's Expedition swung across the living room.

"It's Grayson." Emma's voice reflected the comfort we both felt.

I jerked open the front door as Ridge bounded up the steps, a squirming quilt-covered bundle in one arm, a bag in the other.

"Figured you might be missing her."

"Ivy!" Emma squealed.

He unwrapped Ivy from the soaking wet quilt and handed her to me. She was warm and dry and cranky. I squeezed her tight then planted kisses all over her chubby cheeks. She reached for Emma, and Emma was more than happy to take her. They disappeared through the archway heading toward the sunroom while Cole and Brady headed upstairs, apparently eager to end our game of Life.

I opened the door wider as an invitation for Ridge to come in. He handed me Ivy's diaper bag then shed a plastic poncho with the sheriff's department logo on the chest. He tossed it and his ball cap on one of the porch rocking chairs.

"Do you want a cup of coffee or something? It's miserable out there."

"I'm fine, but thanks anyway."

"How were you able to—"

Ridge raised his hand to hush me. "Look, I know you and the kids had nothing to do with what happened to Trish. You just happened to be in the wrong place at the wrong time."

How many times had we said that to one another? I chewed on

my bottom lip, suddenly uncomfortable. "Yeah. I have a knack for that, don't I?"

He reached out to touch my cheek, but I turned away.

"So how long am I going to get to keep her?"

Ridge cleared his throat then sighed heavily. "At least until the grandparents get here."

I nodded quickly, like I was okay with it. Or at least understood it was just a visit. "Are you going to do a press release?"

"You're the only press within a hundred-mile radius. Do I need to do one?"

I tried my hardest not to smile but in the end just couldn't hold it back. "It would be nice to have an official statement from the Sheriff. Might even score a couple votes."

He let out a laugh. I'd forgotten how nice the sound was. Deep, from the belly. Truthful. And he was so damn good-looking. Perpetually messed-up hair so black it shimmered blue, light blue eyes...I forced my thoughts back to the reasons I hated him, then took a deep breath. "If you're going to make a statement, I'll need it by Tuesday. I go to print Wednesday."

"You'll have it Monday."

CHAPTER 4

On Monday, I dropped Cole and Emma at school and headed to the office with Ivy and a pack-n-play. Since Cole had football practice and wouldn't be heading home right after school, Emma would ride the bus to Doretha's house. Last week and the week before and every day since school started this year, Emma stayed by herself the hour before I got home. Now, she was scared to, and I was scared to let her.

I could have left Ivy with Doretha, but the poor kid had gone through a tragic change in a short amount of time. I didn't want to upset her more than necessary. Not sure how having a toddler underfoot while putting together a newspaper was going to work, but we were going to find out. Her diaper bag was packed with butter cookies, apple slices, and several packs of gummy snacks. Another bag held her lunch, a sippy cup, half gallon of apple juice, and enough toys to keep her occupied for at least half an hour.

The Jackson Creek Chronicle was housed in the old Milton's Mercantile building. An aluminum ice cream box still occupied one corner, unplugged, its sides dinged here and there. The airtight seal made a perfect container for archived copies of the *Chronicle*. A wood-burning stove we named Betsy protruded from the back wall like an unsightly growth, but it kept us warm on chilly days. The back storage room had been transformed into a break room mini-kitchen while a smaller room made a good private office, although I spent most of the time out front with Nola, the office manager, and the rest of the staff.

I split the investigative reporting and human interest features with Quinn Carter, although, truthfully, he carried more of the responsibility than I did. The little paper had grown through the years from a one-person staff—me—to a full staff, office, and impressive circulation and profit numbers.

In the parking lot, I unlatched Ivy from the car seat, slung her bags over my shoulder, closed the door with my hip, then headed inside.

"Oh my goodness," Nola said, hopping up from her seat to help. She relieved me of the bags but Ivy wasn't having anything to do with letting go. She lay her head on my shoulder, her thumb stuck in her mouth. "Is this...the Givens baby?"

"This is Ivy." I wondered if she'd be forever known around Jackson Creek as the Givens baby. Whispered behind her back like it was something she should be ashamed of.

"Bless her little heart." Pansy got up from her desk chair just to ruffle Ivy's hair. The grandmother of six, she couldn't resist a toddler. "She's precious."

Nola made a tsk-tsk sound while shaking her head. She carried the bags over to my desk. "She's beautiful. Just like Trish was. Sad. Just plain sad. The phone's been ringing off the hook."

"I can imagine." I tried to put Ivy down, but she clung tighter, partly leery of Pansy still stroking her hair. "Okay, we can wait for the pack-n-play." I toted her over to my desk where I rummaged through her diaper bag for the stuff that needed to go in the fridge. She pulled her thumb out of her mouth long enough to say "juish."

Quinn gave her a look like a lot of twenty-something single guys—like he wasn't sure what she was.

Nola hurried over to her desk to catch an incoming call. "Sheriff Ridge faxed over a press release this morning. I put it on your desk. Jackson Creek Chronicle, how may I help you?"

It always amazed me how she could switch voices from mountain twang to perfect office professional in the next sentence.

"No, Ava's not in yet. May I take a message?" She grabbed her message pad and pen, flipped to a clean page armed and ready. "Oh. Hold on a minute."

She turned to me and rolled her eyes. "Mayor. He just drove by and saw your car."

I sat down at my desk, put Ivy in my lap, and stared at the phone. I refused to be at the mayor's beck and call. "Tell him I just got in and promise to call him back in a few minutes."

"Justin—Ava just walked in. She said she'd call you back in just a minute. She promises. Okay, I'll hold her to it." She rolled her eyes again before hanging up. Nola was the queen of eye-rollers. At fifty-six, she worked because she knew no better. It was what people around here did. She didn't need the money. Her husband died in a mill accident years ago and left her well taken care of. She was all of five feet tall with baby-making hips and frosted hair that made her look taller.

Ivy took an interest in her toys so I sat her on the plank floor beside my desk. While she played, I read Ridge's fax. Two paragraphs. He assured the public of their safety. Victim appeared to be a white female, early to mid-thirties, cause of death pending.

Pending?

I grabbed the phone and called his office. His secretary, Annie Thompson, transferred me straight in.

"Cause of death pending?" I asked as soon as he answered. "Did you see her face?"

He cleared his throat. "Good morning, Ava. And yes."

"Or maybe I should say what was left of her face?" I immediately regretted saying it and glanced down at Ivy, playing with her stacking toy. Nola had become interested in the conversation, which meant I would have to remind her about the paper's confidentiality clause. Not that we even had one, but now was a good time to implement it.

He cleared his throat and hem-hawed. "Um...I don't want to release that just yet."

"But that's an important detail."

"Ah, yeah. And that's why I don't want it released. Didn't we have this conversation at the crime scene?"

Crime scene. It was still hard to wrap my brain around it. I twirled my finger around a stray lock of hair, contemplating how I was going to write this article.

Ridge interpreted my silence. Damn him. "I need you to think like a witness, Ava. Not a publisher. Please?"

"I don't know how to not think like a publisher, Grayson. Any more than you can't not think like a cop."

Ivy toddled over and handed me a cloth book, grunted something in baby talk, then attempted to climb my leg. I picked her up one-handed and plopped her in my lap. She jerked around and shoved the book in my face with something that sounded very much like a demand to read. "In a minute, baby," I said softly.

"You have Ivy at the office?"

Her goofy grin made me smile. "What else was I supposed to do with her?"

"Why can't Doretha babysit?"

"I don't know. I mean, I'm sure she could. I just thought it might be best for a few days to have some degree of stability, you know?"

"Doretha's not stable?" He was smiling. I could see it in my mind.

"You know what I mean. Look, I've got to go. Thanks for the *press release*." He had some nerve to even call it that.

"Hey—why don't you meet me for lunch and we'll go over this, um...situation."

My mind raced with thoughts. We had several situations between us. Which one was he referring to? "You mean Ivy?"

"Well, no, not really. About the witness versus publisher thing."

"Oh, *that* situation."

My throat tightened at the thought of sitting across from him in a booth. Then I cursed myself for letting our past creep back into the present.

"Bring your notepad. It'll be a working lunch. I'm meeting Trish's parents at the morgue at two, so how does noon sound?"

I pushed away the thought of Trish's bloody body lying in the basement of Jackson Creek Hospital. "Noon's fine. Minnie's Cafe?"

"I'll see you there."

I held the phone a moment after he hung up. I had to find a way to let go of this hurt before it dragged me so far down, I'd never find my way back.

Ivy squealed, bringing me back to reality, and pointed to the baggie of cookies in her diaper bag. "Ookie!"

I gave her a cookie for each hand then kissed the top of her head and sat her back on the ground, hoping she'd stay there long enough for me to call Justin Baker before he did another drive-by.

"Trish was beat to death?" Nola spun around in her seat, seizing the opportunity.

What was I going to do? It was out there. I had said it, I couldn't deny it now. I slowly nodded. "Yeah, but...that's not public knowledge so we need to keep it under wraps. At least for now."

"Oh sure. Sure." She nodded so fast her hair bounced. "Of course. She had such a pretty face." She grimaced as if she was being tortured.

I watched Ivy eating her cookies for a moment, not wanting to have this conversation. Once everything was made public, it was one I was going to have to get used to having. "It's a real sensitive situation. I have more knowledge of the case than I normally would, so we have to be careful what we let out. Make sense?"

Nola pinched her lips together in a tight smile then gestured as if she were zipping her mouth closed. "Me, you, and Betsy."

The phone rang, giving me a reprieve for the moment. As Nola spun around in her chair to grab the call, I rifled through the stack of messages on my desk. Justin, the mayor, had called several times. I wondered what that was about. The town council was always in one crisis or another, but they usually behaved during tourist season and election time. Just as I picked up the phone to call Justin, Rick burst through the front door. He hurriedly approached my desk, all but tripping over Ivy. He stared at her for a moment like Quinn had, like he wasn't sure what she was.

He finally peeled his eyes away from her. "Why haven't you returned any of my calls?"

His abruptness ruffled a feather. "I just didn't feel like talking with anyone."

He was in lawyer mode, probably on his way to court in his coat and tie. He glanced back down at Ivy then over at Nola, then back to me. "Can we talk in your office, please?"

Nola cleared her throat then came over and scooped up Ivy. "Aunt Nola's got something fun for this little girl. We're going to make a paper clip bracelet."

The verdict was still out on whether or not I should thank her. I foresaw an argument with Rick coming and I wasn't in the mood. Still, I turned and headed down the short hallway to the smaller storage room, also known as my office. Rick followed at my heels and closed the door behind us.

"What the hell's going on, Ava? I have to hear it from Judge Hoffler that you're the one who found the body?"

"Judge Hoffler?"

"Yeah. Seems everyone in town except me knew it."

I leaned against the secondhand desk and exhaled until there was no breath left. "Rick, I'm sorry. I really am. I just wanted it to—not be real. And I sure didn't want to have to talk about it again."

"Again?" His brows arched. "Who'd you talk to?"

"Detective Sullivan, Sheriff Ridge…"

"You talked to…" He rolled his eyes, then his shoulders, then took a deep breath. "You talked to the Sheriff without an attorney present?"

He was making way more out of this than I was comfortable with. "Rick—I literally tripped over Trish's body. I didn't do anything wrong. I didn't feel the need for an attorney."

He put off enough steam to power a small engine. "Ava! You just said it yourself—you found the body. From now on, you don't talk to Grayson or Sullivan without me there. Got it?"

"No—I don't *got it.* I didn't do anything wrong, Rick. I'm not a suspect. I'm a witness "

"Oh. Thanks for the clarification. I wasn't sure about the difference." He spun around and faced the door.

I watched his shoulders rise and fall underneath his suit coat before I looked away. He was a good man with a bad habit of telling people what to do. He'd make a good husband for someone who didn't mind that sort of thing. I did.

He turned around slowly and opened his arms, offering an invitation I hesitated to accept. "I'm sorry. I was just really worried about you."

Nodding, I relented and accepted his embrace. Despite my best effort to not sink into his comfort, I did. His arms felt good around me. Sometimes he treated me like a child, him an authority, a take-control type. Sometimes I let him. He stroked my hair then lightly kissed my forehead. "I need to get to court. Can I come by tonight?"

"Sure."

"Okay. Then I'll see you later." He gave me a quick kiss before opening the door.

Justin Baker was at Nola's desk when we returned to the front office. He was thirty-eight years old, married with two adorable kids, and owned a quaint bed and breakfast nestled in downtown Jackson Creek. He and his wife moved here from Cleveland before their kids were born. The fact he wasn't born here made him forever thought of as an outsider. A damn Yankee. But he still managed to get himself elected mayor.

"Ava. We've got a problem." He gave Rick a pleasant smile as he left.

My energy drained like I'd sprung a slow leak. "What kind of problem do *we* have, Justin?"

He patted Ivy on the head, mussing her hair, then came over and helped himself to the guest chair beside my desk. "Residents are wanting to know what's being done about the murder."

I glanced over at Ivy. Still at Nola's desk, she scribbled on copy paper with different colors of highlighters. Pushing my fingers through my hair, I sat down across from Justin. "The sheriff's department is handling it, Justin."

"But it's been a long time since there was a murder in Jackson Creek. Has Sheriff Ridge ever even investigated a murder?"

Honestly, I didn't know. But I'd never let Justin be the wiser. "Justin—Sheriff Ridge and his detectives are more than capable. I really don't think the residents have anything to worry about."

He studied me for a moment. "So they don't think it was random?"

I fought back the urge to smile, even the slightest hint of a grin. "I didn't say that."

We stared at one another as if we were in a contest. Finally, he nodded. "I guess there's not much we can do but wait."

"I'm glad you see it that way. As mayor, I'm sure Sheriff Ridge will keep you informed." I looked at the messages on my desk, tapping them with my finger. "Is there anything else? I really do need to get to work."

He cleared his throat. "Yeah, now that you mention it. Calvin Cooper is going to be contacting you about the poaching on his land again. He's got his panties all in a wad and wants something done about it."

My brows lowered on their own. "Why did he contact you about it? Calvin's property isn't even in the town limits."

Justin rolled his eyes, more exasperated than sarcastic. "I don't know. I'm just relaying the message. He wants you to investigate it. Nothing against Quinn."

That was a common request. I founded the paper so people assumed I was a star reporter. Truth was, Quinn was top notch. "Why doesn't he contact the sheriff's department?"

"He has. At least he says he has. He said Ridge told him they didn't have the manpower to look into poaching."

Ivy toddled over and plopped her empty juice cup in my lap with a demand for more. Nola started over but I waved her off. "I'll get it." I swung Ivy up on my hip and carried her to the kitchen.

One-handed, I refilled her cup with apple juice from the fridge then carried her back to the front. Justin was still at my desk.

As Ivy played in the floor, he gazed at her with sympathetic eyes, the eyes of a father with young daughters at home. "If the sheriff was too busy to investigate the poaching problem before..." he said, speaking slow and deliberate. "I imagine now that they have a murder on their hands, it's really going to take a backseat."

What he said was probably true, but I could smell an attempt to manipulate an election story brewing.

"I'm not telling you what to write, but poaching has been a problem in the past."

If I had a dime for every time someone had told me they weren't telling me what to write, I could retire a very rich woman. I sucked in a deep breath then smiled politely. "I'll look into it."

He pursed his lips as he stared at me. "Fair enough."

Ivy lifted her arms, wanting in my lap. I lifted her up, brushing my fingers through her curls.

"What's going to happen to her?" Justin asked, his voice softer, speaking as a father and not the mayor.

I continued stroking her hair while she sipped her juice. "I don't know. Trish's parents are coming in today to identify the body. I guess it'll be up to them."

He reached out and gently touched Ivy's cheek. "So sad. She looks about the same age as my youngest."

I hugged her a little tighter then kissed the top of her head. "Yeah," I whispered. "So sad."

CHAPTER 5

Around noon, I walked into Minnie's Cafe carrying Ivy on my hip. Sympathetic stares and sad smiles greeted us. I knew Ivy didn't understand but still wanted to tell her she would be okay, after a while the sympathy would fade and she'd just be the girl with the murdered mom, as I had always been the girl with the mom in prison.

The diner was a cinderblock building with a blue tin roof folks said they could spot from a mountain summit. The daily specials, including fish on Thursdays rather than Fridays because Minnie liked being different, were handwritten on copy paper and taped to the front door.

Ridge was in the last booth and waved me over. A highchair was positioned at the end of the booth, even though I'd told him I would drop Ivy off at Doretha's. It was scary how well he knew me.

He stood and held the highchair while I slid Ivy into it then buckled the strap. "How's she doing?"

"Good, I guess. She's asked for Mommy a couple times."

"And how are you answering her?"

I shrugged. "I don't. I just kinda ignore it. Probably not the correct thing to do, but right now it's all I've got."

He smiled. "I won't report you. How're Emma and Cole?"

"Cole seems fine. Emma slept with me Saturday night and again last night. She says Ivy wants her to." I lifted a brow.

He grinned. "Did you confirm that with Ivy?"

Before I could respond, Diane, part-owner and head waitress, dropped two menus and napkin-wrapped silverware on the table. She lightly stroked Ivy's hair. "So sorry to hear about Trish. Such a tragedy."

She took our drink order without further conversation. When she returned with our drinks, Ridge ordered the steak and cheese and I ordered the chicken wrap for me and nuggets for Ivy. What kid didn't like nuggets?

"Any leads?" I took a sip of water.

Ridge half smiled, one corner of his lip arching upward in a noncommittal way. "We were able to get some pretty decent prints."

The horrific image of Trish's bloodied face would be with me for a long while, stuck in my head like something you couldn't un-see. I knew enough to know who ever did it was in a rage. "I'm sure you'll find my and Cole's prints everywhere."

"Do you remember touching anything in particular?"

After some thought, I shook my head. "Nothing comes to mind except the counter. I remember grabbing the kitchen counter to keep from falling in all the blood."

Ivy pointed at my cup and said "juish." I dug her sippy cup out of my bag and when I handed it to her, she clapped. Such a happy little kid.

Ridge playfully drummed his fingers on the highchair tray, playing a silly game of snatch with Ivy. She'd cackle and grab for his fingers just as he pulled them back. About every third try, he'd let her grab hold. He used to play the same game with Emma.

I took a big gulp of water to drown the memories. Of Tommy, of Grayson Ridge, and of a place we never should have been.

"So." I was anxious to put that thought aside. "What information are you going to release to the public? I pulled my notepad and pen from my bag.

He stopped drumming his fingers and glanced at me, my pen poised and ready. "Well, although we'll have to wait for the coroner's official report, the death does appear to be suspicious."

If my stare held toxins, he'd be paralyzed. "Seriously?"

He nodded. "Seriously."

Diane balanced our plates as well as two from the next table on her arms. "Need anything else?" She sat our orders down in front of us.

"I'm good. Ava?"

My reply was a curt nod, the sharpness directed more at Ridge than Diane. She quickly moved on the next table. I plucked a nugget from Ivy's plate and laid it on the tray along with a couple of fries. Did she want ketchup for her fries? Sauce for her nuggets? So many things about this child yet to be learned.

Once Ivy was settled and content with her food, I turned back to Ridge. He was already a couple bites into his sandwich.

"The death *appears* to be suspicious? What kind of B.S. is that?"

He swallowed a mouthful then looked up at me. "It's not B.S. It's a fact."

"Oh, come on, Grayson—it certainly wasn't accidental. We *know* it was suspicious."

"See. You just admitted it was a fact."

The man infuriated me to no end. I sank my teeth into the chicken wrap and tore off a chunk. He handed Ivy another nugget, then sighed and leaned back in the booth. "I'm sorry. I'm really not trying to be a smart ass—"

"Oh, you don't have to try. It comes pretty natural for you."

He raked a hand through his hair while struggling to curtail a wicked grin. "As I was saying, until the coroner confirms the cause of death, I can't *officially* offer anything else."

He was right, as much as it pained me to admit it. Nothing would be published that wasn't official anyway, so why did I get so worked up about it? The man had a knack for confusing my every thought.

Ivy pointed to the plate of nuggets and babbled something only she understood. I handed her another one, along with a few more fries.

After a deep cleansing breath and concession of what I knew to be true, I gave in. "Can I call a truce?"

Although his smile was slight, the sincerity in his eyes ran deep. "Sure. I don't want to be the enemy, Ava."

Ten years of pushing him away landed square in my chest, crushing the breath right out of me. *You never were the enemy.*

"Look, we'll have more information after we meet with Trish's parents and the coroner. Your deadline is Wednesday, right?" Those eyes of his bore straight through me.

"I go to print Wednesday. I have to have it tomorrow."

We let the weight of the deadline settle over us with silence. I was about to take another bite of my chicken wrap when Ed Stinger, Ridge's opponent, slid beside me into the booth. He was fifty-four, stick thin with a bracelet of age spots around his bony wrist.

"Ava. Grayson." He offered a nod in each of our directions. "I hope you're not giving my opponent free press time." He laughed, but he was grossly serious.

Ridge pushed his tongue into the side of his cheek and grinned.

Would the feeling of needing to defend being within a thirty-mile radius of Grayson Ridge ever go away? "No free press, Ed. Just discussing a case."

Stinger partially turned in the booth, draping an arm across the back. His hand rested on my shoulder. "Good. That's what I wanted to talk to you about. Calvin contacted me about the poaching problem on his property. Seems it's really getting out of hand and nothing's being done about it. No disrespect, Grayson."

Ridge smiled but the truth shone in his eyes. He loathed Ed Stinger almost as much as I did. "None taken."

"Calvin and I were thinking if we could get you personally to do an article on it, it might draw some attention to it. Maybe someone's seen something and it might give them a little nudge to come forward. Know what I mean?"

His breath smelled of hot dogs and chili. I folded and unfolded my paper napkin, repeating the process a few times while contemplating what I should say. Telling him to go to hell was a thought, but it would have to remain just that. Aside from the money he'd spent with me on his campaign, he was one of my biggest contract advertisers.

Stinger Realty owned a slew of rental cabins proudly displayed in a full-color half-page ad every week. He, like other local businesses, thrived on tourists. Mountain-lovers from surrounding states flocked to our tiny town for the three weeks in October known as "peak season." A time when leaves showed their colors in dazzling displays of reds, oranges, and golds. Quaint shops and small businesses, including Stinger's rental cabins, often carried their high earnings during the time through the rest of the year and often into spring.

He'd also put the moves on me while his sickly wife looked the other way. Sometimes I hated this business.

"I had planned to call Calvin this afternoon, as a matter of fact."

"Good! Glad to know it's not going to be swept under the rug."

I was curious why the problem had lately become such an issue. Poaching was as old as the hills themselves. The mere fact Ed Stinger was involved meant it had become political.

Ivy grew restless so Ridge entertained her again with his drumming fingers. She grabbed for his hand and cackled.

Stinger offered a sad smile. "Horrible about her mother. Any leads?"

Ridge glanced up and shook his head. "None I can discuss."

Diane saved us from more awkwardness. She tore off our ticket from the order pad and handed it to Ridge against my protest. "Ed, your takeout order's ready at the register." She stroked Ivy's hair, making a *tsk-tsk* sound, then turned and hurried to the next table.

When Ridge stood to leave, Stinger slid out of the booth then turned back to me. "I'll let Calvin know you'll be calling him this afternoon."

After Ed slithered away, I stood and lifted Ivy from the high chair. "So—what *about* the poaching problem?" I threw it out there since the article would need an official statement from the sheriff.

"Despite what Ed Stinger thinks, it hasn't been swept under the rug. And yes, you can quote me on that."

"I will." I slung my bag over one shoulder and hoisted Ivy to my hip. One would never know it'd been years since I toted a baby around. For a moment, the thought surfaced I might miss having her around after her grandparents picked her up.

We waded through the maze of occupied tables, making our way to the register. I felt the stares aimed at the baby perched on my hip, heard the hushed whispers. Unlike years past, this time the whispers weren't about me, or Ridge, or my dead husband. For Ivy's sake, I wished they were.

At the register we fell in line behind Brent O'Reilly picking up a takeout order. I wanted to ask him about Brady but didn't. I didn't think the O'Reilly's family troubles needed my interference.

He paid for his order then accidentally bumped my shoulder as he turned to leave. "Sorry," he said in a hurry, but stopped and smiled at Ivy. She wagged her chubby hands and reached for him.

"Whoa," I said, struggling to keep my hold on her.

Brent nearly dropped his lunch as he moved to catch her. "Squirmy little thing, isn't she?" He laughed once she was upright.

He lightly tickled her tummy while making goofy faces at her. "Hey, thanks for letting Brady stay the other night. We're butting heads a lot lately. Teenage stuff."

My day was probably coming with Cole so Brent earned my sympathy. "No problem. Brady's always welcome at the house."

Ridge reached around me and handed the ticket along with a twenty to the cashier.

I wasn't having that. Not in the middle of an election season. "I've got mine. I had the wrap and the nuggets." After fishing my debit card from my bag, I handed it to her.

"Ava—"

"You're not buying my lunch, Grayson. I'm not giving Ed

Stinger ammunition." I smiled at the cashier then wiggled my fingers at her to ring mine up separately.

I signed the receipt then stuffed everything back in my bag. By the time I stepped out of the way, Brent was already gone.

"You ready?" Ridge looked at me, noticing my hesitation.

"What? Oh...yeah, sure." I readjusted Ivy on my hip and turned to the door.

CHAPTER 6

I called Calvin from the parking lot and arranged to meet him at two o'clock. Ivy's eyes were heavy-lidded and her mood sleepily quiet. We could both benefit from a good nap, but it wasn't on my agenda. I called Doretha and asked if she'd mind letting Ivy nap there while I trudged through Calvin's land.

She was at the door waiting when I arrived. "Bless her heart. Bring her in here."

I followed her through the kitchen and into the dining room where she had an old pack-n-play set up. Emma had taken many naps in it when she was a baby. Despite its age, it was in good shape.

I kissed Ivy's forehead then gently laid her down. She squirmed a little but then rolled onto her side and settled into steady breathing. "I appreciate you watching her for me. I forgot what trying to work with a little one around was like."

Doretha smiled. She'd kept Cole and Emma and many others from the time they were in diapers to when they had book bags weighted down with school work. "You know she's always welcome here. Anything new from the sheriff's office?"

I shook my head. "Sheriff Ridge is meeting Trish's parents at the morgue. Once everything's official, he may be able to say more."

Doretha twisted her lips. The motion lifted her eyebrow as well. I'd seen that look my entire life. "Hmph. How much more official can it get? Dead is dead."

There was no use bickering with her about anything to do with Grayson Ridge. She held him personally responsible for Tommy's death. He was my husband's partner. Although Ridge was on vacation that day, Doretha still felt he let Tommy down. Personal issues aside, Ridge was a good sheriff. The people of Jackson County loved him. Everyone except Doretha and apparently Calvin Cooper.

We left it at that. "I better get," I whispered.

Doretha gave me a hug followed by a quick pop on the backside. "Go do your thing, Miss Reporter."

Calvin Cooper owned three hundred acres of farmland and forest that straddled Jackson and Birch Counties. The forested area, the land being poached, was in Jackson County, unfortunately for Ridge.

Two bluetick hounds bounded off the porch and greeted me with howls as I pulled to a stop at the end of the gravel driveway. The A-frame house was in dire need of fresh paint and shutters that actually hung straight instead of lopsided beside the dirt-streaked windows. Two pots of dying mums sat on each side of the rickety steps. Calvin's wife took spells in trying to spruce things up.

Calvin stepped out onto the decaying porch, letting the screen door pop closed behind him. He was a stout man with a bulk that threatened the seams of his Carhartt coveralls.

"'Preciate you coming out like this, Ava. This dang-blamed poaching's got to stop. Some of that 'seng's been here twenty years or more." He spit a stream of tobacco juice off the side of the porch then wiped his mouth with his sleeve.

"Mature plants like that'll bring top dollar." As if I was an authority on the magical plant known as Ginseng. You couldn't grow up in the Appalachians without knowing a little something about it. The old folks, growers, and buyers simply called it 'seng.

"Thought we'd take the four-wheeler so you can see for yourself. Maybe get some pictures."

I slipped out of my loafers and into my extra pair of hiking boots. This wasn't a job for skirts and heels. Calvin cranked up the ATV while I retrieved my notepad and phone from the Tahoe. Despite being there and doing my job, my mind rambled in several directions. My heart wanted to be back at Doretha's with Ivy. Ridge should be with Trish's parents at the morgue by now. And later, they'd take Ivy with them. Maybe for good.

Calvin wheeled the ATV around beside me. "Climb on up here."

I climbed aboard and straddled the seat, scooting closer to his backside than intended. In my defense, his backside took up a good portion of the seat.

"Hold on. It gets pretty bumpy after we clear the pasture."

I sighed, quietly.

A small herd of Black Angus cattle scattered as we passed, interrupting their grazing.

"How's the cattle business this year?" I yelled over the engine.

"'Bout like everything else these days. Seen better times."

When we reached the edge of the pasture, he stopped, climbed off and opened the iron gate separating the farmland from the forest. Once we were on the other side, he closed the gate. He spat another stream of tobacco juice then climbed back onboard.

About a quarter mile into the woods, I was ready to tell him I'd walk the rest of the way. Every internal organ was jostled out of place. He finally stopped and killed the engine. My knees wobbled when I first tried to stand, making me grab for the ATV to steady myself.

"Watch it there." He took hold of my arm until I found my footing. "Can't have our star reporter taking a tumble."

I laughed, shaking off the jello legs. It'd been years since I'd been on an ATV. Tommy, Ridge, and I used to ride on weekends. Once we traveled to West Virginia to ride a mud trail. Not all the memories of my marriage, or of Grayson Ridge, brought tears.

"The first spot's up here a little ways."

I followed him up a steep slope, grabbing hold of sturdy

branches for support. At this time of day, the ribbons of sunlight filtering through the dense woods of the north side of the mountain were few and far between. The damp musty smell from Saturday's rain lingered, trapped beneath the canopy of forest trees. Scratchy thickets grabbed at the hem of my jeans and around my boots.

Calvin stopped about twenty yards off the trail and pointed to a spot under a thick pine. "See here? Look how big that hole is."

The hole was definitely man-made. A few red berries lay scattered around. From the depth of the hole, the ginseng sported decent-sized roots. I stepped closer and snapped a picture with my phone.

"Over here's another one." He walked a few yards from the first hole. "And another. Look real close and you can see footprints."

I followed him, snapping pictures of the larger holes. "How many holes total?"

"Too damn many to count."

I stopped and brushed the hair out of my eyes. Sweat from the climb dampened my forehead and hair. "How much money you think you've lost?"

Calvin stopped walking and propped his foot on a broken stump. "Hard to say for sure, but probably around fifty grand."

The holes dotting Calvin's land justified his anger. Ginseng season often brought out the worst in people, making enemies of friends. "What does Sheriff Ridge say about it?"

Calvin let loose with a deep laugh, filled with more anger than humor. "Said ain't nothing he can do about it unless I catch 'em red-handed. Don't have the man power for *surveillance*. Ain't that a crock of shit?" He spat another stream of tobacco. "I plan to leave this land to my sons and their kids, but what good will it do them if there ain't no crop left?"

"What about other growers? Are they having the same problems?"

"The hobby farmers like me are. Locals who depend on it for income have pickers. They tend to chase the rogue bastards away."

I wasn't sure I'd consider something with potential to earn fifty grand a hobby.

Calvin looked over his shoulder at the crest. "Seen enough or you want to see more? Gonna be getting dark up in here shortly."

"I'm good."

He nodded as he came down from his perch then led the way back to the four-wheeler. "That was something 'bout that girl getting murdered, wasn't it? Did you know her?"

Apparently he hadn't heard the entire story and I wasn't going to be the one to share it with him. "Yes. I knew her. Been a long time since Jackson Creek's had a murder, so I guess everyone's on edge."

"Adaline's locked up the doors every night since it happened. Scared to be in her own house with the door unlocked."

He climbed aboard the ATV and cranked it up. I wedged in behind him, bracing myself for the ride back. As we bumped along, I looked around the land, at the hills and the valleys, and wondered if whomever had killed Trish was out there. Hiding in the shadows like the boogey man, or maybe even walking the streets of Jackson Creek waving hello to friends and neighbors.

Calvin's wife wasn't the only one now locking her door.

When we got back to the house, we sat on the porch, drinking sweet iced tea, and finished the interview. Bug, the smaller of the two hounds, took an interest in my glass, trying a couple of times to take a drink.

Calvin hurled a stick in the hound's direction. "Bug—git on, you crazy dog. Like I was saying, there's two dealers in these parts that I know of. One of 'em, over near Roan Mountain, got a name for buying from anyone. Aster Hastings's done business with him before. The other buyer, Anderson Lee, you might know him."

I did know Anderson. "I want to do some more research on this, Calvin, before rushing to get it to press. It may be an issue or two before it runs." I shooed Bug away from my drink again.

"Long as it runs before the election." He laughed, making me wonder how much Ed Stinger had to do with this. Ginseng had been growing in these mountains for thousands of years, and poachers had been digging it for almost as many. A different sheriff wasn't going to change that.

It was three thirty when I left Calvin's, anxious to get back to Ivy. Hating the thought of her waking up in a strange place, unsure of her surroundings or the people around her, I sped through the curvy roads carefully.

The road leading from Calvin's was free of the tourist traffic clogging Main Street. Tourists loved the changing of the leaves like visitors in England looked forward to the changing of the guard. Most of them kept to the main streets or the parkway, avoiding the winding side roads where most of the locals lived. As I guessed, as soon as I hit the town limits, traffic was at a crawl. Rather than parking and walking along the sidewalks that stretched maybe all of a mile, people drove from one trendy shop to the next. The stoplight at Main and Birch Mountain Road cycled red twice before I inched my way through the intersection. I passed the little art shop where Trish sold her work. A handmade "CLOSED" sign still hung in the window from when she closed up shop on Friday. A few window-shopping tourists stopped and looked in the gallery then moved on, unaware of the tragedy.

When I got to Doretha's, Ivy was not yet awake but she was stirring.

"She's been a little restless," Doretha whispered, gazing at the baby. "Got about thirty minutes before the school bus gets here with Emma. Why don't we have some tea while we wait."

Anger that my daughter was now too scared to stay by herself in her own home made my skin crawl. It made me angry that this murder had stripped away our sense of security.

In the kitchen, Doretha put the kettle on then pulled two mugs from the cabinet. "Did you get what you needed for your story?"

I sat down at the small dinette table where I had eaten many meals. There were still pencil impressions in the soft wood from where I used to do my homework. "I got enough for a start. Someone's poaching ginseng from Calvin Cooper's land."

"Hmph. Poaching 'seng's been going on since before Calvin himself was alive. Must be some other reason he's wanting a story."

I laughed out loud. "You got that right, and his name's Ed Stinger."

She sat the two mugs on the table, folded her arms across her chest and glared at me. "You think Mr. Stinger'd do something like that? Stir up trouble this close to the election?"

I cocked an eyebrow. "Seriously? I told Calvin I wanted to interview a couple other people before the story ran, and you know what he said?"

"What'd he say?"

"He said as long as it runs before the election. Now you want to ask me again if I think Ed Stinger's involved?" I grinned like I had it all figured out.

She narrowed her eyes, probably not so much not believing Stinger would orchestrate something so politically motivated as not wanting to believe Grayson Ridge was the intended victim. Lucky for me, I was saved by the whistle. Defending Grayson was never easy with Doretha. She removed the kettle from the stove and poured the boiling water over the orange spice tea bags in our mugs.

We could drink our tea, talk about the ugliness of small-town politics, or talk about the going price for ginseng. We could talk until neither of us had anything more to say. But the truth was we were dancing around the subject. The baby in the next room faced an uncertain future whether Ed Stinger was elected or not.

"Grayson was meeting Trish's parents at the morgue at two." I spoke in a quiet voice and it had nothing to do with the sleeping baby.

Doretha glanced at the rooster-shaped clock above the table. She stirred her tea without saying anything. After a long moment, she set the spoon aside, closed her eyes, and said, "Lord Jesus, lead and guide them during this difficult time. Give them the strength they will need in the coming days, in Jesus's name I pray, amen."

I closed my mind to the horrible things wanting to fill my head and breathed in the strong scent of the tea.

"Do you think they'll take her back to Raleigh to bury her?"

I shrugged. It was hard to say. "They waited two days to come claim her body." Bitterness churned in my voice.

Doretha shook her head, her braids swinging back and forth. "Don't judge. Could be circumstances we're not aware of."

I sipped my tea to keep from spewing my thoughts like projectile vomit.

Doretha reached across the table and patted my hand. "Calm down. They can't help it if they're assholes."

I started to laugh but my cell rang. Ridge's number came up. "Hey. What's up?"

"I wanted to check and see if it would be okay if I brought Trish's parents by your house around seven to see Ivy."

I picked up the spoon and absently stirred my tea, under-joyed at the possibility Ivy would be headed to Raleigh tonight with her asshole grandparents. But what was I going to tell him? I had no real claim on her. "Seven will be fine."

In the dining room, she was awake now, sleepy-eyed, baby fine hair mussed all over her head. I brushed a tear away.

CHAPTER 7

I picked up a pizza on the way home so we could eat and get cleaned up before Trish's parents arrived. Would they take her with them when they left? Would they come back in the morning to get her? What if they wanted to wait until the weekend or next week? That would be fine with me. She kept Emma's mind occupied and a smile on my daughter's face. Emma was happy to play with the tot while I packed the baby's stuff.

At six thirty, Brady dropped Cole off but didn't come in. Part of me was relieved as I had enough to deal with at the moment.

It didn't stop me from worrying about him though. "How was Brady today at school?"

Cole shrugged as he wolfed down a slice of pizza. "Fine, I guess."

Boys. Or men in general. What was it about a conversation that required more than three sentences they just didn't get? Sometimes Cole responded with nothing but a grunt rather than actual words. Maybe that had more to do with being a teenager than his gender.

I tidied up the kitchen while we waited for Ridge and the Givens.

After downing double the amount of pizza Emma and I ate, Cole cleaned his spot at the table. "Can I get a shower while they're here or do I have to stay downstairs?"

Still in his football uniform, he smelled like sweaty socks. "You can get a shower."

He grabbed another piece of pizza then raced upstairs, either aware of his own stench or that he was about to have an actual conversation with his mother.

I went into the living room to check on Emma and Ivy. Surprise slapped me in the face, flushing my cheeks with embarrassment. Rick looked about as surprised to see Ivy as I was to see him. A replay of this morning's argument with him and the invitation to come over sparked in my brain.

He stopped glaring at her long enough to glare at me. "Shouldn't she be with social services?"

"We were trying to avoid that. Ridge is bringing Trish's parents by in a few minutes. I'm assuming they'll take her back with them."

"Can I fix her hair?" Emma asked.

I agreed but wondered why we were trying to impress the asshole grandparents. Emma ran upstairs then came back down with a brush and hair bow. Emma put the hair bow in, Ivy took it out. They did this a few times until Emma finally gave up.

A minute later, Finn's ears perked up, then came the bark. Ivy clambered up my leg, afraid of the suddenness of noise and activity. I picked her up and hugged her, watching Ridge's Expedition come up the driveway.

Rick lightly squeezed my arm. "Look, I don't want you saying anything to Ridge. I'm your lawyer so—"

"Rick, please." I flicked my hand, brushing him off.

I greeted them at the door, the perfect hostess. And immediately disliked them. Rupert Givens was a massively intimidating man with a bulbous nose dominating his face. His wife, Ann, was scary thin with sharp angles and taut lips that had never smiled. They were dressed like their dinner at the country club had been interrupted. Ridge looked as uncomfortable as I felt.

After Ridge introduced everyone, I invited them to the sofa. Ivy laid her head on my shoulder. Her sudden shyness probably had more to do with the late hour than the Givens.

Neither Rupert nor his wife said anything, but they did offer a curt nod. They sat side by side, both as stiff as the plank wood flooring. Ridge sat beside Rupert, his ball cap in his hand.

"I'm so sorry for your loss." It was a go-to statement when I failed to have something more meaningful to say. Of course, they weren't sitting on my sofa in my home to hear the condolences I offered. They were there for Ivy. I tried to turn her so they could at least see their granddaughter's face, but she'd have none of it. She buried her cuteness in the crook of my shoulder. "She's tired," I said, making excuses for Ivy's lack of interest in the two strangers seated on the sofa.

And that's what they were. Strangers. I remembered Trish telling me they didn't even come to Ivy's first birthday party.

Since neither made any effort to hold her, I sat in the wingback chair across from the sofa and put Ivy in my lap. Emma sat on the floor beside the chair, quietly worrying with a cloth doll. Ivy squirmed to get down and join Emma so I let her.

Ridge cleared his throat. "Mr. and Mrs. Givens are going to take Trish's body back to Raleigh for burial."

"We have plots at Capital Lawn." The timbre of Rupert's voice was bullying in itself. "We'll make arrangements to have her *trailer* cleaned out once the sheriff releases it." He said the word "trailer" as if it were moldy and rancid. His wife turned her face down and stared at the floor.

I clenched my hands into fists, feeling the sharpness of my nails against my palms. "Of course," I said, just to say something.

Ivy made her baby doll clap. She cackled and showed Emma. Mrs. Givens watched her a moment then turned her gaze back to the floor.

I seized the moment. "Ann, would you like to hold her?"

"No thank you," Rupert answered for his wife. "We'll meet with the lawyers next week and set up a trust. It can be drawn from for her monthly expenses."

The air in my lungs evaporated. After an awkward silence, I finally managed to say, "Pardon?"

Ridge took a deep breath. He rarely showed emotion while on

official duty. This wasn't going to be good. "Mr. and Mrs. Givens don't want to take custody of the baby. They want to relinquish their rights."

Emma jerked her head up, looking to me for an answer. "What does that mean?"

"It means she'll become a ward of the state." With a mother serving a life sentence, I had my share of experience with social services. Doretha was the only bright spot in those memories.

Ridge opened his hands in an apologetic manner. "We'll work with whatever agency we need to try and locate her father."

I turned to Rick, the lawyer in the group. "What if he's never found?"

"After a certain amount of time, she'll be cleared for adoption. Until then, she'll be fostered." He said it so matter-of-factly.

My blood simmered with rising anger. A child. Discarded. Dust your hands of the burden. First comes fostering, then adoption. Like we'd adopted Finn. Saved him from a life of not belonging to anyone. "Like a rescue dog at a shelter."

"Ava," Ridge said, his voice low.

My insides boiled. "How can you not want her? She's your granddaughter, for God's sake." I sprung up from the chair, the nervous energy biting at my insides like a nest of fire ants.

Ann continued her robot-like stare at the floor while Rupert glared at Ivy, condemning the child with contempt-filled eyes. "Mrs. Logan—we did not approve of Trish's lifestyle. She was reckless."

Furious, I pointed my finger at Ivy. "And that's the result of her recklessness? A baby? A living, breathing baby that, unfortunately, has your genes. Your only child is dead. You'll never have another grandchild." If I'd been within striking distance, I would have lashed out at the monster.

Rick moved in between me and Rupert Givens. Although firm, he knew better than to speak around me in a condescending tone. Moments like this, telling me to calm down was useless. "Take a step back, Ava. Regroup."

I turned away from the bastard on my couch. Unspilled tears stung my eyes, but I'd be damned if I'd let Rupert Givens see me cry. "Emma, will you take Ivy in the sunroom, please?"

I knew Ivy didn't understand the words, but I still wanted to protect her. I didn't want Emma to hear all this either. How unwanted children became foster kids, how the system worked. How her own mother fought to have a name other than nobody's baby.

Emma gathered a few toys then scooped Ivy up in her arms. My daughter looked scared, like she wasn't sure what was going to happen to Ivy, this child she'd grown to love and want. I disliked Rupert Givens even more for scaring *my* baby.

Ann, the grandmother, still hadn't said anything. She continued staring at the floor, allowing her husband to speak for her. Her face was stoic, yet somber. Maybe she was afraid of him. Maybe she feared his brute force, the raised hand of a bully. Maybe she wasn't as bad as her husband.

No, I wouldn't feel empathy for her. I wouldn't allow myself to relate.

Rupert Givens leaned forward, massive hands clasped like he was negotiating a deal. "Sheriff Ridge said there's an excellent foster home in town. Run, I believe, by a colored woman?"

My stomach knotted with anger, churning nasty bile into my throat. "A *colored* woman? What century did you walk out of?"

Rick slipped his arm around my waist. "Ava, Mr. And Mrs. Givens have suffered a tragic loss. Let's not—"

I jerked away from him. My heart was beating so fast I could feel the thumping in my ears. "A colored woman? Is that the term *you* used, Grayson? Why was the color of Doretha's skin even mentioned?"

Ridge shot up from the sofa, pointing a stern finger in my direction. "Don't go there, Ava. You know me better than that."

I held my hands in front of myself to steady my nerves and quiet the words threatening to spill from my mouth. After a moment, I took a deep breath. "Have a safe trip back to Raleigh."

It was all I could manage.

I brushed by Rick as I headed for the sun room. There, Emma was on the floor with Ivy in her lap, a coloring book spread before them. Ivy was coloring a bluebird pink but what the hell. She could color it any color she wanted.

Emma looked up at me. Her eyes were wet with tears. "What's going to happen to her, Momma?"

I reached down and stroked Emma's hair. "Don't you worry about it. We'll figure something out."

"But what if nobody wants her?"

My heart shattered into a million pieces. "Oh, honey—she's wanted. Besides, if that's how those people really feel about her, it's probably for the best they don't have a hand in raising her. Right?"

She sniffled and nodded, assured for the moment Ivy's future wasn't as bleak as her twelve-year-old mind had imagined. Now if I could just reassure myself of the same.

Grayson poked his head in the sunroom. "Ava, can I see you a minute in the kitchen?"

I wasn't looking forward to this conversation. Between him and Rick, I was certain I'd be chastised like a kid on her way to the principal's office. I gave Emma and Ivy each a kiss on the top of the head. "I'll be right back. Maybe with some cookies and milk."

In the kitchen, Ridge leaned against the counter, shifting his ball cap between his hands. Rick leaned against the opposite counter, arms folded against his chest. I did owe Ridge an apology, knowing he'd never refer to Doretha in such a manner. It wasn't in him. I'd apologize to him, but Rupert Givens could be planted six feet under before I'd say another word to him. And then it would be "So long, bastard."

"Are they gone?"

Ridge lifted his eyes to glare at me. "They're in a safe place."

Rick exhaled a loud breath. "They're waiting in the sheriff's car. You weren't exactly hospitable."

I glared hard at him, afraid if I said anything he'd see how inhospitable I felt at that moment.

Ridge cleared his throat. "Can Ivy stay here tonight? I'll get the ball rolling with Doretha tomorrow."

I pushed both hands through my hair, suddenly feeling exhaustion settling in my bones. "Of course she can. What are we going to do, Grayson, if Doretha doesn't have room for her? She's already got five that I know of."

Rick didn't wait for Ridge to respond. "I can check with our juvenile attorney. I'm sure there are other foster homes that can take her."

His eagerness to send her away rubbed me the wrong way. "That's not going to happen. I'll adopt her before I let her go into the system."

Rick chuckled. "Ava—you're upset. You're talking crazy. Let's just sleep on it and we'll take a fresh look at our options tomorrow."

I wasn't much of a drinker, but at the moment I could have downed a shot of something then used the bottle over his head. Truth was, I was exhausted. Mentally, physically, and emotionally. Rick wasn't helping with his anger-inducing comments either.

Ridge put on his ball cap, adjusted the brim. "We're going to do a search of Trish's studio. Since you knew her as well as anyone else, would you mind being there? Maybe you could identify some names, clients, anything that could help."

I slowly nodded. "Let me know when."

Rick wagged his fingers at either me or Ridge. Or maybe both. "As Miss Logan's attorney, I don't recommend that."

Ridge threw a death-ray look at me. "You hired an attorney?"

I held my hands up in my own defense. "No. I don't need an attorney. Do I?"

He continued staring at me, slowly shaking his head, never breaking eye contact. "I don't know. Do you?"

"Sheriff, she did find the body. I think it would be best if she had legal representation present before speaking again to you or any of your deputies."

Ridge's eyes could have seared glass. "Is that how *you* feel, Ava?"

I had done nothing wrong. I simply stumbled into a horrible situation. A situation Ivy would carry with her the rest of her life. I owed it to her and her dead mother to do everything I could to help find the person responsible. "I want to do whatever I can to help."

Rick blew air out his nose. "I don't recommend it."

"Duly noted." I turned back to Ridge. "What time?"

"We'll get it lined up in the morning and I'll call you."

The dread of going through Trish's shop and picking apart her privacy weighed heavy on my heart. But it was something that had to be done. For Ivy's sake.

CHAPTER 8

After everyone had left, Emma and I took Ivy upstairs for a bath. Emma dug Ivy's bath supplies from her diaper bag then sat on the floor beside the tub and ran the water. I gathered Cole's dirty clothes from the bathroom floor and yelled at him to come get them. "I'm your mother, not your maid." I handed off the dirty laundry.

He started to stuff the smelly wad into the hamper but I jammed my hand on the lid. "Downstairs. I don't want them up here all week smelling up the bathroom."

Emma laughed as he grumbled something then tromped downstairs with his handful of laundry. "Do all boys smell that bad when they sweat?"

I couldn't help but laugh. "Oh, he's mild compared to some."

She scrunched up her nose which made Ivy cackle. Emma laughed too and of course repeated the scrunchy nose thing until they both lost interest. Ivy found the bubbles surrounding her in the tub more entertaining. Emma splashed her hand in the water a moment but that, too, fizzled out.

I propped against the counter, reached out and stroked my daughter's hair. "You want to talk about it?"

She shrugged and continued to gently wiggle her fingers in the water. After a long moment, the words finally flowed like the water swirling around her fingers. "Why don't they want her?"

I pushed out a deep breath. "I don't know, baby. It's their loss."

She nodded. She took her hand out of the water and blotted it with the towel. "What would happen to me and Cole if something ever happened to you?" She asked it so plainly, it threw me. Emma was a smart child, sometimes too smart for her own good. "I mean, we don't have a dad. Kinda like Ivy."

"Ivy has a father. We just don't know who he is." I wasn't ready to have this conversation with my daughter. She'd already started her period and that was hard enough on me. Truthfully, I knew she probably knew way more than I did at her age, but as her mother I found it hard to talk about it with her.

"Me and Cole don't have a father." She watched Ivy play in the water, avoiding looking directly at me.

"But you have a grandmother that loves you very much."

Tommy's mother, Catherine, was an active part of my kids' lives. I went out of my way to keep her involved. I had Doretha, but I never knew my grandparents. I had barely known my own parents.

"Why don't you go ahead and get her bathed. It's getting late."

She answered with a curt nod and I hated the sudden silence. I didn't know how to talk to my own daughter, how to reassure her she would always be loved and cared for.

I carried Ivy's diaper bag into my room, a room I once shared with Emma's father. I stood staring at the bed until the memories became so real, the pain burned my chest. Forcing myself to look away, I opened the pack-n-play and tried to set it up at the foot of the bed. One of the sides wouldn't lock into place, trying my patience. Angry, I tried shoving the side down then caught myself before kicking the damn thing. I pushed back the tears welling in my eyes and took a deep breath.

"Mom?"

I wiped my face and spun around, forcing myself to smile. Emma was at the door with Ivy wrapped in a towel. "I forgot her pajamas."

"Oh. Uh—yeah. I think she has one clean pair left." I opened her bag and dug out a tiny pair of pajamas covered with purple and green fairies.

Emma looked at me suspiciously. "You okay?"

My heart swelled with a multitude of emotions. Love, fear, anger...way too much to burden a twelve-year-old with. "I'm fine, sweetie." I took Ivy from her and laid the toddler on the bed for a fresh diaper.

Emma climbed up on the bed and sat beside Ivy, her feet barely touching the floor. "Does she have to sleep in the pack-n-play?"

I knew where this was headed. Although I didn't want to make it a habit, tonight I didn't mind. "Go get your pillow."

She hopped off the bed, ran down the hallway, and returned a moment later with her pillow and a Dr. Seuss book. While she and Ivy snuggled down in my bed, I went back downstairs and locked up. Finn followed me from room to room. I stood in the sunroom a moment, imagining the fluid movement of the river stroking the darkness. A darkness I now questioned. The woods on the other side of the glass were black and filled with threats I'd never considered before. Anger gnawed my insides like a cancer each time I felt the fear of knowing a murderer was so close by. Homes were supposed to bring comfort and security, not fear every time you heard a branch snap.

For the first time in ages, I lowered the roman blinds covering the windows, closing us off to the world outside. Finn and I headed back upstairs to turn in for the night, shrouded in a certain sadness like a too-big coat.

At Cole's room, I opened the door and popped my head in to say goodnight. The dirty laundry I'd told him to take downstairs was now piled in his floor. I was too tired to work myself up over a bunch of smelly clothes so I let it go. I learned a long time ago when it came to kids to choose my battles wisely. I didn't care how much dirty laundry was on his floor as long as the clean stuff was put away in a drawer or closet. The rest of his room was passably neat in the grand scheme of things. Schoolbooks spilled from his open backpack thrown on his desk. Two empty glasses with tea crust in their bottoms were on his nightstand. A couple of old sports posters promoting shoes or energy drinks hung crooked on the walls along with a poster of Johnny Cash, dressed in black of course. His dresser was covered with dust, trophies from little league days, and spare change dumped from a pocket.

He was sitting up in the double bed with his back against the headboard, laptop balanced on his knees, with headphones covering his ears. I waved in an exaggerated motion to catch his attention. He looked up and pulled one side of the headphones aside.

"Yeah?"

"I'm turning in. Don't be up much longer."

He nodded then put the headphones back on. I blew him a kiss and nearly fainted when he returned the gesture. His act of affection was probably out of reflex, but whatever it was, I'd accept it.

Before heading back to my bedroom, I went into the kids' bathroom at the end of the hallway and dug around in the vanity drawers for the night light. The last time I used a night light, Emma was a baby. But with Trish's murderer still out there, I felt safer with even just a hint of light peeping from a room at the end of the hall.

I plugged it in, hoping it still worked. The tiny light bulb glowed soft yellow so I turned off the hall light and went to my room. Finn stretched out on the hardwood floor at my bedroom door, more interested in a good night's sleep than guarding his castle.

Ivy was fast asleep in the middle of my bed, both arms and legs splayed in different directions. I supposed one more night of clinging to the edge of my queen-sized bed wasn't going to kill me. Emma was still awake, on her back, staring at the ceiling. Her hands were behind her head, propping it on the pillow. Lying there beside Ivy, Emma looked older than she was. More mature than her twelve years. Yet she was in my bed, afraid to sleep in her own room.

I turned on the bedside lamp then changed into my favorite t-shirt and flannel pants. Emma watched me in the dim light and heavy silence.

"You okay?" I glanced at her over my shoulder.

She hesitated before answering but then dropped her bomb. "Why'd you have to live with Doretha when you were a kid?"

My breath hitched in my chest. I had known before they were born the day would come when my children would want to know about their grandparents. It was like watching someone die of cancer when the end was near—you knew it was inevitable, but it didn't lessen the pain.

I finished dressing and sat on the end of the bed, legs crossed Indian style, facing her. She sat up and scooted up against the headboard. My daughter was ready for this conversation whether I was or not. She stared at me with such a trusting face, waiting on the words I was still searching for.

"I know Grandpa Logan died before I was born. But what about your mom and dad? Where are they?"

My brain grew weary of trying to find the right words. I didn't know if I was trying to protect myself from the truth or my daughter. After a long moment, I figured it was best to just put it out there, ugly warts and all.

I took a deep breath and began the whole sordid story, or at least what she had a right to know. "My father wasn't a nice man. He drank a lot and when he was drunk, he was mean. He wasn't someone a little girl would be proud of."

"Like I was of my daddy?"

I knew she meant no harm in her statement, but it didn't stop the sting. At least I knew now she was too young to remember all the times Tommy raised his hand to me. "Yeah...like you were with your daddy." I forced a deep breath and continued. "My dad was a bully and he liked to hit my mother."

"Why? Why would he do something like that?" Her soft eyes

clouded with questions there was no real answer to. We could guess until we got lucky, but the answer changed with every punch, every bottle.

"Some people are just born to be mean, Emma." I turned my head down, staring at my hands like they carried their own shame.

Ivy stirred. Emma reached over and gently rubbed her back. So loving and caring. Although my father's blood flowed through her veins, there wasn't anything mean about this child. Once Ivy had settled back down, Emma turned her attention back to me. "So what happened to him?"

I cleared my throat. "One day when I was eight, he beat me with a belt."

She flinched and I hesitated telling her more, wondering if she could handle the truth.

Emma gnawed on her bottom lip, contemplating this revelation. "Was it like a *spanking*?" Her voice was quiet and unsure. The mere word "spanking" was foreign to her, something she'd heard about but had never experienced herself. A good firm "no" had always been the only discipline this child had ever needed.

I pushed my hand through my hair, moving it away from my eyes. "It wasn't a spanking. I accidentally dropped a plate and it broke."

"But if it was an accident..." Although her jaw was set firm, uncertainty filled her face.

"He was just a mean man."

After a moment, acceptance replaced the uncertainty on her face. "What happened after that?"

"That was the one and only time he hit me with a belt. Later that night, my mother took his gun and shot him."

My mother wouldn't tolerate him beating me the way he had beat her.

Emma's expression never wavered. No surprise. No shock. Just trust I'd tell her the truth. "She killed him?"

"Yes." Although it was a long time ago, the pain bubbled up like oil rising to the surface.

"So he wasn't just mean. He was abusive."

There was part of me that wanted to smile at how clever this daughter of mine was. But I wouldn't allow myself even a small amount of joy that she was familiar with such a word. For a brief moment I wondered if she remembered my own bruises. She couldn't. She wasn't even two when Tommy died. And to this day, she was proud of him.

I forced myself to remember we were talking about my father, not hers. I hung my head, like it was still my shame to carry. "Yes. He was abusive."

"What happened to Grandma?"

Although most everyone in Jackson Creek knew the story, I had verbalized it to few. "She's in prison."

"Will she ever get out?"

I shrugged. "She's eligible for parole in a few years so she might."

"Do you ever visit her?"

Maybe it was the fact my twelve-year-old daughter knew about these things, or the line of questions she was asking, but my comfort level with the subject had evaporated. "I haven't been in a while."

That was all she needed to know. Doretha used to take me about once a month when I was a kid, but as it often does, the once a month became twice a year and on holidays.

"Does she know about me and Cole?"

I shook my head slowly. I stopped visiting when I got married. Truth was, Tommy stopped me from visiting. We barely had enough money for gas to get around town; running two hundred miles down the road was a waste of resources.

Emma twisted her lips and furrowed her brow, putting the pieces of my life together in her adolescent mind. "And after she went to prison, Doretha became your family then?"

Whether my birth mother was incarcerated or walking free wasn't going to change the fact I considered Doretha my surrogate mother. She'd saved me from myself just as my birth mother saved me from my father. "My mother's still my mother. I just don't have much contact with her. But it doesn't change anything. You, and Cole, and yes, Doretha—you're the family my life revolves around."

"And Ivy." She smiled.

I leaned across the bed and wrapped my arms around her, kissing her all over. "Yes, and Ivy."

CHAPTER 9

The next morning, I dropped the kids at school and Ivy by Doretha's then headed for the office. Nola already had the office toasty with a fire going in the stove. The rich aroma of brewed coffee wafted to the front office from the break room.

Nola handed me my messages before I dropped my bags on my desk. "Justin's looking for you. He's already called twice."

I laughed as I headed to the break room for coffee. There, I pulled a yard sale mug from the cabinet, added cream and sugar, then went back to my desk. "So what did the mayor want this morning?"

Nola stopped typing up the classifieds for print and turned her chair to face me. She had a sour expression on her face. "Some of the folks in town are causing a stink over Trish's murder. Justin's going to have a heart attack worrying himself to death the tourists will find out."

I shook my head. "They're not here long enough to find out anything. They drive through, stop and shop and grab something to eat, then they're gone. He's working himself all up for nothing."

Ever the social butterfly with a manicured nail on the pulse of the town, Nola frowned. "But it's not just Justin. There're rumblings in town. People are scared."

The paper's ads manager dropped the revision report on my desk. "Hardware store wants to make sure we get their ad revised to show they have deadbolts on sale. And Security Plus wants to offer a coupon to new clients."

I looked over the report, understanding their fear. I had closed the world out last night from my own sunroom for the same reason.

Quinn plopped down in my guest chair. He was a good-looking kid with cheekbones that could cut glass. With his looks and deep baritone voice, he would fit nicely in the broadcast news realm, but he preferred print.

He continued to sit there, clearly mulling over something. Just as I was about to ask if there was something he needed, he breached the silence. "I've been thinking about the murder. Considering your involvement, do you think it might be better if I covered that one?"

I took a drink of coffee while giving honest thought to his suggestion. "Any other time, Quinn, I'd agree with you. Sheriff Ridge and I've discussed how the paper's going to approach this story." I stared into my coffee, questioning my own judgment on the matter. "The paper won't be doing any kind of investigation on its own. I need to be a witness in this, not a publisher."

"Then why not let me take it over? You wouldn't have to be involved at all."

The reason why hung in my throat like a bad pill that wouldn't go down. "Sheriff Ridge asked me not to print anything unless it comes from his office and I agreed. So anything we write about Trish Givens' murder will be from press releases or interviews with Detective Sullivan or Sheriff Ridge."

"You agreed to that?"

I exhaled a deep breath. "It's a unique situation, Quinn. There's no easy answer with this one."

The look in his eyes varied from disappointment to unbelieving. "The people have a right to know what happened in their own backyard."

"What do you want us to report on, Quinn? You want me to detail what I saw? The condition of her body?" Leaning in, I whispered between my teeth. "You want me to tell how much blood there was? That she had no face? Just because they have a right to know doesn't mean they need to know."

My mind searched for a mirror to check my reflection. To make sure I was still Ava Logan, headstrong and determined. If Ed Stinger was sheriff instead of Grayson Ridge, would I have been as accommodating?

Quinn clearly still had concerns. If I weren't the owner and publisher of the paper and was young and hungry and wanting to make a mark, I'd have the same misgivings.

He was a good reporter, and for whatever reason, he hung around in the mountains of North Carolina rather than heading for larger cities and markets. I didn't want to lose him. "We'll compromise. Get what information the sheriff's department will release—and don't balk if it's bland and generic—and put together a feature piece on how long it's been since the last murder in Jackson Creek. Deal?"

He mulled it over then slowly nodded. "I like it. I can make that work."

After he returned to his desk with new energy, I turned to Nola. "While I call the mayor, will you call Aster Hastings for me and see if we can set up an interview for this morning?"

I didn't want to deal with the mayor this early but he'd track me down if I didn't. I punched the number for the town hall in the phone. The town clerk answered on the first ring.

"Hey Ava—Justin's waiting on your call. I'll put you through."

"Good morning," I said to empty air.

A few seconds later, Justin was on the line. "Good morning, Ava. Have you gone to print yet?"

I took another sip of coffee on purpose before answering. "No, Justin, I haven't. What's up?"

"What did you write about the Givens' murder?"

Another sip of coffee followed by a pause to let him wonder even longer. "I haven't written anything yet. And what I do write will probably be taken from the press release the sheriff issued, and that wasn't very detailed. Just the basic info."

From his desk across the room, Quinn and I locked eyes.

"Oh, good. I was worried about the details. I heard she was

bludgeoned to death. Stuff like that doesn't really need to be publicized. We don't need all the gory stuff. Know what I mean?"

My mind whirled with questions. The rumor mill of Jackson Creek was already at work. Except it wasn't a rumor. "Where'd you hear that she was bludgeoned to death?"

"Oh, one of the EMS workers told his cousin and—"

"Well, they're jumping the gun. The cause of death won't be determined until the autopsy is complete so please don't repeat that, Justin. It just causes more fear."

"Sure. No problem. I get it. But, I mean, you were there. Are you going to report what you saw?"

I finished the coffee and stewed. As I had told Quinn, writing about the gory stuff was the last thing I planned to do. There were no words to describe what I had seen.

"Ava? You there?"

I drummed a pen on my desk. "I'm here, Justin. And no, I'm not going to write what I saw."

"Has Sheriff Ridge said anything about the investigation? Are they close to making an arrest?"

Nola got up from her desk, carrying her coffee cup, and grabbed mine on her way to the break room. I rolled my eyes and she giggled as she passed. "I haven't heard anything about an arrest, but I'm sure when one is made, everyone in town will know about it." Considering they already knew she was bludgeoned to death, I didn't doubt they'd know about an arrest too.

"Has he said if he thinks it's someone local?"

I shoved my hand through my hair. "If you have all these questions for Grayson, why don't you ask him?"

He coughed, then cleared his throat. "That's your job."

"Then let me do it."

An awkward silence fell over the line as we each waited for the other to make the next move. I picked up the pen and doodled on my desk calendar. He broke first. "Maybe you could do a special issue when they make an arrest. You know, let the people know they're safe."

"And who's going to pay to have it printed?" It amazed me how people thought I snapped my fingers and a paper appeared, with no cost.

"I'm sure the advertisers wouldn't mind an extra edition in this case."

I laid the pen down. "I know everyone's a little jumpy with what happened. But even if we had twenty-four-hour news coverage on it, it's not going to change the process. Besides, people around here are going to know as soon as an arrest is made without the paper telling them so."

The sound of his breath filtered through the line. After a moment he exhaled long and slow. "I guess you're right. This murder's got everyone spooked. We're even keeping the door to the town hall locked during the day. You have to ring the bell for Cathy to open the door."

I thought of my sunroom and the blinds now covering the windows. "Hopefully the sheriff's department will make an arrest soon and we can all rest easier."

"Yeah, I guess." He sounded disappointed, like he'd resolved himself to the fact there wasn't much he could do about the situation. "Have they made any arrangements yet? I mean for Trish."

"Her parents are taking her back to Raleigh for burial once the autopsy's complete. They didn't mention anything about a service." I didn't want to go into detail about the situation with Rupert and Ann Givens so I cut the conversation short. Nola returned with fresh coffee. "Hey, Justin, I've got to get to work. If I hear anything, I'll let you know. Okay?"

"I'd appreciate it. Have a good day."

I hung up and took a long drink from my mug. Nola spun her chair around to face me. She clutched her coffee mug with both hands, staring at me with expectant eyes. "The murder?"

"There's probably more locked doors now in Jackson Creek than ever before."

"Sheriff Ridge still doesn't have a suspect?"

I shrugged. "I haven't heard of one. It's still pretty early in the investigation though. Did you get in touch with Aster?"

She slapped a hand to her head as if I'd reminded her. "Yes. Ten o'clock."

The clock on my computer read 9:10. It was a twenty-minute ride to Aster's, thirty if tourists were already clogging the roads. I had time to call my graphic designer to tell him to save space for another obit. I didn't know what I'd write, but Trish's life deserved as much space as her murder.

Gray smoke rose from the chimney of Aster Hasting's log house and dissipated into a cloudless Carolina blue sky. Miles behind the house, colorful peaks of the Blue Ridge Mountains framed the cabin like a picture. The wooden steps to the porch were lined with pots of gorgeous mums in full bloom. Aster's wife, Sue, met me at the door and welcomed me in. She'd been my Sunday school teacher at church when I was a kid and never failed to offer a hug as an adult.

"How are the kids?" She released her tight embrace, freeing my ribs from the squeeze.

"They're good. Growing up too fast."

The small house was suffocatingly hot thanks to a wood-burning stove that dominated the living room. Sweat beads popped out along my hairline. Sue seemed immune to the heat, comfortable in her cable-knit sweater with an orange pumpkin stretched across her heavy breasts.

Aster came into the living room from the hallway, wearing a plaid flannel shirt and blue trousers left over from his days underneath cars at the Jackson Creek Auto Shop. He was a small-boned man with hunched shoulders that made him look even shorter than he was. His eyes were sunken and ringed with dark circles, making me question his health.

"I liked that article last month on the pumpkin patch. Used to take our kids every year." His voice was wheezy and forced. He offered me a seat in a rocking chair next to the stove.

I used to take Cole and Emma every year too. They'd outgrown the tradition, but maybe next year Ivy might enjoy it.

Balancing my notepad on my knees while wiping a trickle of sweat rolling down my neck, I purposely moved the chair a few inches from the inferno.

"Would you like some coffee?" Sue asked. "Maybe hot tea?"

The mere thought made me want to dive headfirst into a frozen river. "No, I'm fine, but thank you." I smiled politely.

"So I'm supposed to tell you about selling 'seng." Aster labored for breath. He opened the cast-iron door of the stove and tossed in another log before taking a seat on the slipcovered sofa.

"If y'all excuse me, I've got to get the breakfast dishes cleaned up. Aster, you want more coffee?"

After he shook his head, she disappeared into the kitchen. I wondered if it was as hot in there as it was in the tiny living room.

I flipped my notepad open to a clean page. "Calvin told me you've done business with a new buyer over in Roan Mountain. Can you give me his name?"

"Tiny Cormack. Don't let the name fool you—ain't nothing about him *tiny*." He wheezed out a laugh.

I jotted down the name. "Does he have a business name?"

"Got a scrap metal yard he runs his 'seng business out of." He scrunched his face in thought, then continued, "Mack's Metals, maybe? Sounds about right." He sucked in another wheezing breath.

"How'd you hear about him?"

He shrugged and opened his hands in an apologetic manner. "Talk." He coughed up a painful hacking sound and took a moment to recover.

"Can I get you some water?" Drawing attention to his struggle wasn't on my agenda, but I didn't want the man to die in front of me either. I'd had enough of that for this lifetime.

He held a boy-sized hand up and shook his head. "She'll be in here in a minute." His words pulled at his diaphragm, lifting his sunken chest with each breath.

Sue came in the living room carrying a glass of water and a pill of some sort. She handed them to him and waited while he downed them both. "Ava, you sure I can't get you something?"

"I'm sure."

Aster handed the empty glass back to her. His breathing had relaxed enough for him to talk. He started slow, but picked up speed as breathing became easier. "Last year, Anderson Lee was the only one 'round here buying, so he could set his prices as low as he wanted and weren't much the growers could do about it."

Sue headed back to her dishes while Aster resumed his story. "He set his prices so low, the only one making any profit on ginseng was him. Then this season we hear tell 'bout this Cormack fella over the mountain paying good money so some of us took our 'seng over the ridge."

"You do your own picking?"

He coughed again then sucked in a deep breath. "Did last year. Don't quite feel up to it this year."

"Did you hire someone?"

"My son, Greg, and a couple of his friends are helping me out."

"You ever had problems with poachers?"

He bobbed his head. "Poaching's been going on since these mountains were formed. Some years it's worse than others."

"What about this year?"

Aster puckered his lips, scrunching them against toothless gums. "Can't say it's any worse."

I replayed my conversation with Calvin and wondered if he had said Aster was being poached too. If he had, he was either lying or Aster didn't put the same amount of importance on the crime as Calvin. If Calvin was the only one being poached, it was a shame for him, but I could understand Ridge's reluctance to put manpower and tax dollars on it. My political radar went up and zeroed in on Ed Stinger. I scribbled *check notes from Calvin* on my notepad.

"You wouldn't happen to have the address for Mack's Metals, would you?"

He dug his well-worn wallet from his back pocket and fished

out a business card. "He's a right nice fella. Big as a house, but nice just the same."

I took the card from him and wrote down the needed information then handed it back. Sue returned to the living room, carrying a small breathing nebulizer and face mask. "Hate to cut this short, but it's time for his treatment."

Aster smiled a soft smile and gave me a wink. "Are we through?"

"I think I have enough. You've been very helpful." I returned his smile and closed my notepad.

Sue plugged in the small machine and sat it on the end table beside the sofa. She handed him the face mask and waited while he slipped it over his nose and mouth. Soon after, the machine hissed to life, pushing much-needed air into Aster's lungs.

I stood to leave then reached out and patted his bony knee. He was a good man and it pained me to see him struggling for something most take for granted. "Thank you, Aster. You take care."

He didn't try to speak but nodded and waved goodbye. Sue walked with me outside, stopping on the front porch.

"How long's he been sick?"

"Early spring. Mesothelioma. I think that's how you pronounce it."

"I'm so sorry, Sue."

She smiled as she watched a blaze-red cardinal at a feeder in the yard. "He has good days and he has bad days."

"Is he doing chemo?"

She shook her head. "He chose not to. A 'quality of life' thing." She pinched the head off a dying mum and tossed it in the yard. "I didn't mean to run you out in there. If you need to talk to him some more about your story, you're welcome to come back anytime. We're here all the time now. Well, my daughter-in-law, Sherry, comes Mondays so I can run errands, but other than that, we don't get out much."

"Thank you, but I think I got what I needed."

"I don't know what you're going to write, but that man over in Roan Mountain is a good man in my book. Without that extra money our boy's been getting for the 'seng, I don't know what we'd do."

CHAPTER 10

Anderson Lee owned a wholesale produce market near the Virginia state line, about ten miles north of Aster's place. I called to make sure he was in before heading that way, then called Nola to check in. Justin hadn't called again but Ed Stinger had. I wouldn't waste my cell minutes on Stinger and told Nola to just leave a reminder on my desk.

I then called Doretha to check on Ivy.

"She's playing with those old baby dolls been around here for years," Doretha said. "She's a right happy little baby."

I wondered if Ivy would remember anything about all the blood, about the sirens and emergency vehicles. If it was a memory she'd carry in the far recesses of her mind, where it would lay dormant like a monster under the bed. I pushed the thought out of my mind and focused on the here and now—she was a happy baby. That was what I cared about at that moment.

After I hung up with Doretha, I called Ridge. It hadn't been twenty-four hours since Rupert and Ann Givens discarded their granddaughter like a stray dog dropped off on the side of the road. But until Ivy's immediate future was settled, I was uneasy about it.

Ridge's secretary transferred the call to his cell. "Hey. What's up?" There were voices in the background, loud at first, then fading as he must have walked away.

"Have you talked to the D.S.S. yet?"

"Yeah. Hang on a minute—Sullivan, did they dust the baby's room for prints?" There was faint chatter in the background then Ridge came back on the line. "Sorry. We're at the crime scene. Okay, to answer your question, yes. I was going to call you in a little bit."

"What'd they say?"

"They'll need to do a home inspection and an interview and you'll need to fill out a pretty detailed application. In the interim, until you're approved, I'm vouching for you."

I didn't understand. "What do you mean until I'm approved? Approved for what?"

"As a foster mom. We'll worry about the adoption later. Who knows? The Givens may change their mind at some point."

Every thought in my head bounced off one another. I pulled off the road onto one of the graveled scenic overlooks along the Parkway to try and grasp a single thought. An elderly couple was there, their Buick parked beside me. They sat at a picnic table sipping from a thermos. "I thought you were going to see about Doretha taking her?"

Total silence on the other end. He must have walked farther away from the investigation. Finally, Ridge cleared his throat. "I did, and like you said last night, Doretha doesn't have room. Do you want her, or do you want me to withdraw your application?"

Tears spilled down my cheeks. I didn't bother to brush them away. "Yes," I whispered. "I want her."

"Good. Marsha Thomas is the director. She'll assign a caseworker and they'll be giving you a call to get the paperwork started. It'll probably be later in the week before they call."

I sniffled. "And until then?"

"I vouched for you so she'll be staying with you. Looks like you're back to changing diapers."

"Ridge..." I didn't know what to say. I swallowed a torrent of tears, collecting my thoughts. "Thank you," was all I could muster and that was in a tiny voice.

"Thank me in a few weeks if you're still excited about it. Hey, look, I've got to get back in there. We're hoping to wrap this up today."

I shook off the shock of being Ivy's foster mom as my brain shifted gears. "You're making an arrest?" I scrambled for my notepad.

Ridge laughed. "Relax, Ace. I meant wrapping up the crime scene."

"Oh. I knew that."

I could picture him smiling, his head turned slightly downward, his eyes hidden beneath his ball cap. "I'll check in with you later."

After we hung up, I sat there on the side of the road and cried. I cried for Trish. I cried for Ivy. I cried for Emma and the fear she now lived with, along with the knowledge I had burdened her with last night. And I cried for Grayson Ridge. The longing that never seemed to go away. The want to feel his arms around me again. His hands on my waist. His lips..."Stop it," I said out loud. "Stop it. Stop it. Stop it!"

I jerked the door open and leapt out onto the gravel, sobbing and frantic for fresh air. The elderly couple at the picnic table stared at me, alarmed.

"Honey, are you okay?" The woman stood and started toward me.

"Do we need to call someone?" the man asked, following his wife's lead and stepping closer.

I shook my head and leaned over, clutching my knees, fighting back the hyperventilation coming on. The woman was suddenly at my side. "Harold, grab a bottle of water out of the car. Honey, you need to sit down." She wrapped a supportive arm around my waist and led me to the picnic table, forcing me to sit. "Are you in pain?"

I shook my head wildly, fighting as hard as Aster had for breath.

"Look here," the woman said. "Purse your lips like you're blowing a kiss." She knelt in front of me and demonstrated. "Deep, deep breath."

Harold returned from the car, clutching a bottled water. The woman continued the breathing demonstration until my breath matched hers. My heart rate slowed, quieting the jackhammer in my chest.

"I'm Helen. This is my husband, Harold." Kindness radiated from her sun-wrinkled face.

I sipped the water she'd offered. And felt like a fool. Embarrassment flushed my cheeks. "I'm so sorry. I...uh, just got some news I wasn't expecting."

"Must have been pretty bad." Helen put her hand on my shoulder.

I shook my head. "No. Not...really." But I couldn't say that it was good news either. How do you explain something you don't understand yourself? I didn't want Ivy in the foster system being raised by people who never knew her mother. At least I could give her that. I could tell her what a beautiful smile her mother had. I could tell her how much she looked like her mother when and if the time came. And I could tell her how much her mother loved her and it wouldn't be just words coming from a stranger. It would be the truth because I knew it to be, and I would be the one telling her.

Still, I felt a twinge of guilt, feeling happy about it. How could I be happy about the result of Trish being dead? It was like being glad your husband was dead so you could escape a bad marriage.

I sat with Helen and Harold at the picnic table long enough to settle the thoughts running rampant in my head. Helen offered me a wet napkin to wipe away the streaked mascara. I didn't carry makeup with me so Anderson Lee was getting blotched cheeks and red eyes.

And I was getting Ivy.

The thought still terrified me but at least I could breathe now. Once my heart settled into a more natural rhythm, I called Rick to tell him the news.

His cell forwarded to his office. "I'm sorry, Ava, he's in court," his secretary said. "Do you want me to put you through to his voicemail?"

This wasn't news I wanted to leave in a message. "No, but thanks. I'll get with him later."

I sat there another minute, gathering my thoughts, then got back to work. At Anderson's produce market, I parked near the entrance. The market looked like an airport hangar with roll-up sides, open and airy surrounded by a gray metal frame. Pickup trucks were on one side with farmers unloading their goods, while on the other side, delivery drivers were loading their trucks with pumpkins, sweet potatoes, and the last of the apple harvest.

I checked my face in the rearview mirror one more time before getting out. Eyes were still puffy, but the redness had faded. My cheeks were still blotchy, but it was the best I could offer at the moment.

One of Anderson's helpers, a skinny kid with a tattoo on his neck, motioned toward the back when I asked where his boss was. The market smelled like autumn, rich and sweet. Like Doretha's kitchen filled with pumpkin pies and apple crisps, the warm scent of vanilla and roasted pecans. Would Ivy remember the smell of my kitchen like I remembered Doretha's?

Anderson's office was little more than a partitioned area in the back corner. One wall was windowed, allowing a good view of the goings on out on the floor.

He stood to greet me as I entered the cubicle. "Hey, Ava. It's been a while. The paper looks like it's doing well."

"We're still plugging along." I sat down in a plastic chair across from his surplus-sale desk.

Anderson was in his early forties, graying around the temples, with permanently calloused hands from years of work. His son and Cole had played baseball together. Anderson was banned from the field one season for threatening the umpire. He had a temper and he liked being right. Telling him no wasn't an option.

He leaned back in his chair and propped his feet on the edge of his desk. He locked his hands behind his head. "So you want to talk about the ginseng market. What do you want to know?"

"How's the season been?"

He shrugged. "Been better. Like about everything these days."

I opened my notepad to a clean page and scribbled the date and Anderson's name, stalling for time. I had no idea where this story was going, or if it was even worth the time. If Anderson Lee wanted to lowball his growers, that was his business. It wasn't right, but it wasn't newsworthy either. The poaching was the story and unfortunately, Ed Stinger had his hands all over that.

I chewed on that for another moment, feeling like I was being bullied into a story that wasn't there. The least I could do was finish the interview since Anderson had agreed to do it in the first place. "Have you heard tales of poaching being a problem again this year?"

"Poaching's always a problem. Can't really say whether it's any worse this season than in the past or not. I don't really involve myself too much on that end of the business."

"So you don't really know where the ginseng comes from?"

He dropped his feet then leaned into his desk, his elbows propped on a grungy desk calendar with pencil smudges and coffee stains. "Look, I know my growers. Once in a while, I'll have somebody new show up selling roots and when they do, I don't ask where they dug it from. Not really my business. Understand?" He opened his hands like he was making an offer of the truth, whether I liked it or not.

"Have you had any new sellers this season?"

His lips pulled back into a tight grin. "Now you know I ain't going to give you names, right?"

I returned the grin and nodded. "Just wondering."

He glanced out the window at the action on the floor. After watching a moment, he turned back to me. "To be honest with you, Ava, this season has sucked. A lot of my regulars been taking their business to some prick over in Roan Mountain. He's paying three times what I can give."

"Can give or will give?"

He grinned again and turned back to the window. "You see those two guys out there loading and unloading? Those are the only two I've got left. Used to have ten employees. Even had a secretary. Man can't hardly afford to stay in business these days." He turned back to me and for a moment, I felt sorry for him.

"I thought ginseng was a money maker."

He shrugged. "It is. But if I can't afford to buy it from the growers, I ain't got nothing to resale."

I glanced down at my notepad, knowing the answer before asking. "Do you know the guy over in Roan Mountain?"

"I don't know his name. But he's doing business out of some scrap metal place called Mack's Metals."

Tiny Cormack. Just like Aster had said.

I pretended to write the name then closed my notepad. "I appreciate your time, Anderson. And I hope business picks up for you again." I stood to leave and he followed suit.

We walked through the warehouse to the parking lot. At my car, he leaned against the hood. "You asked me about new pickers."

"Did you have many?"

He shook his head. "Just one. Woman 'bout your age."

"A woman? That's a little unusual, isn't it?"

"Not really. Sally Thomas used to be one of the best diggers around."

"Don't suppose you have a record with this woman's name on it you could show me, do you?"

"Would if I could, but she didn't want to take what I offered. Took her business over to the metal shop."

CHAPTER 11

After picking up Emma and Ivy from Doretha's, we went home and I fixed Salisbury steak and mashed potatoes for dinner. It was Emma's favorite. I wasn't sure how she was going to react to having Ivy around on a semi-permanent basis. Maybe I was sucking up. Emma was still shell-shocked over Trish's murder and her current attachment to Ivy was a result. Would she still be as willing to fill that big sister role six months from now? Or would the interest wear off like it often does with a new puppy or a new toy?

Emma was at the table doing her homework while I fixed dinner. Ivy played with a baby doll and stroller she refused to leave at Doretha's. Cole would be home from football practice anytime.

I turned the steaks, adding a little water to help with the steaming. Turning around so I could see her, I leaned against the counter, shuffling the spatula between my hands. "Hey, Em—I got some news today."

Emma continued her homework without looking up. "Uh-huh."

"Grayson's arranged for Ivy to live with us for a while."

She stopped writing and looked up at me, her eyes wide and searching mine. "For how long?" Her voice was quiet, unsure.

I lifted my shoulders in a drawn-out shrug. "I don't know. Maybe for a long time. I mean, if you and Cole don't mind."

Confusion spread across her face. "Why would we mind?"

"Well, it's a big commitment. I want to make sure y'all are

okay with it. It'll be like having a baby sister—one who's around all the time. One that never goes home." I lifted my brows, hoping she'd understand the seriousness of the matter. Ivy wasn't just staying overnight anymore.

To my surprise, Emma leapt up and rushed to me. She threw her arms around my waist and hugged me so tight it was almost painful. "Can she share my room? She can sleep with me until we can get another bed."

I laughed, stroking her hair. "We have an extra bedroom. You don't have to give up having your own room."

"Not even if I want to?"

She was so kindhearted and sweet natured, there were times it worried me. This wasn't one of them though. "We'll see. But I'd feel better if she was in a crib rather than a regular bed. At least until she adjusts."

A smile dominated her face as she walked over to where Ivy was playing. Ivy shoved the stroller and baby doll at her with toddler-like instructions to "play." Emma giggled as she happily obliged.

"Have you told Cole yet?"

"I'm going to tell him at dinner. But, Emma, he has to agree to it too. Okay?"

Her wide grin told me she wasn't concerned with the possibility he might object. I wasn't prepared for the possibility he would.

We were halfway through dinner when Brady's truck pulled into the driveway. Finn's ears perked up and Emma's smile broadened. "Can I tell him?"

Finn barked and nudged the blind over the glass back door out of the way so he could see outside. He continued to bark even after Cole and Brady were inside. Cole stroked the dog and shushed him.

"Y'all grab a plate." I assumed Brady was staying.

Emma was about to burst but held it in until the boys were seated at the table. Once they were, it poured out of her like water from a spigot. "We're going to be Ivy's foster family. At least for a little while. Since we have an extra bedroom, no one will have to give up their bedroom. We'll have to share a bathroom, but she's not even potty trained yet so that shouldn't be an issue—"

"Emma." I held my hand up to slow her down, or at least quiet her a moment. "Catch your breath."

Cole looked at Emma then at me. "Are you going to adopt her?"

My chest expanded with a needed breath. I wasn't sure how to read his question. "Possibly. There's a lot we need to talk about as a family before any decisions like that are made."

He shoved a bite of steak into his mouth and nodded. Brady looked over at Ivy still happily playing and smiled. "She is kinda cute."

Finally, Cole shrugged. "So I'll have two bratty little sisters to pick on instead of one."

Emma's smile spread across her entire face. "I told you he wouldn't care."

Cole laughed and elbowed Brady in the arm. "You're lucky, man. No kid sisters to bug the crap out of you."

Brady smiled at Emma then went back to shoveling his meal. I wondered how long it had been since the kid had eaten.

Cole watched Ivy with more interest than he'd shown since Trish's death. "So what about her grandparents?"

"Right now, her grandparents aren't an issue. At least her mother's parents, anyway. Since we don't know anything about her father, I guess we'll cross that road when we get to it."

"No one knows who her father is?" Brady asked.

"Trish never said." I grew uncomfortable with the direction the conversation was headed so I changed the subject. "Thought we might try hiking Porter's Peak again Saturday if y'all want."

Cole waved his fork at Ivy. "She got hiking boots?"

I chuckled. "I was going to see if Doretha would keep her for a little while."

"Bet I can beat you to the top," Emma said, taunting her brother.

"Ha! You're on...Noodle head."

"Noodle head?" Laughing, I glared at him. "Where'd that come from?"

"I figured you'd get pissed if I called her asswipe."

"Thomas Coleman Logan, Junior—you watch your mouth."

He elbowed Brady again, grinning. "See what you're missing?"

Brady watched the goings on with an amused expression. I wondered how long it had been since he and his parents had laughed about something silly. Although I had no way of knowing, my guess was it had been a while. On the spur of the moment, I broke my own rule of family time and invited someone other than family to join us Saturday. "You ought to come with us hiking, Brady."

The invitation caught him off guard, surprise showing on his face.

"Yeah, you ought to come," Cole said. "Clear your head, get all those thoughts of girls outta there."

His blush quickly faded as they fell into good-natured laughter. I laughed along with them, then confirmed how cleansing a good hike could be. "It really does clear your mind. The fresh air, blue skies. Does wonders."

"Especially after this week," Cole said. "Not every day you find a dead body."

"Cole...not at the table, please." I glanced at Ivy, who, oblivious to the conversation, probably couldn't even understand the words used. Still, Emma could.

Brady finished his dinner, the blush from the earlier joke long gone. "Rough week, huh? I guess that's gonna be front-page news?"

A sigh escaped my lips. "Unfortunately, that's the nature of the business. There's not too much in this issue, but I'm sure as the investigation continues there will be more."

All of a sudden, Finn leapt up, letting out an ear-shattering *woof*, and bolted to the living room. My heart caught between my chest and throat as there was a loud knock on the front door. I steeled my nerves, telling myself if whoever was at the door intended us harm, they probably wouldn't have knocked. Trish's killer had taken more than just her life. They had taken my peace of mind as well.

A second knock made me hurry my step. Emma was right behind me, carrying Ivy. Finn was barking and turning circles at the door.

"It's Grayson." Cole stood between the kitchen and living room, looking out the picture window. Satisfied his protective services weren't needed, he went back to his supper.

I finally let out a breath and relaxed when I saw for myself Ridge's SUV in the driveway. I opened the door as he was about to knock again. "Was beginning to wonder if anyone was home."

Emma sidled up beside him as he stepped inside and hugged him with her free arm. "Mom told me what you did."

He tickled Ivy's cheek then mussed Emma's hair. "Just did what's best for the baby."

I smiled warmly, afraid to let myself say anything. He returned the gesture, then asked Emma, "Would you mind watching her a few minutes? I need to speak with your mom in private."

Emma glanced at me to confirm her role of semi-permanent babysitter.

"That's fine. Why don't you take her in the sunroom where her toys are?"

As she went through the kitchen, I heard her tell Cole to clean off the table when he and Brady were finished and to load the dishwasher. He balked but I couldn't make out his exact words.

Ridge's mouth spread into a wide grin. "I do believe you have a mini-me."

I rolled my eyes. "I prefer to think of it as developing leadership skills rather than being bossy." I sat down in the corner of the sofa, leaving ample room for him to join me. I assumed he wanted to talk privately, and the wingbacks were too far away to guarantee teenaged ears wouldn't hear. "So what's up?"

He sat on the sofa, close enough to speak quietly. "Do you know if Trish owned any firearms?"

My stomach knotted with apprehension. Why would he ask that? "It wasn't something we discussed, so I can't say for sure. Why?"

"Just need it for the report. That's all. And you have no idea who she was with Friday night?"

I slowly shook my head, more out of confusion than as an answer to his question. "Honest, Ridge—I never asked. I respected her privacy. If she wanted to tell me, she would have."

"How many times have you kept Ivy overnight?"

"Not many. Maybe four or five."

"Do you know if Trish stayed at home or would she go out of town?"

"No, she always stayed at home. She was too conscientious about being far away from Ivy."

"What about anyone hanging around her shop? Do you recall seeing the same person on multiple occasions?"

"The few times I was there, she was alone. But the guy next door, the jeweler—he might remember seeing someone."

"What about Ivy's birthday party? Do you remember who all came?"

I dropped my face into my hands, hoping the brief forehead massage would stir the memories. "It was us and maybe two or three other people."

"Do you remember who they were?"

I opened my mouth but nothing came out. Had I been so self-absorbed in my own little world I couldn't name the handful of people at a child's first birthday party? It was a small town, for God's sake. Finally, a spark took hold. "Her clients. There were two ladies there with toddlers. Trish had painted a mural for one and had done some canvas work for the other."

"Do you remember their names?"

I shook my head. "But I'm sure she kept a client list." I was still bothered by his original question and didn't buy his earlier answer. I knew him too well. "Why did you ask about the firearms?"

"Just a routine question, that's all."

My mind raced with memories of that morning as I fought to grab an image that might shed some light on the matter. And then it hit me. There was blood spatter everywhere. On the walls, on the closed bedroom door at the end of the hallway. I had assumed it was from the force of the beating. "Oh my God...She was shot."

His face displayed concern he rarely showed. He took a deeper breath than normal. "Ava—this *has* to be off the record. Agreed?"

I slowly nodded, more concerned with the information he was about to spill than what I was going to do with it.

"I knew it at the scene, but wanted to wait for the autopsy report. She probably died instantly with the first shot."

Words stuck in my throat, unmoved by the rapid-fire thoughts shooting through my brain. Finally, I forced them out. "She was shot more than once?"

"It appears so, yes."

I wasn't sure how to react. I just sat there, stupid, unsure of what to do. I was glad she hadn't suffered.

"Ava, the multiple gunshots, the beating—all of that is personal. I need you to think hard about conversations you had with her. Even the smallest details will help. Was she having problems with anyone, even another woman? We don't have to assume it was a man."

My mind raced with snippets of talks Trish and I'd had, but nothing grabbed me as important. "I...I don't know."

"Think back to your most recent conversations. Did she say anything about having trouble with anyone? An argument, maybe?"

I shook my head. "Nothing jumps out at me. Could someone have broken in without knowing she was home, and she surprised them?"

Ridge ran his hand over his hair. "There was a lot of rage in the way she was killed."

Reaching for straws, I didn't want to think anyone could be that angry with Trish. "Maybe they broke in then panicked when she surprised them?"

He shook his head. "It's a thought, but burglars don't normally carry a long gun with them. If there was already one in the house, it would be more plausible."

My heart jumped as a memory exploded in my thoughts. "Her father! I remember her telling me about the country club they belonged to and how they were on some father-daughter skeet shooting team."

"When was that?"

"It would have had to have been when she was a kid. She went to college at Appalachian and never moved back home."

Ridge shuffled his ball cap back and forth between his hands. "Yet she didn't have a close circle of friends. There has to be a reason she stayed."

Whatever the reason, it didn't change the fact she was dead. Nor that she had died from a gunshot wound. Whoever had killed her was still out there, maybe even still in Jackson Creek. I didn't want to think someone that angry could be that close.

CHAPTER 12

I was anxious to get to the office the next morning. Hopefully, get in and get out before Quinn showed up. I didn't want to lie to him, but couldn't tell him the new development in Trish's murder. She wasn't beaten to death. She died of a gunshot wound to the face. Ridge would withhold that information from the public, and I couldn't break his trust.

Luckily, Quinn wasn't in yet. I went over the day's schedule with Nola then left to meet Ridge at Trish's studio. The shop was in a strip of retail businesses along Main Street, catering to the arts and crafts crowd. The buildings had been there since the turn of the century and carried every weathered scar with pride. Trish's shop, called Pretty Paintings, was sandwiched between a homemade jewelry shop and a bookstore. The windows were still shuttered, the blinds still drawn over the glass in the door.

I parked across the street in one of the small gravel lots and waited for Ridge. While I waited, I called Lacy Duggins, my graphic designer, to see how the layout was coming.

Lacy was an old-school advertising guy who, unlike others in his profession, changed with the times. He knew his way around graphics programs and knew better than to put Taylor's Funeral Service on the same page as the wedding announcements. "Should be ready to transmit by early afternoon."

We were laughing about Judge Hoffler's corny ad when movement at Trish's shop caught my attention. Brent O'Reilly stood at the door, peering in. I watched him a moment, then got out and sprinted across the street.

He jerked around and stared at me, as surprised to see me as I was to see him. He clutched a small bouquet of yellow lilies in his hand, their stems wrapped in a wet paper towel. Glancing down at the flowers, he then looked across the street, anywhere but at me. "I worked with her at the school. She was a sweet girl."

The school? "I hadn't realized Trish worked at the school."

He nodded, staring at the flowers he held. "She was a sub. What's going to happen to the baby?"

"We're looking for her father. I'll run some notices in the paper. See what comes of it. Did she ever say anything at school about him?"

After giving it a thought, Brent shook his head. "Not that I know of."

"Was she friends with any of the other teachers?"

Again, he shook his head. "She was friendly to everybody but I don't remember seeing anyone in particular that she hung out with."

At that moment, Ridge pulled his Expedition beside the curb, followed by another SUV and the mobile crime scene van. He got out, adjusted his ball cap, then offered his hand to Brent. "Brent—good to see you."

Brent shuffled the flowers from one hand to the other, then shook Ridge's hand. "Sheriff. I was just dropping some flowers by. She was a nice girl. I bought one of her paintings a while back. It was a doe, in the middle of a patch of mountain laurel. It was pretty. I liked it."

"You still have it?"

Brent shook his head and grinned. "Nah. Wife redecorated and it didn't fit the new *decor*."

They laughed like they were sitting on barstools swapping wife stories. I didn't know how long Ridge planned on scouring Trish's studio, but I needed to get over to Roan Mountain sometime today. Tiny Cormack was on my list of people to see.

"Brent said Trish subbed at the school," I said to Ridge, anxious to get back to the investigation and kill the small talk.

Brent confirmed my statement with a nod.

Ridge mulled it over before asking, "How often?"

He hem-hawed. "Maybe once a week? I'm not sure. The office would be able to tell you better." He glanced at this watch. "I've got to get. Have a class starting soon."

"I'll take the flowers to Ivy if you want. I mean, unless you wanted to leave them here."

"No. That would be great." He handed me the bouquet before heading off.

We watched him jog away, neither of us saying anything. The cluster of lilies emanated a gentle fragrance that caught the wind, trailing off into the more dominate smells of autumn.

As we were about to head inside, Merritt Sawyer, the owner of the jewelry store next door, rushed outside. He was red-faced and flustered. "Oh good lord. Has something else happened?"

Ridge held his hands up in a futile effort to calm the man. "Everything's good, Merritt. We're here to process Trish's studio. I would like to ask you a few questions though, if you don't mind."

Merritt was a small man with small hands, perfect for the delicate work his job required. But right now, they were flailing about. "Sure, sure. Be glad to help. But come on, Sheriff. Do you have to park right in front of the store? Can't your men park across the street in the lot? Doesn't look good for business."

Ridge looked across the street at the parking lot then motioned for his men to move their vehicles, probably scoring himself a vote from Merritt. "Unload your equipment first."

"Thank you, Sheriff. Such a shame what happened to her."

"Did you have much contact with her?"

Merritt shook his head. "Not really. Sometimes if we opened and closed at the same time, we'd say hello at the doors, but other than that, can't say that I did."

"Did you notice anyone visiting more than usual? Like a repeat customer, or just a friend dropping by?"

He gave it some thought, then shook his head again. "Can't say that I did."

Detective Steve Sullivan joined us after jogging over from across the street. Sullivan was married with four little kids and always looked like he could use another hour of sleep. He was one of those in law enforcement whose mistrust of the media carried over to even a casual greeting. The scowl on his face told me he wasn't happy about me being there.

Ridge offered Merritt his hand. "Thanks for your time, Merritt. If I have anything else, I'll be in touch."

Merritt disappeared into his jewelry shop as Sullivan opened the door to the studio. He rolled his eyes when Ridge handed me a pair of latex gloves. The air in the studio was full of tension and Sullivan added to it.

The silence was overbearing, the stillness, intimidating. The walls held the air captive, refusing to allow it to circulate. Paintings on display that a few days ago illuminated the room with life had lost their glow. The figures on the canvas now seemed frozen in time. A framed photo of Ivy sat on an antique desk along with scattered work orders and invoices. I snapped on the gloves and picked up the frame, running my finger over the image of Ivy's chubby cheeks.

"You okay?" Ridge stood behind me, speaking in a quiet voice.

I exhaled and returned the frame to its place on the desk. "Yeah."

"What exactly is she supposed to do?" Sullivan glared at Ridge. It was a fair question. I didn't know myself.

Ridge gathered the papers scattered on the desk and handed them to me. "See if you recognize any names. You know more people in town than the average person. Look for repeats and anyone you know who owns a rifle. And the two mothers you told me about last night who came to Ivy's birthday party. Sullivan, check the file drawers and see if you can find more work orders." He pulled the chair out from under the desk and motioned for me to sit.

I sat down at the desk and began looking through the slips of paper, concentrating on the customer names. I recognized several, some even as gun owners. I set those slips aside. Sullivan handed me a file folder with more. As I thumbed through them, one caught my attention. *Mack's Metals?* The slip was signed by Tiny Cormack, Roan Mountain, Tennessee.

I left Trish's studio around eleven and picked up Highway 221 South, destined for Roan Mountain. I called Doretha from the road to check on Ivy. "She's a little fussy. But nothing we can't handle."

"Is she running a fever?"

"Don't seem to be. She's just a little out of sorts, that's all."

"Maybe she's teething?" It'd been so long since I'd had a little one around, I no longer knew the schedule for those things.

"Could be, but you stop worrying about her. She'll be fine. I'll call you if I need you."

Just as I was about to tell her goodbye, I rounded a peak and lost the signal. *Great.* Roan Mountain was an hour and a half drive from Jackson Creek in regular traffic, probably two during leaf season. I had no idea if I would be able or not to pick up the signal again on the other side of the mountain. Uncomfortable with being out of touch that long, not only for Ivy's sake but for Cole and Emma too, I pressed the gas a little harder.

I ran over the names of Trish's customers in my mind. Dale and Linda Tilly were repeat customers. Dale was also an avid gun collector. I did an article for the paper about his collection a few years back. Karen Summers and Becca Gladney were the two mothers who attended Ivy's birthday party. Karen worked at the bank and Becca owned a bakery. Trish had provided original artwork for each business. Wesley Morris, the local hunter safety instructor, paid $3,500 for an original oil painting. Ridge balked at the amount and had me set the work order aside. He also had me set aside Brent O'Reilly's invoice. Like Brent had said, it was for a doe in a thicket of mountain laurel.

It was pushing one o'clock when I reached the gravel parking lot of Mack's Metals. A chain-link fence topped with razor wire enclosed the south side of the property, protecting small mountains of scrap metal. *Mack's Metals* was hand painted in blue on the side of an aluminum-sided building. It reminded me of a homemade yard sign where someone paints *cucs and maters for sale* in black paint on a cut-to-size piece of plywood.

An *OPEN* sign hung from the inside against a dirty window. I gathered my notepad and bag then headed in to meet Mr. Tiny Cormack. And hopefully find out how he knew Trish.

From the description Aster Hastings had given of Mr. Cormack, I assumed the giant of a man behind the counter was Tiny. "Tiny Cormack?"

He rose from behind the counter to his full height, which had to be around six-seven. "That's me. What can I do for you?"

"I'm Ava Logan with *The Jackson Creek Chronicle.* We spoke on the phone earlier."

"Oh yeah—the reporter lady. Good to meet you." He extended a hand that could easily hold four of mine. Surprisingly, his handshake was gentle. He wasn't a bad-looking man, if you liked them big. His eyes were the color of warmed chocolate and radiated the same warmth. Blond curls poked from beneath a Tennessee Titans ball cap. There was no doubt Tiny Cormack was stout, but there appeared to be much more muscle than fat.

"Is now a good time to talk?"

"Sure. I can spare a few minutes. Let me get you a stool." He disappeared around a cloth partition then returned a moment later with a simple bar stool. The kind one would be more likely to find at a breakfast bar in a home rather than a drinking bar. He placed it behind the counter near his. "So what do you want to know about the ginseng market?"

I opened my notepad and turned to a clean page. "There's talk over in Jackson Creek that you're undercutting the other dealers."

He let out a loud guffaw and slapped his knee. "Damn Anderson Lee. I knew he was behind this."

I grinned. "Anderson's not behind it. Look, as long as whatever price war you and Anderson are in doesn't turn real ugly and become news, it doesn't concern me. My real question concerns your pickers."

He tilted his head back, glaring at me, the warm chocolate eyes now chilled with a hint of suspicion. "What do you want to know about the pickers?"

"Do they tell you where they're digging?"

"Not my concern. I pay for the product. Doesn't matter if they dug it out of a moon crater."

"And you sell what they bring you to dealers in China?"

He nodded then took a long sip of a diet soda that looked like it had been sitting on the counter since morning. He swallowed, then continued, "Mainly Korea. I do most of my business with Korea."

"What do you consider a good haul for a picker?"

He shrugged. "Depends. I guess if you have to put an average on it, most pickers earn three hundred to five hundred dollars per pound. Seen some walk out of here with ten grand in their pocket. Had a picker hit a honey hole the start of the season and got a grand per pound. Trish lucked up on that. Choice roots, at least fifteen years old."

I raised an eyebrow. "You said 'Trish.' Wouldn't have been Trish Givens, would it?"

From the look on his face, he was taken aback. "Yeah. Trish. Pretty little thing. She's an artist over in your neck of the woods. Painted a picture of the shop for me. I've got it hanging in the back office. She usually comes in on Fridays."

Apparently, news from Jackson Creek hadn't made it over the mountain yet. "Trish won't be coming in this Friday, Mr. Cormack. She was killed in her home over the weekend."

Like one of the fresh canvases in her studio, Cormack's face was blank. After a long moment, he finally blinked. "Killed like murdered? Did they catch who did it?"

I shook my head. "Not yet. Was Trish here last Friday?"

Cormack took off his ball cap and scratched his head like it would help him remember. "She came in that afternoon. I can look up what I bought from her if you need me to."

"Sure. If you wouldn't mind."

He pulled a ledger book from under the counter and flipped through the pages. On Friday's entries, he used his finger as a guide and followed the numbers. "Looks like she did pretty good that day. I paid her three grand."

I wrote down the date and dollar amount. "Was anyone else here when you paid her?"

He looked over the ledger again. "Yeah, looks like Greg Hastings was right behind her, and then Lester Paine. I remember Lester commenting on wanting to know her 'secret.'"

Greg Hastings? "Aster Hastings' boy?"

Cormack nodded. "From what Greg tells me, ol' Aster ain't doing so well these days."

I thought of the whirring sound the nebulizer made as it pushed air into his damaged lungs. I tried to smile but my mouth just wouldn't cooperate. "He's seen better days. How much did you pay Greg Hastings that day?"

He glanced at the numbers. "Looks like four hundred dollars. Not a great day. But it's four hundred dollars they didn't have, right?"

I forced a smile. "Right. This, ah...Lester Paine. Does he live around here? Don't believe I've heard that name before."

"Yep. Lester's 'bout two miles up the road. On a little side road called Perkins Place. Got his phone number if you want it."

I jotted it down as he recited it. I was much more interested in talking with Greg Hastings than Lester Paine, but I didn't want to overlook anything either. "Tiny, one other thing and then I'll let you get back to your work. Do you know where Trish was digging?"

"Pisgah Forest."

My eyes widened. "She was digging on federal land?"

Cormack shrugged his massive shoulders. "Said she had a permit. I didn't question it."

CHAPTER 13

I called Lester Paine from the parking lot of Mack's Metals. The call went to voicemail. I didn't leave a message. It would have been nice to interview him in person, but my instinct told me Greg Hastings was the one I needed to talk to. If I needed to, I'd call Lester again and do an interview over the phone. Right now, I needed to get back to Jackson Creek. I had a paper at the printers and a cranky toddler to deal with.

Nola answered the phone on the second ring, which meant things were slow at the office. "Lacy called and said, get this, Ed Stinger called *him* and wanted to know if you ran the poaching story."

What the hell? Why would Ed call Lacy for that information? Why didn't he just call the office? My face flushed with anger. "Call Lacy and tell him *I'll* deal with Ed. Anything else?"

"Gladys Boatright called and said the church is holding a spaghetti supper for families in need. She wanted to know if Pansy'd do an article on it. I got the basic information and said we'd call her later in the week."

"I guess paying for an ad is out of the question."

Nola snickered. "You know Gladys. You'd be doing a public service for a public service event."

I sighed. "Uh-huh. And printing the paper doesn't cost anything these days either."

Stories like New Hope Baptist Church's fundraising dinner

teetered on a wobbly line. Was it newsworthy? On a slow day, maybe. Give me the name of a family the church has helped in the past, a father out of work, a sick mother—there's the story. Like the whole poaching thing. Calvin's land being poached wasn't the real story. But if the poaching had ties to a murder...Ed Stinger might have just opened a shitload of stink.

I wanted to call Ridge and tell him what I'd learned but lost the signal in a valley outside of Blowing Rock. I wanted to call Ed Stinger too, but needed to sit on that call until I calmed down.

Being out of touch even for an hour made worse-case scenarios swirl like tiny tornadoes in my head. Maybe I was a slave to modern technology. But it had been years since I had a little one to worry about. Although it didn't lessen the worry, there wasn't much I could do at the moment so I queued a Carolina Chocolate Drops CD in the player for the ride home.

The late afternoon sky peered over the mountain peaks in a brilliant shade of blue. Trish couldn't have painted the landscape any prettier. The layers of rich autumn colors against the cloudless sky infused a relaxing air into my jumbled thoughts. Ed Stinger...Greg Hastings...and Grayson Ridge were occupying too much space in my head. I cranked up the volume on the CD player to drown them out.

It was after four when I got to Doretha's. Emma met me at the door and told me everything that had happened to her at school in one breath. Nothing big, no bad grades, no girlfriend drama. Just a whole bunch of little things she wanted to share in one glorious spiel. I retained about 50 percent of the information but nodded and smiled like I was hanging on to every word. She'd probably quiz me on it later, in which case, I'd fail.

In the kitchen, Doretha grinned knowingly. Ivy was at the small kitchen table eating a graham cracker.

"Still fussy?" I sat down beside Ivy at the table.

"She's been better this afternoon. She has been asking for Mommy though." Doretha pursed her lips and lifted her brow. "I told her Mommy was in heaven."

I stroked Ivy's hair then tickled underneath her chin. "Then that's what we'll tell her when she asks."

Emma stood beside me, twisting the hem of her shirt around her finger. "I think Mason Walker asked me out." She caught my full attention with that one.

I stared at her with raised brows as I nibbled a bite of Ivy's cracker. "Oh? How so?"

"He asked if I was going to the football game Friday night. Said maybe he'd see me there." She sucked on her lips in a bashful smile.

"Uh-huh." I wasn't sure in this day and time if that constituted a *date*. In my book, it didn't and I didn't want her to think of it as such if that wasn't his intention.

"We are going, right? I mean, I told him we usually go because of Cole and all, but now with Ivy, I wasn't sure if that was going to change. We didn't go last Friday when we had her."

I slightly shook my head and shrugged, wondering if she'd already ditched the big sister role. For a boy no less. "We didn't take her last week when we were babysitting because there wasn't a game. They had a bye week. We can take her with us. Go ahead and get your stuff together. I'm ready for a do-nothing night." I still wanted to call Ed Stinger and bite him a new one but refused to allow him into my down time.

Emma turned and went downstairs to the playroom while I started packing Ivy's diaper bag. "She's way too young to be that excited about a boy."

Doretha laughed as she handed me Ivy's sippy cup. "I say she's about the right age if you ask me."

"I didn't ask you." I wrapped my arms around Doretha's neck in a comforting embrace, breathing in the scent of fried potatoes and green beans. I missed those suppers. I missed her.

She kissed me on the cheek after smoothing my hair. "So it's a do-nothing night. I like the sound of that."

"I hope so anyway. Why don't you come to the ballgame with us Friday night?"

She bobbed her head back and forth, sending her beaded

braids clacking against each other. "I might just do that. I can load the kids up in the van and we can get our groove on. Did I ever tell you I was in the marching band?" Laughing, she bumped her hip against mine.

"Only about a thousand times. But what's one more, right?" My giggle turned into a full-on cackle and there we stood, laughing until we both had to pee.

Doretha thumped her hand on her chest in a dramatic fashion. "Oh Lordy! I can't wait 'til Friday night. We gonna rock those stands."

"What do you mean *rock the stands*?" Emma stood in the doorway, her book bag slung across her shoulder, a concerned expression frozen on her face. "Y'all aren't going to embarrass me or anything, are you?"

Doretha patted her braids to stop the swinging motion. "Probably."

"That's what mothers are for." I stifled another chuckle and handed the diaper bag to Emma. "And as you get older, it gets worse. Just preparing you."

Emma tried hard not to smile but the muscles in her jaw betrayed her. "Whatever." She rolled her eyes then kissed Doretha goodbye. "Come on, Brat. Let's go home."

Brat. I liked that. It sounded like something a big sister would say.

Dinner was takeout pizza I grabbed on the way home. Emma and I sat on pillows around the coffee table in the sunroom and ate off of paper plates while Cole was still at practice. A fire burned in the fireplace while Finn slept at Emma's feet. Ivy sat in my lap and nibbled at the sausage and pepperoni. I felt her forehead often, waiting for a fever to come.

"Maybe she misses her mom." Emma's voice was sprinkled with sadness. She must have noticed my numerous forehead checks.

"I'm sure she does. I'm just not sure if that's the problem or if she's coming down with something." The fact I knew so little about this child now in my care weighed heavily on my mind. I didn't know who her doctor was, if she was current on her shots, or if she'd ever been to the dentist. Certainly Trish would have mentioned any allergies to me the few times Ivy was in my care. There were no "oh by the way, she's allergic to peanut butter"-type conversations.

"Is she old enough to understand her mommy's not coming back?" Emma spoke in a hushed voice, like she was afraid Ivy *would* understand.

I slowly shrugged, handing Ivy another pepperoni. "Probably not, but I'm sure she senses something's not right."

Finn's ears perked up followed by a loud succession of barks. He stood to his full height and stared into the kitchen. There was a *rap, rap, rap* at the back door then Rick's voice.

"Ava?"

"In the sunroom." I shushed Finn then treated him with a hunk of sausage.

Judging by his coat and tie, Rick must have come straight from his office. A black and yellow campaign button for Ed Stinger clashed with the navy pinstripe. Rick stared at Ivy as he removed his jacket and loosened his tie. "I thought she was going to stay with Doretha?" The soft firelight did little to hide the glowing concern shadowing his face.

"Mom didn't tell you? Sheriff Ridge arranged for us to be her foster family."

Rick looked at Emma longer than necessary, the surprise obvious in his eyes. He then moved his attention to me. "Wasn't that nice of him."

The anticipation of another argument settled in the pit of my stomach like a lead weight. "I tried to call. You were in court."

"And how long is *little Ivy* going to be here?" His sarcastic tone was lost on Emma but I got the message. Loud and clear.

"Mom's thinking about adopting her. Won't that be cool?"

He grinned so big his eyes nearly closed. "Yeah, that's pretty cool."

"Emma, why don't you take Ivy upstairs and go ahead and give her a bath. Maybe a warm bath will make her feel better."

She didn't argue. I stood up, stretching the kinks out of my legs, then sat on the sofa. Once certain Emma was safely out of earshot, I attempted an explanation. "Doretha didn't have room, and I didn't want her going into the system."

Rick shoved a hand through his hair and exhaled louder than needed. "You didn't think this was something we should have talked about?"

"I tried calling, Rick. I didn't want to leave a message."

"Ava, we should have talked about it."

"We as in me and you, or we as client attorney?"

He scoffed. "Either. You don't think even *thinking* about adopting a baby is something we should have discussed before you put the wheels in motion?"

"I haven't put any wheels in motion. I just didn't want her in the system, Rick."

He huffed then sat down beside me on the sofa. "Well, unless we can find her father, she is going to be *part of the system*. That's just the hard truth, Ava." Although his tone had softened, his words stung.

"But she doesn't have to be. That's the whole point of her staying with me."

"For how long?"

I didn't know how to answer. The reality of the fact I didn't consult with him about a life-changing event smacked me in the face. This was a child I was talking about bringing into my life, *our* lives. Seeking his opinion had never entered my mind.

I didn't know if that little fact spoke more about my stubbornness or the state of this relationship.

"I'm sorry, Rick. It all just happened so fast and—"

"Shh." He draped his arm around my shoulder and pulled me to him. "It's okay. We'll figure a way out of it."

I turned and glared at him. "Out of it? What do you want me to do—take her back like a shirt that doesn't fit?"

He huffed, bordering on frustration. "That's not what I meant."

I put more space between us on the sofa. "Then what *did* you mean?"

He was the one now searching for words. I felt like a pregnant teenager sharing the news with my boyfriend. And it was pretty evident we weren't on the same page with this issue.

"All I meant was maybe we shouldn't jump to action just yet. Doretha's always shuffling kids around. She'll probably have an opening soon."

I sprang up from the sofa. Finn lifted his head and stared at me, probably waiting for his cue to attack. I was prepared to do enough for both of us. "That's exactly what I want to avoid, Rick. I don't want her shuffled around. I want her to have a home. A *real* home."

That truth stung my own being more than I ever imagined. Was there something buried deep that prevented me from thinking of Doretha's house as a *real* home? There was so much more than four walls, a covered floor, and a ceiling.

Rick blew a troubled sigh and leaned back on the cushions, resting his head against the pillow. "It's a noble thought, Ava. I just wish you would have considered *us*, me and you, before you thought it. Maybe there's some hidden reason you didn't." He leaned forward and shrugged, looking at me with confusion showing on his face.

"Don't read more into this than is there, Rick. Me, you—*us*—wasn't on my mind. That little girl who just lost her mother was. And I'm sorry if you think I acted impulsively. It was never my intention to *hurt you*."

He laughed. "Well, you're right on that. You never thought about me at all."

I moved away from him, needing to put distance between us. "Look, I need to check on the girls. Why don't you let yourself out."

I went upstairs, leaving him in the sunroom, and waited in the hallway until the back door closed. When his headlights shone through the upstairs window, I finally cried.

CHAPTER 14

Morning came too early as I rushed the kids out of the house, hurrying to get them to Doretha's. A dense wet fog enveloped the mountain, wrapping itself around me like a damp blanket. Ivy didn't want to put on her coat so I bribed her with a pack of fruit snacks.

John Mark from WebPress Printers delivered the newest issue of *The Jackson Creek Chronicle* to the office promptly at seven a.m. I liked to look it over before sending it out to the world. On these early mornings, Cole never forgot to remind me that school didn't start for another hour and a half.

Despite the coat, Ivy was the only one bright-eyed. Cole grumbled about being fifteen and having to ride to school with Doretha, a.k.a. *the babysitter*; Emma didn't have time to do anything with her hair so if Mason Walker quit liking her, it was my fault. I couldn't argue with them. It was a rushed morning following a sleepless night that left me with red-streaked eyes and a headache.

After dropping the kids off with the *babysitter*, I went to the office and waited for John Mark. A pot of brewing coffee and a fire in Betsy kept me company until he got there. I stood in front of the wood-burning stove, warming my hands and thinking about Rick, and Ed Stinger's gall at calling Lacy.

My anger was no longer boiling with Rick but it was still on a slow simmer. Maybe it was with myself I found the most anger. He wasn't a bad man. In girly terms, he'd make a nice catch. Why did I seem so determined to ruin it with him?

Maybe he was more invested in the relationship than I was. Truthfully, I'd never thought of him in a long-term way. My kids didn't see him as a future stepdad. Not that they had issues with him. They just didn't think of him in that manner and neither had I. Maybe that's why he never crossed my mind where Ivy was concerned.

The bell over the front door jingled, startling me out of my thoughts of Rick and our nonexistent future. John Mark called from the doorway. "Morning, beautiful lady!"

No matter how bad I felt or how sad I was, the balding stump of a man could make me smile. The day's burdens lifted from my shoulders. "Coffee?"

"If you've got a spare, I'd love a cup." He followed me to the breakroom, leaning against the counter while I poured a cup. I slid the sugar and creamer toward him.

"How's it look?" I peered at the paper in his hands.

"It would be a lot better without all the political ads, but what do I know?"

I laughed out loud and it was a welcome change. It felt much better than last night's crying spell. "Those political ads pay for the printing which pays your salary which allows you to keep the missus happy."

I took the paper from him and looked through it, happy to not find anything questionable. "Looks good. As always." I smiled then took a sip of my coffee.

"Good. Got to keep all my women happy. If I leave the missus, will you marry me?"

"No."

We laughed ourselves silly as we had this conversation the same time each week. It was our routine. I'd met his wife on several occasions and she'd fight back a smile and roll her eyes at the things he'd say. I couldn't imagine my life without John Mark any more than I could imagine my life with Rick.

"Words going 'round town you're the one who found the body." The laughter had settled and his tone was now somber.

I slowly nodded, not surprised that news had spread. Especially given the 911 operator loved her role as the town gossip. "I was."

He raised his bushy old-man eyebrows. "I was a little surprised there wasn't much about it in the paper."

I leaned against the counter and sipped my coffee, allowing the steam to warm my face. "It's like walking a tightrope, John Mark. I know things that could possibly jeopardize the investigation, but does the public have a right to know too?"

"It's a tough situation. I don't know that there are any clear answers. You're damned if you do and damned if you don't."

John Mark was an old newspaper guy who moved from reporting the news to printing it along with store inserts, college admissions pamphlets, and the occasional yearbook.

"But," he continued, "your job is to inform the public. If there's a serial killer on the loose, they need to know that. If it was a random murder and it was just her unlucky day, they need to know that—so they can be on the lookout. But if it wasn't random, if it was something personal, the public doesn't need the details until the suspect is caught."

The bell jingled again followed by Rayne Holbrook's youthful voice. "Ava, you in?"

John Mark and I took our coffee to the front. Rayne was a sweet kid working his way through college since his mom and dad were a little off center. They lived in a nice tent deep in the forest and thought the mother ship would have picked them up long before their kid needed college money. Rayne scheduled his classes around delivering *The Jackson Creek Chronicle*.

I didn't bother to ask if he wanted coffee, knowing he'd have a high-powered energy drink in his hand.

"Those things are going to kill you one day, Rayne." I pointed to the drink he was holding.

He grinned. "No worse than that pot of coffee you'll drink

today. I'm just getting my caffeine in one large dose." He moved to the stove and held his empty hand over it. "Bit nipply out there this morning. Wonder if the wooly warm will get it right this year?"

"You mean will you be able to hit the slopes more than usual?" John Mark cut me a glance coupled with a wink.

Rayne smiled. "Living up here has its perks. That was until we had an actual *crime* rate. Guess the murder made the front page, huh?"

John Mark and I looked at one another. I answered the question, knowing I'd be asked the same thing a thousand times over. "There's not a lot of information at the moment. I'm sure it will come in due time."

John Mark rubbed his hands together. "Well, let's get this show on the road. The missus is expecting me to take her to breakfast."

I helped transfer papers from one van to the other then sent them on their way. Nola pulled up in her silver Mercedes as we finished. I was glad we lived in a small town where people knew her dead husband's life insurance paid for the expensive little car rather than her salary as my office manager.

No matter how friendly a small town can be, they're chock full of people who begrudge another's success. Advertisers, like Ed Stinger, would argue that if the paper was doing well enough to pay Nola the big bucks, then I should be able to cut the advertising rates.

Nola dragged her oversized Dooney & Burke bag from the front seat and slung it over her shoulder. "Good morning," she chirped in an I've-been-up-for-hours voice. It probably took her that long to apply her makeup and do her hair. "Another edition hits the streets. The phone will be burning this afternoon."

I grinned. "Nothing too controversial this time. The town council didn't meet."

We went in and both huddled around Betsy. I had been in such a rush to get the kids out the door and to Doretha's, I hadn't paid much attention to how really cold it was. Emma was wearing a short-sleeved shirt and no jacket. I made a mental note to change out their seasonal clothes before the soccer moms cast judgment. I had enough change of clothes for Ivy to last a few days but would have to eventually go back to Trish's for her things. That was one trip I wasn't looking forward to.

While Nola checked messages, I scoured the paper for the tiniest of errors council member Nancy Farmer would find. A retired schoolteacher, she thrived on pointing out the typos.

Not finding any, I put the paper away and called Ridge. His secretary put me right through.

"Good morning." His voice was still fighting off morning dryness.

"Can I come by? I need to talk to you about something. There's a connection between Trish and the ginseng."

He cleared his throat. "I'm scheduled to speak at the Kiwanis meeting today at lunch. I'll be leaving around eleven thirty, but if you can make it before then, I'm all yours."

"Hot on the campaign trail, huh?"

He scoffed. "I'll just be glad when it's over."

On a smaller scale, I understood where he was coming from. No one liked having every facet of their life scrutinized. Being the owner and publisher of *The Jackson Creek Chronicle* brought a small amount of name recognition with it, which I despised.

I did a quick scan of my schedule. "I'll see you around nine."

"See you then."

I stared at the phone after we hung up. This case was forcing us together even if we didn't want it to. Funny thing was, the pain that had accumulated over the years had lost its edge. It wasn't as sharp or debilitating as it used to be. More like a dull ache you learned to live with. Maybe it was finally time to let go of a few things.

Nola breezed past me, heading to her desk. "So how did Ivy make out last night?"

Jolted back to the here and now, I forced a sad smile. "Okay, I guess. She started asking for her mommy."

Nola's expression turned sour. "Oh no. How are you going to handle that?"

I shrugged. "I said her mommy was in heaven and left it at that. I'm sure the more her language skills improve, the harder the questions will get though."

Nola frowned then sighed deeply. "Poor thing."

The phone rang, putting an end to the conversation. I was glad. If I never had to say another thing about how a toddler was coping with the death of her mother, I'd be happy. With Nola busy, I opened the public records database program on my computer and did a search for Greg Hastings. Four were listed from the area, two in Tennessee and two in North Carolina. My bet was the two North Carolinians were one and the same. Gregory Aster Hastings and Greg A. Hastings.

I scanned over his information then slammed the brakes as if the light had suddenly gone from yellow to red. Greg had three arrests with one conviction for assault and battery. Got a suspended sentence with two years of probation. All three instances were domestic disturbances with the last one allegedly occurring about three years ago.

Bile burned my insides so bad I wanted to vomit. I forced myself to breathe then leaned back in my chair and studied the screen. I knew Sherry. She and Greg had a daughter in the same grade as Emma. We had chaperoned several school field trips together. Apparently, daughters in the same grade weren't the only thing we'd had in common.

This new twist made me even more anxious to talk to Ridge. There was a connection, no matter how small, between Greg, Trish, and the ginseng. Finding out how deep the connection ran was suddenly a target. At eight thirty, I gathered my notepad and bag and told Nola I was going to the sheriff's office.

The Jackson County Sheriff's office was in the former Jackson Creek Bank & Trust's ancient three-story clapboard building with yellowed windows. Three vaults tucked away in the dank basement were made into seldom used six by eight holding cells. The real prisoners, those who would be staying more than a night, were transported down to Ashe County. Minnie's Cafe delivered meals to anyone needing overnight accommodations.

Ridge's office was on the ground floor down a short hallway fronted by a green marble counter that was once used by the bank's tellers. It was now Annie Thompson's desk, where she sat overlooking the small lobby. She'd been the secretary to four sheriffs, including Ridge. While most department employees worked at the discretion of the sheriff, Annie came with the job. It was something that was understood from one sheriff to another.

She glanced up from the computer monitor. Her lips arched upward in a welcoming smile. "Why Ava Logan—haven't seen you in a while. You've cut your hair." She removed her glasses, pushing the end of one of the pink arms between her teeth. "I like it. Very flattering."

"Thank you. It's a whole lot easier to manage. Just wash and go." I tucked a stray lock behind my ear.

"You get it cut down at Clip-N-Curls?"

"Yes ma'am. Even used the coupon they run in the paper."

She giggled followed by a little wink. "Grayson's in his office. You can go on back."

"Thank you." I smiled then headed to Ridge's office, surprised to find Detective Sullivan already there. I could have used the bags under Sullivan's eyes as a purse.

Ridge's office was small and in need of a good dusting. Forever at the mercy of the county commissioner's budget, Ridge was a master at pinching pennies, especially during an election year. The cleaning crew must have been the first to go. The office was sparsely decorated with certificates and awards and an old framed photo of the Atlanta Braves pitchers known as the Fab Five. He did love his baseball.

He was seated at his desk with Sullivan standing beside him. Crime scene photos were splayed out in front of them. Like a horrific car accident, I couldn't look away from a photo of Trish's twisted body.

"Hope you don't mind, I asked Steve to sit in with us." Apparently he noticed me staring at the picture and gathered it and the others into a stack. He handed it off to Sullivan.

I finally blinked, burying the images. "No, of course I don't mind." I did, but what could I say? It was hard to explain something you didn't understand yourself. Sullivan had every right to sit in on the conversation. Trish's murder was his case and the poaching now seemed connected.

"How's Ivy?"

"She was cranky yesterday. I don't know if she didn't feel well or what."

Sullivan sighed. "Strep throat's going around. Two of mine have it. We're waiting for the other two to get it." He shrugged in a what-can-you-do-about-it manner.

For a moment, I almost felt sorry for him. He always looked so damn tired. I don't remember Cole or Emma requiring *that* much energy. But I had been a lot younger back then too. Sullivan was pushing forty with four under the age of eight. If the adoption with Ivy worked out, I might look as tired in a few years.

I sat down in one of the two visitor's chairs across from Ridge's desk then took out my notepad. "Is this an I'll-show-you-mine-if-you-show-me-yours thing?"

Ridge laughed. Sullivan didn't. I flipped open my notepad. "I met with a ginseng buyer named Tiny Cormack yesterday in Roan Mountain. He said Trish was one of his best diggers."

Ridge and Sullivan glanced at one another. I couldn't gauge if the information was new to them or not. I continued, "Cormack said Trish told him she had a permit to dig Pisgah Forest. I haven't checked yet if she did, but I can't see any reason why she would lie about that."

Sullivan clicked his tongue. "Digging on federal land carries jail time. That's reason enough to lie."

"Yeah, but why even admit that's where it came from? I mean, if she didn't have a permit, why didn't she just say she dug it at Joe Blow's? Why lie about it?"

Sullivan blew a sharp breath and stuffed his hands into his jeans pockets. "Is this going in the paper?"

The sharpness of the question caught me off guard. It took me a moment to recover. In that moment, I wasn't sure why I was even there. Who was helping whom with what? Since Ridge wasn't jumping in to referee, or to defend me, I went for it myself. "Okay— here's the deal, Steve. I had planned to interview your boss about the annual poaching problem—yes, for the paper, if there was a story there. In *my* investigation about the poaching problem, I discovered Trish had a connection to ginseng, primarily to this Tiny Cormack. I was told by a source to talk to Aster Hastings about the poaching on his land—"

"Aster's pretty sick from what I hear." Ridge's voice registered true concern.

I nodded. "He is. His boy, Greg, is picking for him now. Sue told me without that extra money they got for the 'seng, she didn't know how they'd make it."

Sullivan crossed his arms, glaring at me. "So how is this connected to Trish?"

"When I interviewed Tiny Cormack, he told me Trish was in there last Friday and she hit big. There were two men in line behind her waiting to cash in and one of them was Greg Hastings, Aster's son."

Ridge leaned into his desk, his eyes locked on mine. "Greg Hastings has a short fuse. He's been a guest here a couple times. His prints will be on file." He looked up at Sullivan, who quickly gathered up his case file.

"I'm on it," he said, a new spark of energy in his eyes. He hurried out and cussed the old caged-door elevator in the hallway loud enough his voice carried back into Ridge's office.

I sat back in the chair, satisfied with myself.

CHAPTER 15

Late that Friday afternoon, I learned to never underestimate the time it took a twelve-year-old to get ready for what she considered a date. A shower followed by blow-dried hair followed by a flat iron, coupled with three outfit changes and enough makeup to qualify as a Covergirl spokesperson and she was finally ready.

I was in the bedroom packing Ivy's diaper bag when Emma came in and asked if I needed help. I stared at the girl that used to be my daughter, then pointed a stern finger toward the bathroom. "Off, Emma. The whole purpose of makeup is to enhance, not hide."

"Is the red lipstick too much?"

I shoved a handful of diapers in the bag then turned around and cut Emma an I'm-not-happy look. "Well, that and the entire tube of mascara is a bit much."

"It's not mascara. They're false lashes. Look." She turned sideways and batted the fake lashes so I could get a better view.

They looked like long skinny spider legs growing out of her eyelids. "Where in the...where'd you get those?"

"Abby Reynolds gave them to me."

"Okay, well, they need to come off. You're not wearing fake anything."

"But Mom—"

"Take them off, Emma." I stuffed Ivy's blanket in the bag while my irritation rose. I did not want an argument to precede our family fun night.

Her child-like eyes, so happy seconds ago framed by fake lashes, were now wet with tears. My heart cried for her. I remembered being twelve and having no one explain why some things were the way they were. *Just the way things are*, Doretha would say. "Look...Emma—"

"I know, you think I'm too young. But I'm twelve, Mom." She wasn't being defiant, just a kid trying to speak honestly.

I motioned for her to sit down on the bed. "Age isn't it, Emma. This boy—Mason. He asked Emma-with-no-makeup if she was going to the football game, not Emma with false eyelashes. Don't you think it would be better if the Emma he goes to school with shows up rather than someone ready for the runway?"

Her adolescent mind was processing the information while her lips were turned upside down in a pout. She huffed, admitting in her own way I was right.

"Besides," I continued, "boys Mason's age can be intimidated very easily by a pretty girl. It might be best to hold back a little. Know what I mean?"

"You mean it might overwhelm him?"

I bit my lip to trap the chuckle and prevent it from escaping. "Yeah. No need to overwhelm him."

She seemed to accept that it was for Mason's own good she go bare-faced and headed to the bathroom to wash the makeup off. I finished packing Ivy's diaper bag, having no idea what I had already packed and what was still needed. A couple more diapers wouldn't hurt anything. Ivy sat at my feet in the floor force-feeding a teddy bear and protested when I wrestled her into a jacket.

A few minutes later, I had her buckled into her car seat with a fresh-faced Emma beside her. "Have you got her stroller?" Emma asked.

We shared a dumbfounded expression. I didn't have the child's stroller, a high chair, or all the other staples that came with a toddler. "I'll just have to carry her, I guess."

"Are we ever going to get her stuff from her house? She'd probably like her own toys."

"As soon as Ridge gives the all clear, I'll go back over there." If I had the money, I'd just buy everything new.

Jackson Creek High School was as old as the mountains surrounding it. The campus had been well maintained over the years, adding an annex along with a math and science building. A football field had been carved into the side of a slope years ago. Brent petitioned the school board every year for a new field, saying the field goal was too close to the wall of granite and players could be injured having to come to an abrupt halt from a full run.

Doretha and her litter of kids were waiting on us in the school parking lot. A black Jackson Creek Panther stretched across her chest, making it look like the cat on the sweatshirt was taking a bite out of her breast. She swiveled her hips and pointed at Emma. I laughed as Emma rolled her eyes.

Despite the restraints of a car seat, Ivy had managed to take her shoes off during the short ride, so I hurriedly put them back on her kicking feet then hoisted her to my hip. She was squirmy with excitement and clapped wildly at the sight of Doretha.

"Sweet precious baby." Doretha kissed her on the forehead.

The sweet precious baby grew heavy as we tromped through the parking lot toward the gate. Energy blasted from the stadium like a fast-acting drug, seeping deep into my bones with each beat of the drum. A cornucopia of smells from the concession stand filled the night air, making me fully aware at some point during the game I was going to have to buy hot dogs, popcorn, and possibly cotton candy.

Near the concession stand, I spotted Greg and Sherry Hastings in line. I turned to Doretha. "Why don't you take the kids on in and get a seat. I'll be there in just a second."

She gave me an odd look but didn't question anything then herded the kids toward the bleachers. With Ivy still on my hip, I approached Greg and Sherry. After discovering he was a wife beater, I'd never understand why she was still with him. But I wasn't exactly one to give advice in that department.

"Hey, Greg. Sherry," I said, offering my best smile.

"Hey, girl. Haven't seen you in ages." Sherry reached out and lightly tickled Ivy's chin. She yelled over the thumping music, leaning in closer to be heard. "How have you been?"

"Can't complain. Y'all?"

She nodded all was well, but her face said otherwise. Although the bruises were hidden, they were there.

"Greg, I interviewed your father the other day about the 'seng market. He said you were picking for him now."

He grunted as they moved up in line. "I help 'em out a little bit."

I moved up with them. The closer we got to the window, the stronger the smells of Friday night games became. "I think you and Trish Givens used the same buyer."

Sherry glanced at Greg, then at me. She reached out again and stroked Ivy's hair. "Wasn't that her mother? I didn't know she dug 'seng."

"I saw her some over at the metal shop," Greg said.

My arms ached from the twenty pounds I wasn't used to carrying. I shifted her on my hip. "That would be Tiny Cormack's place?"

Greg chomped on a piece of gum like he was growing bored. "Yeah. Tiny Cormack."

He stepped up to the concession window then ordered two hot dogs all the way, an order of fries, and two bottled waters. He seemed in no hurry to return to our conversation.

"Hey, Greg, mind if I come by one evening next week to talk about the 'seng market? The poaching is heating up again."

Shrugging, he showed way more interest in the fixing of his hot dogs than discussing ginseng. "I guess. We ain't had much of a poaching problem this year though, so I don't know why you need to talk to me."

Sherry sidled beside me so she didn't have to scream. "We'll be home later tomorrow if you want to come over then."

For a moment, I considered canceling our hiking trip. I'd be too tired to even think about interviewing anyone afterward. Still balanced on my hip, Ivy was growing heavy, and restless. Canceling wouldn't be fair to Cole and Emma. They'd given enough, including peace of mind, to Trish's murder. They didn't need to give up another day as a family too.

"Can't do it tomorrow. We're hiking Porter's Peak."

Greg handed Sherry a hot dog and drink. "You still have our number, don't you?" she asked me.

"I do. I'll call first of the week."

She nodded before Greg tugged her toward the bleachers. Knowing what I knew about him now, I despised every movement. I saw a controlling cowardly sonofabitch in his every breath.

Whether he was a sonofabitch enough to kill Trish was the question.

I joined my crew in the stands. Emma had directed our entourage where to sit according to where her friends were seated. Close enough, yet not so close we would embarrass her. She craned her neck looking for her "date."

The Friday night home games had become a ritual, but this was the first that I had a toddler in tow. I was suddenly aware of the steepness of the concrete stands and how the crowd moved around one another. And now very afraid of letting Ivy out of my sight, or even off my lap for that matter.

She bounced up and down in my lap to the rhythm of the marching band and clapped her chubby hands. Emma elbowed my arm, lobbing her head to one side in a not-so nonchalant manner. "There he is," she mouthed.

There were no less than ten boys in the direction she had bobbed her head. I didn't want to just nod and say "nice"—this boy had my daughter's heart, temporarily, so I wanted to know which one he was. "Which one?" I whispered, although there was no need. The marching band was louder than any conversation hoped to be.

"Red shirt, brown hair."

"Glasses?"

She rolled her eyes. "Of course, Mom. He plays violin. Isn't he *hot*?"

Hot wasn't the word I would have chosen. Grayson Ridge was hot. Mason Walker was a little on the geeky side. A lot on the geeky side. I supposed, in his own twelve-year-old geeky style, he *was* cute. The more I watched him, the cuter he became.

"You do know around these parts, it's not called a violin. It's a fiddle," I said, sharing my limited knowledge of mountain music.

"Lindsey Stirling doesn't play the *fiddle*." She grinned, then gasped and held her breath when he looked over and waved.

"Wave back," I said between my teeth so he wouldn't see me giving her instructions.

She offered a tiny wave as redness crept up her neck and spread over her cheeks. When Mason motioned for her to come join the group, she turned to me for permission and my heart melted. I was proud that she was still considerate enough to seek my permission. My own insides fluttered with memories of the heart-thumping light-headed feeling a boy could bring. Such a wonderfully confusing time.

"Go on. Just don't leave my sight."

She leapt up and rushed to join her friends a few rows down from us. It made me happy to see her glide so easily into a group of her peers. She was well liked and genuinely accepted into a large cluster of friends, yet didn't depend on the acceptance to define her. Maybe I hadn't done such a bad job of raising this kid of mine after all.

"You know he'll be the first of many. She's a cute girl." Doretha leaned in so she didn't have to shout over the band.

My eyes grew moist with thoughts of the years, and heartaches, to come. I wanted to save her from the broken heart of a teenage crush, from the emptiness when he doesn't call.

The crowd erupted with cheers and shouts as Brady O'Reilly scored the night's first touchdown. Doretha leapt up and shimmied her hips, hooting and hollering for the Panthers. The kids with her did the same. Even Ivy clapped crazily, although she had no idea what she was clapping for. Laughing, I wrapped her in a hug and kissed the top of her head.

A tap at my shoulder startled me for a second, then surprise took over as Rick sat down in Emma's empty spot. "Mind if I sit here until Emma comes back?"

"Of course not." I smiled, trying to remember what we had fought about the night before. And then Ivy squirmed, bringing everything back in clear focus. I pushed the argument back down and hoped it stayed there. Tonight was about having fun.

He held out a small bag of popcorn in Ivy's direction. "Can she have it?"

"Sure." I took the peace offering from him then offered her a handful. "Can you say *thank you*?"

She scooped a few pieces out of my hand and jammed them in her open mouth, eyeing Rick suspiciously. I couldn't really blame her; he hadn't been exactly warm and cuddly toward her.

Doretha looked over and smiled her approval. She leaned forward, speaking across me. "Hey, Rick, thanks for dropping off those new campaign signs."

"Thanks for asking for them."

They went back and forth, carrying on a conversation around me that I wasn't a part of. I wondered if Doretha hadn't opened this wound on purpose. Anything to demonstrate how much she preferred Rick over anyone else I might have a soft spot for.

I lifted Ivy off my lap and stood. "I'm going to bow out of talking politics if y'all don't mind. I'm going to let her stretch a little."

Rick looked blindsided. "Want me to come with you?"

I shook my head, then smiled my best smile hoping he'd know I wasn't angry. I just didn't want to be part of the politics. "No, you're fine. Keep Doretha straight for me. I'm just going to walk up here with Ivy for a minute. Stretch our legs a little."

With Ivy on my hip, I climbed the steps and headed for the exit. I put her down behind the chest-high concrete wall and let her play in the gravel a moment. From my vantage point, I could still keep an eye on Emma and see the game. I could also see Cole keeping the bench warm. But my gaze kept going back to Doretha and Rick, who had slid into my place. They had their heads together in a conspiratorial way, although I knew if they were chatting it was hard to hear over the band. Still, something about it bugged me.

I zipped my jacket to ward off the night air, wondering if I needed to pull Ivy's hood up. It had been years since I worried about stuff like ear infections and sore throats. Maybe part of Rick's argument had been valid. It had been a long time since there had been a little one to worry about. Just as I was about to reach for her, Ivy picked up a tiny handful of gravel and flung it in the air. A small group of women standing against the wall turned and looked my way.

"Ivy—no, no." I brushed the rocks from her hand while embarrassment flushed my face. Hopefully, the surrounding darkness cloaked the reddened cheeks.

One of the women, Lori Abbott, reached down and stroked Ivy's hair. "She's adorable. So sad about her mother."

Another said, "It was so hard to believe. I'm scared to be alone in my own house now."

Megan O'Reilly, Brady's mother, gazed at Ivy. "Do they have any suspects yet?" Although looking at Ivy, I assumed she directed the question to me.

"I don't think so. If they do, they're not sharing that information yet." I picked Ivy up and propped her on my hip.

Megan reached out and tickled under Ivy's chin. "It must have been horrible. Finding her mother like you did."

Before I could answer, the crowd erupted in cheers. Brady's name and number flashed across the scoreboard.

Lori clapped wildly, punching the air with her fist. Chanting like she had as head cheerleader during our high school days. She grabbed Megan in a hug. "That's your boy."

I wanted to thank Megan for letting Brady bring Cole home every day from practice but didn't. Their small group was too wrapped up in their celebration to remember I was still standing there.

When you peeled away the superficial layers, wiped away the

mascara and lip gloss, they weren't bad people. We probably all wanted the same things—our kids to be healthy and happy, a safe home. The things that mattered. At least that's what I told myself as I headed back to the bleachers unnoticed. I reclaimed my seat, sliding in between Rick and Doretha, then plopped Ivy back on my lap.

"Everything okay?" Rick asked. He slipped his arm around my waist, and I didn't pull back. In that moment, I liked what he was offering.

"It's all good." I kissed him lightly on the cheek and settled in for the rest of the game.

CHAPTER 16

The next morning, Cole bounded down the stairs and into the kitchen already dressed in his hiking gear. He snatched a piece of freshly cooked bacon from the platter and did a silly little jig around Finn.

"You're full of energy this morning." I poured myself a second cup of coffee.

"Ready to get my hike on. Y'all ready?" He popped Emma on the top of the head.

"Ouch!"

"Cole—settle please." I pulled a plate from the cabinet then filled it with scrambled eggs, bacon, and a piece of toast. He poured himself a glass of milk then took the offered plate.

He sat down beside Ivy and pretended to grab a piece of her bacon. She giggled then offered it to him anyway. A smile tickled my lips. I knew not every day would be idyllic, but I wasn't going to let the moment slip away without appreciation.

After breakfast, we gathered our gear and loaded the Tahoe. Finn bounded into the backseat, unsure what to make of Ivy and the car seat in his usual claimed spot. He turned his body around in circles, eventually wedging himself between Emma and Ivy. Emma squealed with disgust every time his hairy butt brushed against her. Cole laughed, which made Ivy laugh, which made me chuckle. It was going to be a good day. It was starting out so well, I toyed with the thought of farming the kids off on Doretha for the night and calling Rick when we got back. It'd been a few weeks since we'd been together; maybe it would do us both good.

After dropping Ivy off, we headed for Porter's Peak. It was a moderate-rated trail we had tackled several times, even Emma. Truth was, we had probably met the challenge and should move on. Deep down both Cole and I worried Emma might not be ready for a more advanced trail and leaving her wasn't an option.

Traffic crawled through town with cars filled with out-of-towners hoping to breathe in the fresh air while snapping pictures of the palette of colors the mountains offered. It would only get worse as peak season blossomed, then it would settle back down after the leaves dropped. Sometimes it picked back up in the winter during ski season, but Jackson Creek was only a stopover for snow lovers, having no ski trails of its own to offer.

Cole's cell rang as I passed through the last stop light and pressed the gas, anxious to move away from the traffic. "Yeah," he said as he answered. "What's up?" He listened for a moment then mouthed the word *Brady* to me. "Nah. We're doing the hiking thing. Besides, my mom's not gonna let me go deer hunting without an adult." He burst out laughing then nipped it when I cut him a nasty glance. "Yeah, okay. I'll text you when we get back." He chatted for another minute or two then hung up.

"He didn't want to come hiking?"

"Nah. He's hunting over at the Milters' property. Asked if I could go with him next weekend."

I cut my eyes at him. "And you knew my answer to you deer hunting with no adult without even asking. Smart boy." Dove hunting, squirrel hunting—they were different. The gun was pointed up. With deer hunting, the gun was pointed chest level.

"Well, we've got a whole week to argue about it, don't we?" He grinned wide then punched up his music playlist on his phone and settled in for some of the finest Appalachia music offered. At least I had instilled a love of mountain music in my kids rather than Billboard's Top Forty.

Once we made it through town, we picked up the four-lane highway. Ten miles out, the road grew more curvy and forested as it turned back into a two-lane that led to the trail head. Porter's Peak was a four or eight-mile loop that began and ended at a paved parking lot. The trail's shorter loop, along with a couple picnic tables and a bathroom facility, made it great for families. Today, at least so far, we had the lot to ourselves.

After parking, we climbed out and unloaded the gear. Finn sniffed along the tree line then followed a scent to the trail head a few feet away. He waited anxiously while we slipped into our daypacks. The crisp air smelled fresh and I welcomed it into my lungs and mind, breathing it in through long deep breaths. Although the morning was cool, I knew we wouldn't be long on the trail before I'd be shrugging out of my zippered sweatshirt. The idea of shedding even more clothes charmed my thoughts.

I checked my phone for a signal. "Y'all go ahead. I'm going to call Rick for a second."

Cole rolled his eyes. He nudged Emma toward the trail head. "Come on, dork, Mom needs to make a booty call."

"Cole Logan!"

Emma blushed as much as I did and hurried away, shaking her head like she was trying to dislodge the image. If we survived the hike, I would kill Cole when we got back home.

I prayed for a signal, then breathed a sigh when I saw four bars pop up. "Good morning."

"Good morning to you too. I thought y'all were hiking today." He stumbled over words, the morning grogginess making him thick-tongued.

"We are. I just wanted to see if you wanted to come over tonight. I'm thinking of maybe farming the kids off...if you know what I mean." I gnawed on my bottom lip, anticipating his answer.

He cleared away the morning dryness from his throat. "I'll bring my toothbrush. And a bottle of wine."

"I'll see you around seven?"

"Oh yeah."

A smile dominated my face. I took a deep breath and tried to un-smile before joining the kids. I didn't want to give credence to Cole's remark. I was Supermom. I didn't need booty calls.

I adjusted my daypack and joined them. "Ready?"

"We're spending the night with Doretha." Cole elbowed Emma and they both giggled. He then offered me his hand for a high-five. I reluctantly accepted the gesture, wondering if he was high-fiving because we were ready to hit the trail or because Mom had indeed scored.

We hit the trail with Cole in the lead, flanked by Finn, Emma in the middle, and me bringing up the rear. We hiked a good hour before stopping for a water break. We sat on boulders nestled into a slope overlooking a valley below. The sky faded into the horizon, merging with the mighty Blue Ridge Mountains and created a canvas of varying shades of blue.

"Pretty, isn't it?" Emma said.

"Yes, it is." I slipped my arm around her shoulder, giving her a gentle hug.

"You think they're still out there?"

I pulled back and looked at her. "Who?"

"Whoever killed Trish."

For a moment, the beauty of the mountains, the tranquility of the land evaporated, leaving me feeling violated. I hated the sonofabitch, whoever he was, for taking away that calm.

Cole tossed a rock over the edge of the mountain. "Well yeah, if they haven't made an arrest yet, they're still out there."

I stood, stretching my legs. I'd avoided talking to them in depth about Trish's murder but could now see maybe that had been a mistake. "Okay, here's the deal. Trish's murder probably wasn't random. Whoever killed her probably went there with the intention of killing her."

Emma's face wrenched with confusion. "Why would someone want to kill her?"

"We don't know. My point is, whoever killed Trish had a reason for killing her. Not you. Not me. Whoever went to her house that morning went there with a purpose and killing Trish *was* the purpose. Does that make sense?"

"She means there's probably no psycho serial killer guy lurking around somewhere out there." Cole pointed his water bottle toward the valley.

Emma nodded, apparently more comfortable with her brother's explanation than mine. I ruffled her hair then repacked Finn's portable water bowl. "Ready to get back at it?"

We headed out, moving toward the north face. About two and a half hours in, I was feeling every bit of my age. With about two miles left, I unzipped my sweatshirt and wrapped it around my waist. Sweat already trickled down my face, spilling onto my cheeks and neck. I sucked each breath in deeper and deeper, the chilled air cooling my burning lungs. Emma was doing a better job at keeping up than I was. "Break," I managed to squeak out before Cole and Finn rounded the next bend.

I leaned over, pressing my hands into my aching thighs. Whatever made me think I was able to hike an eight-mile moderate-rated trail with no preparation?

"You okay?" Emma asked. Cole and Finn backtracked a few yards and joined us.

Nodding, I sipped from my near-empty water bottle. I used the sleeve of my sweatshirt to wipe the moisture from my lips. While I stood there catching my breath, I spotted a series of holes in the slope. The forest floor had been dug out in places, leaving several gaping root holes. The trail of cavities grew thin and ended under a bushy cluster of mountain laurel. But on the other side of the laurel was a plentiful bed of ginseng, roots, red berries and all.

I glanced around, trying to get my bearings on our location. Porter's Peak was part of the Pisgah Forest, that much I knew. Whoever was digging this spot of 'seng would have to have a permit to dig on federal land. Trish had told Tiny Cormack she had a permit. I wondered how many permits the Ranger's office issued.

Cole peered over my shoulder. "What's wrong?"

I pointed to the holes. "Someone's been digging ginseng."

"Isn't that illegal on federal land?"

"Unless you have a permit."

Finn's ears perked up then the dog let out a *woof* that rattled us all. Cole reached out to rub his head and quiet him but Finn persisted. Emma moved toward me, fear growing in her eyes.

Suddenly, a blast ripped through the forest, followed by another, shattering the silence. Cole knocked Emma to the ground hard then scrambled to pull me down. Finn barked viciously at the trees, baring teeth between snarling growls. Another shot rang out, this one closer. Emma screamed for me, crying hysterically. Cole was crouching, partially covering Emma with his own body, peering over her shoulder to get a look at the shooter.

My heart was throbbing in my throat, pounding in my ears. Every smell, every sound painfully amplified. Leaves rustled in the distance, footfalls growing nearer.

"We've got to get to better cover." I yanked at the both of them, shoving them toward a massive boulder about twenty yards down the trail.

Shots followed us as we scrambled toward the giant rock, zinging off the trees. I ran alongside Emma, covering her head with my arms while Cole yanked Finn by the leash. We dove behind the makeshift cover with more shots trailing us.

Frantic, I dug the Tahoe keys out of my pocket and shoved them at Cole. "Go!"

"What? No!"

"Cole—go. Take Emma and Finn. Go get the car. I'll be right behind you."

He was shaking his head, crying. My son was crying. "I'm not leaving you."

"Cole—listen to me. Whoever it is can't follow both us if we go in different directions. Go. Get to the car. I'll be right behind you."

Emma sobbed and clutched at me as Cole pulled her away. My heart shattered into a million pieces as I let go of her and pushed her toward her brother. He tugged her down the hill with one hand, and with the other, pulled Finn's leash.

When they disappeared beyond a ridge, I bolted toward an outcrop, sliding in behind it as shots blasted off the rock. The shots followed me down the trail, zapping in their wake leaves and small branches just over my head. I covered my head with my arms as I dove behind a slab of granite.

I couldn't breathe, suffocating on pure fear and adrenaline. My heart exploded in my ears, deafening me to the sound of my own sobs. A bullet flew over my head and exploded on the ground in front of me. Paralyzed with fear, I screamed out. Images of Cole and Emma and the fear that had ravaged their beautiful faces boiled inside of me.

Maybe a mile. That was the distance between me and my kids. Between us and safety. And now we were separated. I scooped up a handful of broken branches and threw them to the opposite side of the trail, hoping to draw fire in that direction. When the shot rang out, I ran with everything in me. My legs exploded into an inferno as white hot pain shot up each limb, burning dormant muscles into action. Yet I ran. I would not stop until I knew my kids were safe. I could not stop.

I ran toward a cluster of pines, then beyond to the next rock. From there, I could see the edge of the parking lot, the asphalt gray and worn. As I blinked back stinging tears, the rear bumper of the Tahoe came into view. As Cole backed it toward the trail head, I leapt up and made a run for it.

Pain skittered up my legs, the muscles cramping with knots. My lungs were on fire with each gasping breath. A series of shots trailed me, finally stopping as I dove into the open passenger door.

"Go!" I screamed at Cole. I barely had time to close the door as he gunned the engine. His knuckles were white from gripping the steering wheel. He had his seatbelt on.

Emma was hunkered down in the backseat, the look of sheer terror on her face permanently etched into my mind. Finn was barking and trying to turn his big frame in circles as he watched out the window.

"The Ranger's station's about two miles north. Turn left out of the parking lot. Hurry!" My words were clipped, the shortness of breath robbing them of syllables.

Before we could make it onto the road, a full-size white SUV with the green stripe and familiar arrowhead logo met us head on. Cole slammed the brakes, sending Emma and Finn into the floorboard. The ranger and I leapt out at the same time, him with his gun drawn.

"Up there—I don't know who it was," I stammered, pointing toward the forest. "They fired several shots...they just kept firing."

CHAPTER 17

Parks Service Ranger Todd Blackwell's office was cramped and cluttered, but being inside the four dingy walls felt safe. My ears still rang with the sounds of gunshots and my own screaming. And Emma's crying. I'd never forget as long as I lived the sound of her fear.

Blackwell took our statements with little emotion, like being shot at while hiking was an everyday occurrence. Maybe he was just being super calm so the terrified family in his office could take a deep breath and focus. My heart rate had yet to return to normal.

My hands shook while I sipped from a cup of tepid water Blackwell had offered. He looked maybe mid-forties, with an athletic build and no-nonsense eyes. I had spoken with him before for an article about an orphaned bear cub. He was pleasant enough, but it didn't take a genius to recognize he was much more comfortable with nature than people.

I sat in a metal folding chair next to his desk while Cole sat in a plastic one a few feet away. Emma sat on the tile floor in front of Blackwell's desk with her arms around Finn's thick neck. She had said very little since our escape to safety.

Cole stared at the floor, picking nervously at his cuticles. "They were using a laser scope." His voice was quiet, reserved.

Blackwell and I looked at one another with our mouths hanging open, then at him. "Pardon?" Blackwell asked for the same confirmation I wanted. Or didn't want. The implication was beyond frightening.

Cole finally lifted his eyes and looked at me, then at Blackwell. "They were using a scope."

Blackwell leaned forward. "How do you know?"

"I saw the green light." He stopped picking at the cuticle and looked up at Blackwell. "It was on my mom's forehead."

Blackwell cleared his throat. "Are you sure that's what you saw?"

Cole nodded then glanced at me. He quickly turned his attention back to the cuticle. The act was more of an aversion than an interest.

"I don't understand. What does that mean?" Emma asked.

Blackwell cleared his throat and began to speak but Cole interrupted. "It means someone was trying to kill Mom."

"That is *not* what it means. Don't scare her like that." My voice was stern. Maybe in an effort to hide my own fear.

"There was a freakin' green dot between your eyes, Mom—what do *you* think it meant?" He jammed his index finger against his forehead to illustrate his point.

I couldn't find my voice. Even if I had been able to speak, I didn't know what to say. I pushed a swell of tears back, refusing to show my kids how vulnerable and scared I felt at that moment.

A bell attached to the outside door jingled followed by a familiar voice. "Ava?"

Ridge? I jerked my head up as he entered Blackwell's office. It was all I could do not to jump up and rush to him, to the safety I knew his arms offered. Emma wasted no time seeking her own comfort. He wrapped her in a tight embrace then lightly kissed the top of her hair as she sobbed into his chest.

"I called him from the car." Cole looked at me, anticipating my question.

Emma wiped her face with the backs of her hands. "Someone was shooting at us. Are you going to arrest them?"

Ridge pulled away from her slightly and looked down into her tear-filled eyes. "Sweetheart, Ranger Blackwell will do everything he can to find out who was out there. It was probably just a hunter with really bad eyesight." He offered her comfort with a warm smile. "Why don't you and Cole take Finn out to the car. Maybe get him some water while I talk to your mom and Ranger Blackwell."

I wasn't too keen on the idea of them being outside these four walls by themselves but knew there were probably questions coming that they didn't need to hear the answers to.

I assumed Cole still had the car keys. "Stay in the car. Do not get out."

Emma tugged Finn's leash as Cole pulled himself up from the hard plastic chair. He stopped in front of Grayson and spoke quietly. "If they were hunting, Mom was the target. They used a green laser scope."

They shared a quick nod before Cole joined Emma and Finn. My breath hung in my throat as the doorbell jingled again and I knew my kids were now outside, exposed.

"I'm not sure what capacity you're here in, Sheriff." Blackwell offered his hand.

Ridge accepted the gesture. "I'm a family friend. Here to offer support."

On the verge...so on the verge, my toes were dangling off a cliff I'd backed away from so many times over the years. I couldn't stop the tears. I didn't want to stop them, allowing them to flow freely from my eyes and down my cheeks. In our moment of need, my son had called Grayson Ridge. Not Rick, nor Doretha.

He knelt in front of me and used his thumbs to gently wipe the tears.

Blackwell retrieved a box of tissues from a desk drawer then pulled one out and handed it to me. "Her son seems to think she was the intended target. Judging from the number of shots fired, I think he may be right."

I dabbed at my eyes then wiped my nose on the tissue. "I found holes along the trail where ginseng had been dug up. We were looking at the holes when the first shots were fired."

Blackwell scrunched his brows. "No one's supposed to be digging on that trail."

But Trish had said she had a permit. "You didn't issue permits this year?"

He shook his head. "No. Not a one."

Why would Trish lie about that? My stomach jumped, twisting and turning with thoughts I didn't want to think.

"You think you might have walked up on a poaching site?" Ridge pulled Cole's vacated seat closer and sat down.

I brushed at my eyes again, wiping away the sentiment-laced fog. "It would have to be if there were no permits issued. But we were the only ones on the trail. At least I thought we were."

"Poachers don't dig right on a trail." Blackwell scratched his chin like he was scratching away his perplexion.

"Ava, who all have you talked to about the poaching problem?" Ridge asked.

Blackwell cocked his head. "What do you mean?"

I sniffled then tossed the tissue in the wastebasket beside Blackwell's desk. "I was asked by someone to look into an alleged poaching problem for the paper. I've talked to a couple local growers and buyers, but none would..." I stumbled on the words. "None would resort to *that*. Besides, they would've had to have known I was going to be here today, right?"

Ridge ran his hand over the dark morning stubble along his jawline. "Unless they followed you."

I heard what he was saying but I couldn't comprehend the implication. "But the ones I've talked to have been buyers or the *victims* of poaching. Why would they want to hurt me?"

"The buyers would have as big a stake in it as anyone," Blackwell offered. "Especially if they have contracts to fill."

My heart jerked as I remembered Greg Hastings. He knew how much Trish had scored on her last dig. Money he needed for his sick father. And he knew I'd be at Porter's Peak.

Ridge followed us home and stayed with us the rest of the day, lying to Emma when necessary. He kept up the deer hunting charade for her sake. Although I had never advocated lying to my kids, I didn't object this time. Convincing Cole would be a bit harder.

Emma played with Ivy in the backyard on a wooden playset Emma had outgrown years ago. The swings and plastic slide had weathered life well. It made me smile knowing Ivy was part of its resurrection, breathing new life into its stagnant existence. On the back patio looking out at the playset and the river just beyond, Ridge taught Cole the fine art of grilling as burgers sizzled over the charcoal. I sat near the fire pit, taking it all in, relaxed in the warmth of the building flames. The river moved slowly, pushing its lifeblood downstream with a gentle hand. The music of the flowing water was subtle, barely there. But it was always there. It was a part of my life I couldn't deny.

Ridge gazed in my direction with eyes softer than the pale-colored sunset. I looked away, afraid to give in. There was still so much hurt, so much guilt that bubbled to the surface every time I looked at him.

The playful banter between him and my son was interrupted by Brady, who joined the impromptu cookout. Dressed in his hunting camo, he and Cole threw a couple teasing punches at one another before Brady walked over beside me, pulled up a chair, and sat down. "Hey, Ms. Logan. Did y'all have a good hike?"

I pushed a lock of hair out of my eyes. I wasn't up to explaining what had happened and how I feared Greg Hastings' infamous temper had gotten the better of him again. Or how Trish might have been poaching and went and got herself killed over it. But the pain of the fear wouldn't let me glamorize today's hike either. "It was good up until the last two miles. You'll have to go with us next time."

He picked up a stick and stoked the fire. "I'd like that. I haven't been hiking in a long time. Me and my dad used to go when I was a kid, but Mom never did. She doesn't like to break a sweat." His grin was sweet and sincere, making him look more like a twelve-year-old than the brawling football player he was.

"I spoke to your mom at the game last night."

He continued poking at the fire without saying anything. After a long moment, he finally spoke. "What'd she have to say?"

"Not much. Just chit chat."

He sighed heavily and leaned back in the chair. "She and my dad are fighting a lot lately. I think they might get a divorce."

"I'm sorry to hear that, Brady. It's always hard for a kid to discover their parents don't always have the answers, you know?" Truth be told, most kids I knew would be surprised at how much this parenting game their parents played was a hit and miss. There was no rule book. No game day plan to follow. Some kids became disillusioned when they learned our terrible secret.

"Burgers are ready." Grayson loaded dinner onto a platter.

I pulled myself up from the chair then stretched the kinks out of my back. My thighs ached and shin splits burnt my shins. Although we were regular hikers, I wasn't used to having to run. Ivy squealed in protest when Emma lifted her out of the swing. "Want to go get a cookie?" My daughter had learned the fine art of bribery from someone, and I was denying claim to that particular talent.

Inside, we ate charbroiled burgers with all the fixings, grilled corn on the cob, and baked potatoes on Styrofoam plates in the dining room. Ivy had her cookie instead of a baked potato and for the moment all was good.

We sat there at the table long after we had finished eating and talked about school, football, and the coming Halloween. Emma asked if she could be in charge of picking Ivy's costume. She asked if the tot could be a princess; Cole told her not to give the toddler false hope—there were no princesses in this house, everyone pulled their own weight. I laughed until my eyes dampened with happy tears.

A few minutes later, the relaxed, comfortable setting gave way as Rick came through the front door, a bottle of wine in his hand. The surprise on his face matched the expression on my own. I had messed up.

I leapt up and made a feeble attempt to welcome him, stumbling over my own words.

Cole looked from me to Rick. "Someone took a couple shots at us today. It was pretty scary for a while."

I wasn't sure if he was trying to rescue me, knowing I'd forgotten about my earlier invitation, or covering my ass because Ridge was there.

Rick stared at me, concern written deep into his face. "She didn't tell me. What happened?"

"Someone shot at you?" Brady asked. "Where at?"

Cole swallowed a mouthful of burger, still enjoying his meal despite the awkwardness. "Up on Porter's Peak."

"Maybe it was a deer hunter." Brady lifted a brow, proposing what we all hoped, but doubted.

"One shot, maybe. But not several."

The expression on Rick's face pricked at my heart. Concern, anger, and hurt showed in his eyes. I took the bottle of wine and gently squeezed his hand, leading him to the table.

"Hey guys, why don't y'all take Ivy in the sunroom and watch a movie."

No one protested. I assumed they welcomed an escape from what had turned into a thick cloud of tension. Rick sat down and stared at the bottle of wine for a moment, then looked directly at Ridge. "So what happened?"

I figured now wasn't the best time to point out I was still in the room. I took a deep breath and sat down beside Rick. "Well—we were hiking and about two miles from the trail head, we heard gunshots."

"And you don't think it was a deer hunter?" he asked Ridge, not me.

Ridge shook his head. "Probably not. Like Cole said, one shot, we could probably assume that. But not several."

"How many shots were there?"

"A lot," I answered, although, again, the question was directed to Ridge.

He glanced at Ridge then turned to me. "Did you report it to the *Ranger's* office?"

"He heard the shots and was on his way when we ran into him."

"What'd he say?"

"We think Ava may have stumbled onto a poaching site," Ridge answered.

"Poaching?" Rick stared at me as if he'd never heard the term. "Poaching what?"

"Ginseng. I'm doing an investigation into a supposed poaching problem and I was showing the kids some holes, right there on the trail, where it looked like it had been dug. That's when the shots started."

Rick pressed his fingers deep into his forehead and massaged the area like he was hoping to rub away a sharp pain. He exhaled a long breath. "You said you were *investigating* a poaching problem. Shouldn't that be something left up to the Sheriff's department?"

Ridge cleared his throat. "We're looking into it."

"Since when? Since shots were fired?"

"Rick—now's not the time." I surprised myself with how controlled my voice was.

He pushed away from the table and stood up, gesturing toward the table and the meal we'd finished. "No, I guess it's *not* the right time. Don't let me interrupt your dinner." He turned, storming through the living room toward the front door.

I leapt up and chased after him, catching him on the front porch. "Rick, please. Just listen to me. It's not what it looks like."

He stopped on the steps and spun around, facing me. The hurt in his eyes shone like a light in the dark. "What *does* it look like, Ava? You tell me."

The words wouldn't come. They clung to the inside of my throat like my heart hanging onto the past. Tears tumbled out of my eyes and spilled down my cheeks.

Rick pushed his hands in his pockets and let out a deep breath. "I can't keep doing this. I've tried, Ava. God knows, I've tried to help, to fix whatever it is that has you so broken."

His words knocked the breath out of me. "Fix me?"

He looked at me, then stared up at the full moon as if the old man held the answer. "Ava—"

"I'm not *broken*."

He sighed softly, shaking his head. "I had an uncle who was an alcoholic. God himself could have come down and said *you need help*, and he wouldn't have believed him. Until he was ready to admit he was...broken...there wasn't anything anyone could do to help him. Just something he had to figure out himself, I guess."

I watched him leave without saying anything. I didn't know what to say. My heart had shattered into a million heavy pieces that burdened my soul. The smothering thought that maybe, just maybe, he was right hummed around me like swarming bees.

Numb, I sat down on the top step, hugging my knees tightly, and cried. I'd lost track of how long I'd been sitting there when Ridge sat down beside me. The sobbing had settled into a tired sniffle. "I'm sorry you had to be in the middle of that." I laid my head on his shoulder.

He slipped an arm around my waist then kissed my tear-streaked cheek. "I'm sorry you're having to go through it."

The night air had turned cold, bringing shivers with it. I pulled the sleeves of my sweatshirt over my hands. Fireplaces scattered throughout the valley offered up the smell of wood burning in the hearths of neighbors. Still, I couldn't quite enjoy the comfort of where I was and whose shoulder I rested my head on.

"How do we move past it, Grayson?" I asked quietly.

"What happened to Tommy wasn't our fault, Ava. It never was."

I wiped a stream of tears from my face with my sleeve.

CHAPTER 18

I stared out the window of the sunroom, gazing into the darkness, mentally visualizing the river beyond the pines while sipping a cup of hot tea. Grayson sat on the sofa drinking a Guinness Stout. He'd already had one. Two was his limit.

"Tell me everything about the poaching again." He was tired. I heard it in his voice.

I turned away from the window, joining him on the sofa. "We know Trish told Tiny Cormack she dug at Pisgah Forest but Blackwell said they didn't issue any permits this year. If she did dig there, she was poaching."

Knowing Trish may have been digging illegally landed heavy on my mind. Especially if it had put her life in jeopardy, and forever altered Ivy's.

"And Greg Hastings fits into this how?"

"He was behind her at Tiny Cormack's when she cashed in. He knew how much she made with that one haul."

Ridge traced a drop of moisture trickling its way down the amber bottle with his finger. His expression rivaled a closed book, no insight. Nothing to gain. "But did he know where she was digging?" His tone was as empty as his expression. He wasn't giving anything away.

"It's possible. She told Tiny Cormack where she was digging and maybe Greg overheard."

He washed his consideration down with a swig of his drink.

"That might explain Trish's murder, but it doesn't connect to someone taking shots at you. Pisgah Forest is a big place. Unless someone told him you were going to be at Porter's Peak—"

"I told him." The memory shot through my mind like a short-circuiting charge. "At the ballgame last night. Right after I told him I was doing a piece on poaching." My voice faltered at the thought I'd put myself and my kids in the line of fire.

His eyes filled with as much anger as question. "Why were you talking to Greg Hastings about poaching?"

The air in the sunroom grew thick, a smothering pause that poorly concealed my hesitation.

"Ava..."

I sucked in the thick air along with my pride. "I am doing an investigation on poaching. Since Greg's picking for Aster this season, I thought he would probably know more about it than his daddy, so—"

"And it just happens he may be someone of interest in Trish's death?" His words bit like an angry hornet. "You knew that, Ava. You're the one who brought it to my and Sullivan's attention."

I wanted to mouth off at him, bite back with comments sharper than a katana, but I froze under the dark truth of his words. The truth wasn't buried in gentle innuendo either. It flapped out there in front of my eyes like a proudly displayed garden flag.

I sank into the sofa, wishing I could melt into the fabric and disappear. "I'm sorry," I whispered.

He sat the empty bottle on the coffee table then leaned back and turned to face me. "I need you to let me handle Trish's death. Can you do that?"

I was being scolded like a chastised child. If I hadn't been so deserving of his scrutiny, I'd have handed him his head. "Yeah. I can do that."

Although his eyes had regained some of their warmth, a shadow of distrust still loomed. "Don't burn me on this."

Taken aback, disbelief held my breath captive but soon gave way to anger. "Have I *ever* burned you, Grayson Ridge?"

Ridge was quiet, like he knew more than he was saying. It was such a delicate tightrope we were walking. Law enforcement and newspapers, or any media for that matter, didn't mesh well.

He took a deep breath, releasing it slowly. "I don't think you understand the complexity—"

"Understand?" I pushed myself up off the sofa and stepped away from it. "How can you say I don't understand the complexity? I *am* the complexity."

"Ava—"

"I'm getting so damn tired of *not understanding*, Ridge. Obviously I don't understand my and Rick's relationship, I don't understand our relationship, I don't understand why you don't trust me—"

"I do trust you. But there are things about Trish's murder you just don't need to know."

"I don't need to know? Or *The Jackson Creek Chronicle* doesn't need to know?"

We stared at one another for a painfully long silent moment.

"Have I ever published anything you asked me not to?" There was a part of me that wanted to tell him I'd rather die than knowingly hurt him again, but I kept the thought to myself. This conversation was about professional choices, not matters of the heart.

"It's not a good time to have my relationship with the media come into question."

So there it was. That's what I was to him. *The media.* I swallowed the bad taste it left in my mouth. "Of course it's not a good time. We're three weeks away from the election."

He closed his eyes for a moment then shook his head. "Ava— can you once, just once, try to see this thing from my point of view? If it was any other reporter, would I even be sitting here having this conversation? No. You know it, and I know it."

"But you said it yourself, I'm not just a reporter with this one. Someone took a shot at me today and I had my kids with me. I'm not just scared, I'm pissed."

He pointed a stern finger at me. "And that's what I'm afraid of. You're going to go out there half-cocked, digging around in something you have no business digging into, and get yourself hurt. Just leave it alone, Ava. Let me and Sullivan handle it. Please?"

I didn't know whether I wanted to choke him or hug him. How two people could be so connected yet so far apart puzzled me still after all these years.

I plopped back down on the sofa beside him and stared at the ceiling. "How are you and Sullivan going to investigate the shooting? It was in a national park. Not your jurisdiction."

"I'm aware of that."

Finn pulled himself up from in front of the fireplace and stretched. He sauntered over to the sofa and rested his head on my leg, staring at me with his huge brown eyes. I softly stroked his head. "Why aren't you upstairs with the girls?"

"Maybe he knows you're the one who needs protecting."

CHAPTER 19

Monday morning, I had the coffee on and a fire going in Betsy before the rest of the crew arrived at the office. The outside temperature was hovering in the mid-thirties with a threat of snow flurries. It wasn't unheard of this early in the season but dampened tourists' excitement over the leaves. Hard to appreciate the fading red and gold when you're bundled in snow gear. It would also put a quick end to the ginseng season, as no one dug after the first frost.

Not that I'd ever given it much thought, but this would be one ginseng season I'd be happy to see end.

I was at my desk, sipping my coffee, reading through emails when Justin Baker came in. We chatted a moment with small talk—he was concerned about how the chance of flurries would impact tourism—then he pulled a chair up beside my desk and sat down.

"Just a heads-up." He handed me the council agenda for tonight's meeting. REVISED was typed under the heading.

I flipped through the folder marked TOWN COUNCIL in my bin and pulled out the original agenda issued last week. Comparing the two, there was only one glaring difference. "Who felt like Trish Givens' murder should be an agenda item?"

Justin half shrugged and rolled his eyes. "You know how Nancy is. She's all up in arms about the citizens' safety."

"More so than you?" With a smirk, I reminded him of his own near panic last week.

He groaned and shook his head. "It's still a concern, but Nancy's making it political. You know how she works."

Indeed I did. Council member Nancy Farmer's great-great-grandparents helped settle Jackson Creek, therefore she felt she shouldered the entire town's wellbeing on her stout shoulders. She always took care enough to call when the new issue of the paper came out so she could point out the errors. I told her once I left them in there just for her.

I placed the revised agenda in my folder. "So why does she feel a murder needs discussing at a town council meeting?"

He squirmed while making a horribly painful look. "That's where it gets complicated. Did you know Nancy's on Ed Stinger's campaign committee?"

I did not see that coming. The dots connecting in my head grew into one giant explosion. "I'll be damned."

"Apparently it was hush-hush until yesterday. A Stinger sign went up in her front yard."

"But that doesn't mean she's part of his election committee."

He shook his head. "That's what I thought too. Maybe she just put his yard sign up, no big deal. So I called her and she admitted she was organizing his phone tree. It wouldn't be that big of a deal if we, as a council, hadn't agreed to not endorse any candidate."

Nancy Farmer was so polarizing, there were plenty of sources who I could depend on to call and tell me about her latest underhanded manipulations. Why did no one call on this one? Ridge was a popular sheriff with a strong support system. It didn't make sense.

I took a long sip of coffee then leaned back in my chair. "Is she going to be called out for going against what the council agreed on?"

Justin massaged the side of his head like a migraine might be forming. "I've talked with the other council members and although no one is happy about it, there's not much we can do since we didn't actually vote on it. It was just a suggestion we all agreed upon. Or seemed to, anyway."

"She doesn't have the authority to revise the agenda, Justin."

"No, but she has the right to request an item be placed on the agenda, which she did. And with the murder still fresh in everyone's minds, other members of the council agreed it might be worth discussing."

The bell above the door jingled as Nola came in. "Good morning." She placed her bag at her desk then warmed her hands over Betsy. "I saw the girls at church yesterday, Justin. They're getting so big."

"They're growing up, that's for sure." After a moment, he turned back to me. "So I guess I'll see you tonight?"

I wanted so bad to tell him no, that I had better things to do other than listen to the Jackson Creek Town Council bicker. But I just nodded, accepting it was all a part of the job.

After he left, I called Doretha to confirm Emma and Ivy could stay later than usual. I didn't anticipate it being a problem.

"Oh, honey, I wish I could help. I have a conference with Amber's teacher at six then I promised her if it's a good report, I'd take her to get ice cream."

"It's okay. No problem. I can take them with me if I have to." I'd taken Emma before, but never a toddler. It wasn't very professional, but it was one of the perks of a small-town newspaper.

Nola turned around in her seat when I hung up with Doretha. "I'll be glad to watch them if you need me to."

Not that I didn't appreciate the offer, but I didn't want to pawn Ivy off on someone she didn't know. "Thanks for offering, but they should be fine. Emma's super good with Ivy."

I sent Cole a text giving him a heads-up that I wouldn't be home until late. I told him to fix himself a sandwich and reminded him to let Finn out. It must be something about being fifteen that required spelled-out directions.

Since someone took a couple shots at us yesterday, I wasn't thrilled about leaving him at home alone, even if he was fifteen. Knowing Brady would more than likely be there was a comfort. Small, but a comfort just the same.

Images of the three of us scrambling to get off the trail while bullets flew overhead assaulted my memories of what should have been a great day. The thought I'd unknowingly invited Greg to tag along with us sent a chill up my spine.

The more I thought about it, the shock gave way to anger. I gathered my notepad and purse. "I've got something I need to take care of. Mind watching the store a little while by yourself?"

"'Course not. Got your cell?"

I flashed it to her then dropped it in my bag. A few minutes later, I was on my way to Aster Hastings'. I remembered Sue saying Sherry came on Mondays to help out. Maybe Sherry could confirm where Greg was on Saturday.

I stopped at Sweet Treats on Main Street and picked up a dozen doughnuts, figuring the gesture would be an excuse to drop in on the Hastings.

"Hear there's going to be trouble at the meeting tonight." Becky, the bakery owner, filled a box with fall-decorated treats.

I raised my brows, wondering if there was more to the story than Justin had eluded to. "What kind of trouble?"

"From what I've heard, Ed Stinger's got something brewing. Supposedly it's not going to reflect too well on Sheriff Ridge." She shrugged then ran my card through the register.

On the way to Aster's, I called the office. If anyone knew scuttlebutt, it was Nola. But she usually told me too.

"Have you heard anything about Ed Stinger having something on Sheriff Ridge?"

"What could anyone have on Sheriff Ridge?"

"I don't know. Supposedly, Stinger has something and is going to make a show of it at the council meeting tonight." A slow burn churned its way from my belly into my throat as I thought of the possibility of having to dig into something Grayson was being accused of. How was I supposed to remain neutral when I was growing to loathe Ed Stinger?

"Sounds like it's going to be an interesting meeting. Why don't I come and help Emma with Ivy?"

I really hated to impose on Nola's off time but it did sound like a good idea. "You wouldn't mind?"

"Of course not."

We chatted until I pulled into Aster and Sue's driveway. An SUV crossover with an *I Love Soccer* decal on the bumper was parked beside Sue's Buick. I remembered Emma playing soccer with Sherry and Greg's daughter so hoped I was right in assuming the vehicle belonged to Sherry.

The view framing the house had already changed in the few days since I had been there. The colors beyond the ridge weren't as vibrant, lacking the take-your-breath-away majesty of the leaves at their peak.

A lot had changed since I had been here last.

With the box of doughnuts tucked under my arm, I climbed the few steps and was greeted by Sue at the door. She had her purse in hand. "I thought I heard a car pull up." She smiled, wrapping me in an embrace as she welcomed me into her home again.

The house was as stifling hot as it had been the other day. Aster was on the sofa with his face buried in an oxygen mask, sucking the much-needed medicine deep into his damaged lungs. His faded eyes did the smiling for him as he waggled the fingers of his free hand in a wave.

I handed Sue the box of doughnuts. "I brought Aster a little treat."

She beamed with joy as she took the simple offering. "Oh, honey, you didn't need to do that. How sweet. Look, Aster. Won't these be good?" She showed him the treats and he responded with an enthusiastic nod.

Sherry came into the cramped living room from the kitchen and offered a tentative smile. She sat a steaming cup of coffee on the side table beside Aster. "Hey, Ava."

I returned the greeting, wondering how I should approach the subject of my visit.

"So what brings you out today?" Sue asked.

My mouth opened, but thank God nothing came out. I smiled,

then finally said, "Actually, I was just following up on our earlier talk. I have a few more questions I'd like to ask."

"Oh, of course. Let Aster finish his treatment and I'm sure he won't mind at all. I've got to go into town for a few errands but Sherry will be here."

Sue bent to give Aster a kiss; he removed the mask for the second it took and the warmth radiating from his smile could have warmed the house.

"Good seeing you again, Ava. Don't you be a stranger now." She patted my shoulder as she left, closing the door behind her.

With Aster continuing his treatment, Sherry asked, "Would you like a cup of coffee? Tea?"

I seized the moment. "Coffee will be fine." I followed her into the outdated kitchen and leaned against a Formica-topped counter while she fixed two cups of coffee.

"He should be finished in a few minutes." She handed me a cup with the number 300 and an embossed bowling ball beneath the numbers indicating Sue's claim to a perfect game.

"Actually, you can probably help me as much as Aster." I sipped the coffee, hoping she wouldn't mind the questions.

"Are you still wanting to talk to Greg too? I think he's working late tonight." She took her coffee to the small table and sat in one of the cane-back chairs.

I joined her at the table. "You can probably answer some of the questions. How long has Greg been digging for Aster?"

Sherry turned her eyes from me to her coffee. She blew a soft breath into the mug as if hoping to cool the hot drink. "Since Aster's been sick. The extra money sure helps them out."

I nodded, not wanting to rush into a barrage of seemingly unrelated questions. "Must be hard. And tiring. Is he still working full time too?"

She swallowed a sip and nodded. "Over at the lumber yard. Fifty hours a week. Monday through Friday, and sometimes on Saturdays too."

So why was he at Tiny Cormack's the Friday before Trish was

killed? I treaded carefully, not wanting to put her on the defensive. "When does he find time to dig?"

"Oh, he does the digging on Saturdays. During season, his boss lets him have Saturdays off."

"So he was digging this past Saturday?"

She furrowed her brow and looked at me like she didn't understand the question. "Yeah, for a little while. But he was done by noon. That's why I said at the game you could come by late Saturday if you needed."

I drank my coffee while thinking of a question that wouldn't raise her suspicion any more than I already had. "How's Brittany? Since she and Emma aren't in the same class anymore, I hardly ever hear about her."

She chuckled. "Yeah, I know, right? Funny how that works out. But she's doing okay. Teenage drama—you know how that goes."

I chuckled too. "Yeah, and I've got *two* of them."

Sherry nodded, still laughing. "Greg asked Brittany if she'd help him dig some—he was going to pay her and everything—but the look she gave him, you'd think he'd asked her to clean an outhouse. Didn't want to get her nails dirty."

"Oh, God forbid they mess up the nail art." I told her about Emma's attempt with the false lashes and thought she was going to spew coffee.

"That is too funny. *Girls*. What are we going to do with them?"

"Just love them through it, I guess. So I guess she didn't help her daddy dig this weekend either, huh?"

"Are you kidding? He was back before she even got up."

"She didn't want to come to Grandma and Grandpa's for one of Sue's home-cooked meals? I'd have helped him for that."

Sherry shook her head. "Oh no. He wasn't digging here Saturday. I'm not sure where he was."

CHAPTER 20

I juggled Ivy, her diaper bag, and her sippy cup in the parking lot of the town hall. Emma carried her own overloaded book bag and an activity bag Doretha had packed full of coloring books, crayons, and toddler-sized puzzles. The parking lot was full; several cars sported bumper stickers showing support for Ed Stinger. Ed's Cadillac donned a black and yellow striped wrap, giving the caddy the appearance of a bumblebee of mammoth proportions. Ridge's Expedition was parked at the far end of the lot. The black Beemer parked in a STAFF parking spot belonged to Rick, the town attorney. The thought of seeing him again so soon after the other night dragged me down like an anchor.

The Jackson Creek town hall used to be the town's three-bay fire station. Citizens decided the volunteer firemen needed more modern facilities more than the mayor and his staff, so they voted to fund construction of a new state-of-the-art firehouse.

A group of Stinger's campaign workers stood outside the door, handing out campaign material to anyone with an open hand.

I stared at the postcard and rubber bracelet the worker handed to Ivy. "I didn't think you could campaign on municipal property."

"Like we really have anyone here who'll actually enforce the law." He shrugged and handed the same to the person behind me.

I nudged Emma inside, pointing her toward two tables near the front. The council "chamber" was the three bays that once housed the firetrucks, but now held fifteen rows of folding chairs, ten chairs to a row. The setup made it easy to approximate the number in attendance. Folding tables on a raised platform stretched end to end to accommodate the seven-member council. Why the tables were on a riser was a sore spot with many, giving some the idea the council thought they were above the average citizen. An old podium scavenged from the high school stood to the right of the makeshift dais with a cardboard copy of the town seal glued to its front. Two tables down front to the left were designated for media and the town attorney—me and Rick. This meeting couldn't be more uncomfortable.

The chamber was filling up fast with a crowd of Ed Stinger supporters. The burning in the pit of my stomach told me this meeting was not going to bode well for Grayson. I spotted him near the front talking with Justin. He was in uniform, full dress blues. I'd only seen him dressed so formally a few times. Tommy's funeral was one of them.

Nola was on the front row, near the "media" desk. The kids and I made our way through the crowd with several people smiling and reaching out to touch Ivy as if she was a golden calf. All the attention made her burrow into my shoulder. Emma sat in the saved seat beside Nola, greeting her with a warm hug.

Nola draped her arm around Emma's shoulder. "Hey there, Sugar. You're more beautiful every time I see you."

With all the touchy-feely sentiments toward Ivy from strangers just getting through the door, there was no way the toddler was going to let me plop her down beside Nola at that moment. I sat down at the table and put Ivy in the chair beside me. For the moment, she was content with a coloring book and crayons.

I was digging in my bag for my notepad and micro-recorder when Ed Stinger himself knelt down beside me. "I was hoping you'd be here tonight."

I turned the recorder on and placed it on the edge of the table. "I'm at every council meeting, Ed."

He draped his arm around the back of my chair and patted my shoulder. "Maybe you can write up a good article and really stir up a bee's nest." He chuckled and my skin felt the tiny prickling legs of a swarm of crawling bugs.

Justin shook Grayson's hand then made his way up to the dais where the rest of the council waited. Ed finally removed his arm from around my shoulder and took a seat behind Nola. The overpowering scent of his aftershave lingered.

Rick was less than ten feet away at the next table and had yet to acknowledge my presence. The crowd settled into their seats as a hushed murmur settled over the room. After Justin called the meeting to order, the council went through the Pledge of Allegiance, a moment of silence rather than prayer because Nancy Farmer was worried about the town being sued for praying, and then approved the revised agenda. With the formalities out of the way, they moved right into the first public speaking session where members of the public had signed up earlier to speak. The second public speaking part at the end of the meeting was first come, first served. Ed Stinger was the first person called to the podium.

After stating his name and address for the record, he pointed toward my table. "That little girl, that beautiful baby is now motherless. That little orphan is a direct product of that man's incompetence." He pointed to Ridge. An uneasy rustling moved through the crowd. "As a concerned citizen, I demand to know what precautions his department is taking to ensure our safety."

Nasty searing bile churned in my stomach while I watched the spectacle. How *dare* this man use Ivy for his political gain. Ridge's expression never wavered. Rock steady.

Stinger turned his pointing finger toward me. "Ava Logan. Found the murder victim's body and can attest to the brutality of Miss Givens' murder. The horrific manner in which that little orphaned child's mother died is indicative of a serial killer. Citizens are afraid for their safety. We'd like to know what you're doing, Sheriff Ridge, to make sure Miss Givens' killer doesn't strike again."

"Yeah, what are you doing, Ridge?" a man shouted from the back.

More call-outs followed and Justin raised his hand for quiet.

"Order, *please*. Can we keep this civil? Sheriff Ridge—would you like to speak?"

"He didn't sign up," Nancy Farmer snapped.

Justin turned and stared at her, his own anger bleeding through. "But he has the right to defend himself and his department."

"This isn't a court of law, Mr. Mayor." Smugness oozed from Nancy's self-righteous pores.

"Really? Sure seems like Grayson's on trial, if you ask me."

Grayson's supporters rallied to life, shouting at Justin to let the sheriff speak.

"I say we let Sheriff Ridge speak," Susan Layton, another council member said. Four of the other members agreed. The lone hold-out, other than Nancy, was Blythe Summers, Stinger's nephew by marriage.

Summers looked at Nancy for approval. "It's breaking protocol. If we do it once, we'll have to do it each time someone wants to rebut a speaker."

Justin turned to Rick. "Are there any laws we'd be breaking if we let the sheriff speak?"

It was like watching a horror movie through splayed fingers. I didn't want to look, but couldn't look away.

After an agonizingly long moment, Rick shook his head. "No. It would show good faith to let the sheriff address Mr. Stinger's complaint."

Ed Stinger's clenched jaw showed his nonverbal disapproval of Rick's fairness. Made me wonder how tight Ed thought his relationship with the town attorney really was. For a moment, my sympathy rose for Rick and the relationships crumbling at his feet, then I realized one of those was with Ed Stinger. My sympathy waned.

"Would you like to speak, Sheriff?" Justin asked.

Ridge strode to the front of the room, bypassing the podium. He stopped at the dais and turned to face the crowd, rather than the council. "Mr. Stinger, I'm not sure where you got your information—maybe you've been watching too many crime shows on television—but I can assure the citizens of Jackson County, Trish Givens' death was not at the hand of a serial killer."

"Have you ever dealt with a serial killer, *Mister* Ridge?" Stinger shot back.

"Have you? I mean, considering all your years in the real estate business?"

A low murmur rippled through the crowd. Stinger shifted his weight from one foot to the other.

"With all due respect, Ed," Ridge continued, much more pleasant than Stinger deserved, "there is no evidence whatsoever to support any fears of a so-called serial killer. Whoever's throwing that term around is contributing to nothing but town gossip."

Nancy Farmer snapped to attention. "Well, maybe the State Bureau of Investigation would feel differently. I propose that the S.B.I. be contacted immediately about overseeing this case."

"You don't control the sheriff's department, lady," a man called from the crowd.

The rumblings were growing louder, with the majority of the crowd throwing support for Ridge.

Justin banged the gavel to quieten the crowd. "Nancy, this council has no say so over the sheriff's department. The county commissioners handle that."

"Then perhaps we should propose it to them."

A man in a khaki work uniform and ball cap stood up in the back. "Why don't you investigate it yourself since you know everything?" The man's statement brought shouts of support.

Justin called for order and banged the gavel again. The suddenness of the *bang* startled Ivy, sending her scampering into my lap, crying. Her pitiful wails and obvious fear hushed the ruckus as the crowd watched what some of them had come to see—a terrified motherless child on full display, clinging to the only safety net she now knew.

Emma rushed over and gently stroked her hair, shushing her in a quiet voice. "It's okay, Ivy."

"That right there is a perfect example of what our citizens are now living with." Stinger adjusted the microphone on the podium to make sure his words were heard over Ivy's crying.

I'd had enough. His comment pushed me over the edge. "Oh, good Lord, Ed. She's crying because the sound of the gavel scared her. It has nothing to do with her mother."

"Do you feel safe, Ava?" Stinger's eyes burnt through my bones. My slight hesitation in answering fueled his fire even more.

"Didn't think so. No one feels safe in our community anymore. And why should they? We have a do-nothing sheriff who comes with a history of doing nothing. Case in point—where was he when your very own husband was killed, Ava? I know where he was and I think it's time the rest of Jackson Creek knows too."

Every molecule of life-sustaining matter that flowed through my body froze in place. My lungs ceased to take in or push out much-needed air; my heart failed to pump blood through my veins. For the smallest of seconds, even my brain failed me, squeezing out rational thought while wrapping itself around a completely new fear. Could Cole and Emma ever forgive me?

The silence that enveloped the crowd was so total, I was certain they could hear my heart pounding in my chest.

Finally, after what seemed like an eternity, Justin spoke. "Mr. Stinger—you're not going to hijack a town council meeting and turn it into your own personal campaign platform. I think your allotted time at the podium is up. Next speaker."

With apprehension, Betty Crowder made her way to the podium, looking back and forth between Ed and Justin as if waiting for one of them to explode. Ed finally stepped aside and relinquished his hold on the microphone, and the audience. I lost Ridge in the crowd; my eyes searched frantically for him, but to no avail. Suddenly, Ed was beside me again, crouching like before.

"So...you want to hear more?" he whispered. "Or maybe I should say, *see* for yourself. I have videotapes."

CHAPTER 21

Ed Stinger had whispered in my ear the ugly truth. Afterward, the council continued with their meeting but my attention was elsewhere. It lingered like memories in a cheap motel room. I double-checked the micro-recorder and checked it again to make sure it was recording. Ivy fidgeted in the chair beside me. I checked the wall clock behind the dais again. Ten minutes had passed since the last check.

I couldn't think, I couldn't take notes, and I didn't give a crap about what new crisis the council had moved on to.

I stuffed Ivy's coloring book and crayons in my bag then turned to Emma. "Get your stuff together." I knelt beside Nola and handed her the recorder. "I've got to get Ivy home. Do you mind staying and minding the recorder?"

She shook her head then spoke in a hushed voice. "Of course not. Leave me your notepad and I'll take notes for you too."

After scooping up Ivy, I slung my bag over my shoulder and motioned for Emma to head toward the door. Nola scooted over into my vacant seat at the table.

I struggled to draw air into my lungs. The building's walls had sucked up every ounce of much-needed oxygen and held it at bay, teasing me. Once outside, I ran to the car, jostling Ivy on my hip, gasping like a drowning victim breaking free of the suffocating water.

"Mom, what's wrong? Why are we running?" Emma was breathless from sprinting the distance to where we were parked.

"Everything's fine, baby. I just need to get home." I threw open the back door and dropped Ivy into her car seat. Fighting the aggravating buckle with one hand, I dug my phone out of my pocket with the other. My hands were shaking so bad, I could barely tap in Ridge's number.

Emma gently nudged my hand out of the way and finished securing Ivy in the seat.

"I need to see you," I said as soon as he answered.

At home, I snuggled Emma and Ivy down in my bed with a movie on Emma's tablet and a bag of microwave popcorn. Cole was in his room with his headphones on, hunkered down at his desk working on a history project. Finn followed me from room to room, aware of my anxiousness. Ridge waited downstairs in the sunroom.

I stopped in the kids' bathroom to gather myself, hiding, clutching the cool vanity for support. Emma was suspicious enough already; I didn't want her to see the trembling I was fighting to control.

Downstairs, Finn trotted ahead of me to the sunroom. Ridge stood at the window, looking out into darkness, his hands stuffed into the pockets of his jeans. He heard us come in and turned toward me. For the first time in many years, a look of worry shadowed his face.

I fell onto the couch, burying my face in my hands, pushing back the sobs that were ready to pour out of me. I steeled my nerves, telling myself to hold it together. Don't break down. Not now, not like this. I rubbed my palms on my jeans, hoping to wipe away the nerves as much as the dampness.

A deep breath helped to push the words out. "Stinger has a videotape of us going into a room at the Parkway Inn the day Tommy was killed." There. I'd finally said it. It had taken me ten years to vocalize the fact I was in a hotel room with Grayson Ridge the day my husband was gunned down. Room 110. Ground floor. Near the ice machine.

"He's bluffing. He has to be."

I shook my head. "Stinger Realty bought the inn last year. Apparently, there's a pending lawsuit where someone was hurt in the parking lot several years ago. The previous owners left a bunch of security tapes and some of them spanned the timeframe of when the person was injured. One of those tapes is the day Tommy was killed. Ed was reviewing the tapes to see if the person's fall was caught on camera, and he saw you and an *unidentified* woman. Going into a room."

I couldn't look at him. I stared at the floor, each fiber of the carpet in clear focus. He sat down on the couch, close enough I felt his warmth. "But he doesn't know the woman was you."

"He said you were with a woman he couldn't identify. I was wearing a hooded sweater that day. I remember it was cold."

Ridge turned to me, draping his arm across my shoulder. "But he doesn't know it was you, Ava. The only thing he has is a video tape of a *single* man and a woman going into a motel room."

I sprang up from the sofa and spun around to face him. "Grayson—whether he can identify me or not, what's it going to say about you? About your character? We messed up that day, Grayson...We both know it."

"No." He leapt up and stood only inches away from me. "What *I* know is I would have killed Tommy myself if he had hit you again. That's what I know, Ava. We didn't mess up. Fate just had other plans that day."

"Like keeping us apart?" Tears stung my eyes and rolled down my cheeks.

"That's not fate's doing." He reached out to wipe the tears but I turned away.

I quickly brushed my hands over my face and sniffled. "We should never have been there that day."

"What happened to Tommy happened, Ava. It wouldn't have mattered if I had gone to the lake by myself that day instead of the Parkway Inn. I wouldn't have been there anyway."

I closed my eyes, wishing I could make him see the things I

saw. "We went there to be together, Ridge. I had every intention of sleeping with you that day. If you hadn't gotten the call when you did, I would have. Whether we did or didn't doesn't matter. We were someplace we never should have been." I moved away from him and walked to the windows. Even through the darkness, I could see leaves swirling in a gusty wind. I could hear the river crashing against the rocky bank. And I could feel him behind me.

"You were going to leave him." His voice was soft, his breath featherlike against my neck.

I wrapped my arms around myself to keep from reaching for him. "It doesn't change the fact I was still married at the time." I wasn't the only one who saw the wrong in that; Doretha had hated Ridge ever since I tearfully confessed my sin.

He sighed heavily. "I wish to God there was a way you could move past the guilt."

I turned around to face him. "Have you?"

After hesitating, he finally shook his head. "The only thing I was ever guilty of was loving you." He lightly touched my cheek, and I let him, holding his hand there with my own.

For the first time in a long, long time, I wanted to give in. I wanted to break free of the crushing guilt and love him openly and wholly. But there was more to consider. My kids, his position...whether or not Ed Stinger had proof of our near-tryst didn't matter. I couldn't take the chance that he did.

"What are we going to do about Stinger?" I pulled away from him then walked back to the couch.

He followed and sat down beside me. "If he knew it was you on the tape, he'd have made a show of it. He'd have made sure you knew it."

"But what about you? Whether you were single or not, it's not going to look good."

He slowly shrugged and smiled, but I saw the worry he was trying to hide. "I've got way too many things right now needing my attention more than Ed Stinger. Like Trish's murder, and someone taking a couple shots at you."

The issue with Stinger dimmed slightly as the sound of gunshots exploded again in my memory. "I spoke with Sherry Hastings this morning."

Ridge stared at me with burning questions then leaned back against the sofa and dropped his head against the pillow. "*Ava*...didn't I ask you to please leave this to me and Sullivan?"

I cleared my throat and spoke quietly. "I had to know, Grayson. I just couldn't *not* do anything."

Ridge guffawed. "And? What did you find out?"

I felt like a scolded child. "Sherry said Greg was digging Saturday morning, but she didn't know where."

He sighed loud enough the kids could have heard him upstairs. He rubbed his fingers hard against his forehead. "So you think he was in Pisgah Forest using you for target practice."

"I don't know what to think. But the only thing Trish and I had in common is ginseng. She dug it and I'm doing an investigative article on it. And the common thread is Greg Hastings."

He slowly shook his head. "You have something else in common, Ava."

I pushed thoughts around in my head, trying to grasp something to hold onto, to see another connection other than a plant with red berries.

Ridge blew a heavy breath, exorcising the tiredness like a demon. "Ivy," he said, his voice slight. "Ivy's a common thread."

I blinked, allowing the words to sink in. And not wanting to believe it. "How is she connected to Greg?"

"Maybe she's not. But she is connected to both you and Trish."

Pushing myself up from the sofa, I stepped away from Ridge and his ideas. I wanted to walk as far away as possible. Could Ivy really be the catalyst for her mother's death and the attempt on my life? The attempt on the life of my own children?

"You're sure you have no idea who her father is?" Ridge asked.

I turned around to look him in the eyes, to comprehend where his thoughts were coming from. "We never talked about it. It was as if one didn't even exist."

Could all this really be domestic-related? *If* Ivy's father even knew about her, was he angry over visitation? Child support perhaps? There were still so many unanswered questions. "I can sort of see how a domestic situation might be behind Trish's death—maybe she was asking for child support or maybe he wanted visitation—but then why try and kill *me*?"

"That brings us back to the 'seng."

Couple all the paternity issues with the fact Trish had made some enemies digging ginseng, it was enough to make anyone doubt the reality of either situation.

"Ginseng's a very lucrative business," I said, growing weary of the subject. It was becoming a bigger problem than just poaching.

"It's lucrative when you're hitting."

"And Trish was hitting. That alone is enough to make other diggers angry. Especially if she's digging where she's not supposed to be." And then thoughts began skittering through my memory like ants scattering from a destroyed mound. "Ridge—who asked me to look into the ginseng poaching?"

"Ed Stinger."

"What if he knew all of this would connect back to Trish?"

He furrowed his brows, glaring at me. "You mean like setting you up?"

I quickly nodded. "Yes. Like a...threat. He asked me weeks ago for an endorsement."

"What'd you tell him?"

There were so many thoughts running through my mind at that moment, it was hard to grasp just one, yet there was *one* that kept inching to the forefront. "I told him no."

Ridge shook his head. "But why kill Trish? One, he would've had to have known you were babysitting Ivy that night. It seems a bit extreme because you refused to endorse him."

I figured now was as good a time as any to come clean. "I also wouldn't sleep with him."

He looked at me with such intensity, I felt his questions. "He made a pass at you? When?"

I hesitated, going over in my own mind the probability that Ed Stinger could truly sink as low as murder. "I don't know...He's always made inappropriate comments but I just ignored them. Then not long after he filed to run for sheriff, he came by the office to pick up a candidates' media kit. He asked me if I'd like to spend the weekend at one of the cabins—with him."

"Was that the only time?"

I slowly shook my head. "No, there were several. The last time was...maybe two or three weeks ago. Each time he was a little more...direct." My body shivered on its own at the memory of his slimy hand on my shoulder. Behind his good ol' boy southern charm and business sense, he was vile to the core. I remembered him tucking a stray lock of hair behind my ear, remembered how my body went stiff at his touch.

Ridge gnawed on his bottom lip while considering Stinger and what I had just told him. "Has he ever made a *romantic* advance toward you? Not just wanting to sleep with you, but more interested in a relationship with you?"

My mouth opened but nothing came out as I replayed every recent encounter with Ed Stinger. They had been awkward and made me want to douse the room with antibacterial spray. "I don't think a *relationship* is what he was wanting."

Ridge slowly shook his head, his brows furrowed. "Stinger's a creep, but murder? And a brutal murder, at that."

"But why send me on this poaching investigation when the only one being poached is Calvin Cooper? It's like he purposely steered me toward that story, and in the end, it had no basis."

"Don't forget the poaching up at Porter's Peak. My guess is Stinger didn't even know it was Trish doing the poaching. And because he knew about Calvin, he wanted to use it to make it look like I'm not doing my job. Anything he can use against me, he will. He's an ass, but he's not a murderer."

Tension tormented every muscle in my body. Crawling into a soft bed and sleeping for a hundred years sounded like a good idea.

I hated to admit it, but he was probably right. Trish's murder,

Ivy, the ginseng, and someone firing off a couple shots at me may be connected. But no matter how I tried to manipulate the pieces, short of forcing it, I couldn't fit Stinger into the puzzle anywhere.

"What are we going to do about the videotape?" I asked.

He ran his hand over his hair and sighed. "All he has is video of me and an unidentified woman going into a motel room together. That unidentified woman could have been an informant, could have been an out-of-town friend visiting...could have been anyone."

But it wasn't anyone. It was me.

CHAPTER 22

After a sleepless night, I was in no mood for grumpy kids and a toddler who refused to eat her breakfast. Even Emma, my perpetually happy child, grumbled over her cereal. And poor Finn ran and hid when Ivy let loose with a wail of rebellion over being plopped in the chair. I'd never had to deal with tantrums. Neither Cole nor Emma ever felt the need to stand in challenge.

But Ivy wasn't my child. And I couldn't send her home to her mother. We'd make this work. I'd figured out what to do with the tantrums, one way or another. No matter how unpleasant.

As much as I tried to put on a happy face to counter all the grumps, I couldn't shake the image of Ed Stinger kneeling beside my table at the council meeting, sharing secrets, dirty little secrets, like a grocery store rag mag. The thoughts made me anxious to get on with the day, to face whatever shitstorm Stinger was trying to create. I hurried the kids along and packed up Ivy's breakfast to finish at Doretha's.

The morning ride was quiet aside from a few mumbles. At school, Cole did say goodbye before rushing off to catch up with Brady, while Emma gave me a quick peck on the cheek. Ivy silently waved at Emma as she watched her walk along the sidewalk to the main building. Watching Ivy in the rearview mirror offer a silent wave to someone who couldn't even see her brought tears to my eyes. Could this child really be the cause for one murder and the attempt at another? Or was it the ginseng that robbed her of her mother? If Trish had been involved with poaching and it had gotten her killed, at least her murder had nothing to do with Ivy. I'd never be able to forgive myself if Ivy's mere presence had put Emma and Cole in danger.

At Doretha's, Ivy clung to me rather than wanting down to go play. She wrapped her tiny arms around my neck and squeezed. Maybe she sensed the tension that had been in everyone that morning. I hugged her a little longer and stroked her hair, and she finally gave way to Doretha's outstretched arms. Ivy offered a slight smile then gently batted at Doretha's braids.

"Mind if I bring Cole and Emma, and of course little Ivy here to church tonight? We're having games and songs night." Doretha made a funny face that made Ivy giggle. "I know it's a school night, but I'll make sure they get their homework done before we go."

"Sure. I'll send Cole a text and have Brady just drop him off here. Do you want me to pick them up afterward?"

Doretha shook her head. The beads on her braids clacked against one another. "I'll bring them home. It'll probably be around ten."

I lowered my brows in question. "You sure you want to take Ivy? She's not used to being up that late."

A raucous laugh escaped Doretha's lips. She put her hand on my shoulder and turned me toward the door. "You go on now, missy. We've got this covered. Go to work then enjoy your few hours alone tonight."

The thought did sound appealing. A roaring fire, a bottle of wine, and one of my nightstand books I could no longer read because of my munchkin bed partners. Whatever fleeting moment of a happy thought I had was blown to pieces as soon as I pulled into the office parking lot. Ed Stinger's Cadillac was parked near the door. Nola wasn't in yet, so Ed had no choice but to sit in his car and wait for whoever showed up first. Unfortunately, it was me.

A sour taste filled my mouth as I unlocked the front door. I could feel him behind me, the stench of his aftershave gagging me.

"Good morning, Ava."

He was one of my biggest advertisers and I loathed every dollar he spent. To lose his money would hurt the paper. Like Ridge had said, the man was a slime ball, but not a killer. I took a deep breath then let it out slow. "Morning, Ed." My voice was barely audible to even myself.

"You got out of there last night before I had the chance to talk about my new ad." Even the tone of his voice made my skin crawl.

I finally jammed the key in the lock and shoved the door open. I hated this man. Every passive-aggressive word that came out of his mouth was aimed at causing someone hurt. "I don't normally carry ad spec sheets to council meetings, so I wouldn't have been able to help you last night anyway."

He followed me inside and stood by the wood stove as I lit the fire. While Betsy cranked up, I went into the kitchen and fixed a pot of coffee, thankful he hadn't followed me back there. I leaned against the counter and waited for the first cup. The image of him kneeling beside the media table last night whispering his secrets would not leave my mind. Like the java, my anger was quickly brewing.

I wrapped my arms around myself to ward off the chill, and to coax out an ounce of inner comfort so I didn't go totally ballistic on the creep. Once the pot was full, I poured myself a cup and headed back into the front office. He was sitting in the guest chair beside my desk with his expensive heavy wool coat draped across the back. I hadn't bothered to ask if he wanted a cup.

"So...I thought for the next two issues, I'd go full page color. And I'd like either the back page or page two. Of course, I'll pay the upcharge for prime placement."

Any other time I would be giddy over a two-issue full page color with placement upcharge ad run—but now wasn't one of those times. I blew a soft cooling breath into the steaming cup. "Is this for Stinger Realty or your campaign?"

"Oh, it's for the campaign. I have a lot to say this time." He winked and I wanted to sling the scalding coffee at him.

After a long moment, I finally put my mug down and pulled out an ad spec sheet. "What do you have in mind?"

He dug into his coat pocket and retrieved a folded piece of paper and an envelope then tossed them onto my desk. "I'd like to use at least one of the pictures if possible. They're not the best quality but hopefully we can make one of them work."

Just as I was about to open the envelope, Nola hurried in and kicked the door closed behind her. "What happened to fall? It's like winter out there." She dropped her bag on her desk then went over to the stove and warmed her hands. "Good morning, Ava. Ed."

Stinger's smile reminded me of a snake slithering across a roadway. "Good morning, Miss Nola. You sure are looking lovely this morning."

Nola chuckled and waved him off. "You always were the charmer."

Whatever they were chatting about couldn't hold my interest as I pulled the photos out of Ed's envelope. They were still shots taken from a grainy video. From the parking lot of the Parkway Inn. Of Grayson Ridge and an *unidentified* woman outside room 110. Ground floor. Near the ice machine. If Nola and Ed were still talking, I didn't know. Their voices melded together in a muted mumble of background noise. The world outside my narrow field of focus disappeared as my eyes zeroed in on the grainy images.

"Ava?" Ed lightly touched my arm to draw my attention. "Like I was saying, I want the ad to look like an actual news story. You know, with a headline and all. Sheriff caught in compromising position...something like that."

I fought to keep from vomiting. One single incident had caused so much pain over the years, and was now resurfacing to cause even more.

"And then in the body of the text," he continued, "I want it to hit on these bullet points..." He slid the piece of paper in front of me. Words like moral character, integrity, and leadership jumped off the page. "And then I'd like to work in the question in bold letters, and maybe a larger font, 'If you can't trust this morally corrupt man with your wife, can you trust him with your life?' What do you think about that?"

Frantic, I shoved away from my desk and ran to the bathroom, making it just in time. I gagged on the vomit as the putrid venom scorched my throat. My heart thundered in my chest as the room spun like a child's toy top.

"Ava?" Nola asked from the hallway. "Honey, are you okay?"

I rested my face against the cool porcelain and cried.

Nola was still on the other side of the door, her perfume slipping under the threshold. "There's a stomach bug going around. Sure hope that's not what it is."

Ridge had been right. Stinger didn't know I was the woman in the pictures. Still, if they were ever made public, it wouldn't shine a good light on Ridge. It could possibly cost him the election.

Nola rapped lightly on the door then poked her head in. "Brought you some water, Sugar." She stepped in and handed me the bottle then rolled off several paper towels from the holder. After dampening them in the sink, she handed them to me. "You poor thing. Think it's a bug?"

I blotted my face with the paper towels, sucking in long deep breaths. "It's a bug alright. Just not a stomach bug."

She lifted her perfectly waxed brows. "Not following, but that's okay. I'm going to go check on Ed if you're sure you're okay."

I stood and squared my shoulders, harboring a newfound approach to Ed Stinger. My knees wobbled a little but I waved Nola off with a nod. "Tell Ed not to leave yet. I'd like to continue our conversation."

She closed the door on her way out, leaving me alone with my reflection in the mirror. At that moment, I didn't see weakness; I saw strength. I washed my face then brushed my teeth and took a deep breath.

Ed was still at my desk, reviewing his ad. He looked up and smiled in a genuinely concerned way. "I hope you're feeling better. Can't have our star reporter coming down with anything this close to the election."

"Nola, would you be a sweetheart and run down to Sweet Treats on Main and grab a box of cinnamon rolls?" I handed her a twenty from my wallet. "And then swing by the post office on your way back. No hurry though. Take your time." Our eyes met as she took the money, and she understood.

When I was certain she was on the road, I locked the door. "We need to discuss your advertisement, Ed."

"Certainly. Sure you're feeling up to it?" He watched me move to my desk and seemed surprised when I didn't sit down. Instead, I leaned up against it, towering over him in the chair.

"I won't be running that particular ad."

The look of surprise on his face was nearly comical, but I wasn't laughing. "Pardon?"

"I said I wouldn't be running your ad. I'm not going to be a part of your smear campaign."

He stood up, his irritation showing in his clenched jaw. "Now wait just a minute, Ava. It's not a smear campaign if it's the truth."

"How do you know it's the truth? All you have is a picture of Sheriff Ridge and a woman in a motel parking lot. She could have been a cousin visiting from out of town, or maybe an informant— you have no idea who she was and no right to judge him for being there with her."

He blew air out his nose then crossed his arms like the pompous ass he was. "Look here, Ava—I'm paying a right nice figure for space in your paper. With that comes the right to say what I want, since I am paying for it."

I shook my head. "Have you ever read that tiny disclaimer in the paper's media kit? It says the publisher has the right to refuse any advertisement they deem inappropriate for a family publication. I'm the publisher, Ed. And I'm refusing your ad."

His face flushed the color of beets. Our eyes were locked in a battle of wills, both of us refusing to look away.

"I suppose you're going to sweep the whole incident under the rug and not do a story on it either?" He was so angry, he radiated heat.

"There is no *story*, Ed, and I'm certainly not going to make it look like there is."

"Does it not bother you to know where he was the day your husband was killed? They were partners, right?"

I pushed by him, got my mug, then went back to the kitchen and poured myself a fresh cup. I counted to ten to steady my nerves, proud of myself so far. I hadn't shed the first tear. When I returned to the front office, he was at the wood stove staring at the black cast iron like it held the answers.

"You didn't answer," he said, turning around to face me.

I returned to my position of leaning against the desk rather than sitting down. It made me feel more in control, stronger. "Tommy and Grayson Ridge were work partners. They weren't joined at the hip. Ridge was on vacation the day Tommy died. If anything, Tommy should have waited for backup before going into a domestic situation. That's basic law enforcement. Surprised you didn't know that, considering you're running for the top law-enforcement position in the county."

He chuckled, but it wasn't a pleasant sound like a child might make. It was dirty and vile and sounded how I imagined Satan himself did. "Why are you protecting him, Ava? Don't you think the people of Jackson Creek deserve to know what kind of man he is?"

I took a slow sip of coffee before responding. "I'm not protecting him, Ed. The truth is—Grayson Ridge is a good man. The people of Jackson Creek already know that."

He nodded, not in agreement with what I'd said but accepting he wasn't going to change my mind about it. "You may be the only newspaper serving Jackson County, but there are other ways to get a message out."

"Are you going to spew your lies through postcards, flyers maybe? Perhaps shout it with a bullhorn while you're riding in the school's Homecoming parade?"

He pursed his pencil-thin lips. "I won't need to go to that extreme. All I really need to do is plant the seed. The gossips in this town will take it from there."

I strolled over to the stove and stood close enough to him I could smell his sweat. "Plant a seed. I like that. I like that a lot. I might have to plant my own seed. Except my seed would be the truth."

"What are you talking about?"

"You, Ed. I wonder how many other women in town would come forward and say you've come on to them too, if I planted that seed?"

A spark in the stove popped and echoed in the silence filling the room at the moment. I finally turned and looked at him, wanting to see the bastard squirm.

"You must have mistaken my friendliness for a romantic gesture. I assure you, Miss Logan, *coming on to you* was never my intention. I'm a very happily married man."

I nodded. "And was your wife going to join us at the cabin you wanted to take me to?"

He sucked in a sharp breath and steeled his jaw as rage filled his eyes. "My wife is a sickly woman—"

"Then it's going to look *real* bad if and when I divulge your dirty little secret, isn't it, Ed?" I folded my arms across my chest, more in control of any situation than I'd ever been. "Here's what we're going to do. I'll run your full page color campaign ad, but instead of trashing your opponent, it's going to tell the voters what you can do for them. And you'll continue to run the Stinger Realty ads just like we've never had this conversation. Does that sound like a good deal to you?"

We stood there staring at one another for a long moment without saying anything. What else really was there to say? He'd played his cards, and I'd played mine. After a moment, he walked over to the chair and put his coat on then cut his eyes at me on his way out. I could see his Cadillac through the window and when I saw it turn out on to the road, I finally let out the breath I'd been holding.

CHAPTER 23

I left the office around four thirty, went home, and soaked in a steaming hot bath until the tips of my fingers were wrinkled. A glass of Chardonnay and Edgar Meyer's "Appalachia Waltz" playing softly on my phone helped erase the tension of the day. After the second glass, I actually giggled, remembering the look on Ed's face when I gave my little speech.

Wrapped in nothing but my fluffy bathrobe, I padded downstairs with Finn at my side. I couldn't remember the last time I had any amount of consecutive hours to myself. Yet I wondered about the kids. Ten o'clock was going to be awfully late for Ivy, and probably Emma too. Would Cole have time to finish his homework? Football practice or not, he still had a good two or three hours' worth of homework every night. I wondered if Brady would go with them. Maybe I should have asked Doretha if she would mind. I couldn't imagine why she would but I'd never been one to assume.

I debated calling just to make sure, then shoved the thought aside. Knowing Doretha, she'd invite him herself.

I heated a plate of leftovers in the microwave then carried it and the bottle of wine into the sunroom. My own private sanctuary. Finn tagged along, anxious for a bite. After starting a fire, I sank into the couch with Finn at my feet and poured another glass of wine. Following a couple bites of my less-than-appetizing supper, I was happy to share it with Finn. While he ate, I flipped through channels on the TV. I wasn't in the mood for the entertainment news shows nor did I have the brain power for Jeopardy. I turned the television off and settled in to browse through the latest issue of *People*.

There was nothing within the slick, glossy covers that interested me. No matter how much I tried to concentrate on someone else's story, or my relaxing night alone, my thoughts kept going back to Trish.

There was so much I didn't know about her. What if she *had* been involved in something that had, ultimately, gotten her killed? Would I shield Ivy from that truth or speak honestly to her when that day came? And where did Ivy fit into this? Was she the cause or was it the ginseng? If it did come down to being all about Ivy, that truth would be better left unsaid. The child would have enough to deal with. Telling her she may have been the reason her mother was murdered would remain off limits, at least in my household. I couldn't always protect her from the outside world, but I'd damn sure protect her in my own home.

Finn's ears perked up at the sound of something only he could hear. He stared out the wall of windows for a moment then decided his food was more interesting. I rubbed his fur before pulling out a notepad and pen from the coffee table drawer.

On one side of the paper I wrote TRISH, in the middle I wrote IVY, and on the right-hand side I wrote, ME. I separated the headings into columns with a line drawn down the length of the paper. I stared at the paper for a good while before writing the first thing, but then the thoughts started coming. One after the other, I jotted down everything I knew to be true that connected the three of us. Ginseng, Ivy's birthday party and the two other women that were there, Minnie's Cafe where we often had lunch, Dale and Linda Tilly—the gun collector I did an article about who had also bought artwork from Trish—and Ed Stinger, who had asked me to investigate a ginseng poaching problem that he'd hoped to turn political.

He had also shown a more-than-average interest in finding

Trish's killer. Was his interest merely campaign related in an effort to make Ridge look bad? Or was he truly interested in the community's wellbeing? Ed Stinger seldom did anything for the betterment of someone else. There was always an ulterior motive.

Finn stopped eating and lifted his head, his ears on alert. I pulled the robe tighter around myself, my nerves flickering with unease. "S'okay, boy." I stroked his neck, more unsettled than I cared to be. Just as I went back to my list, a low growl rolled up from deep in his throat. A swarm of butterflies stomped uneasily in my stomach. I moved over to the side table, feeling for the key taped underneath, then unlocked the drawer. I eased the drawer open and caught the gleam of the Glock.

A soft knock on the back door stopped my heart. Whoever was there knocked again, this time a little harder. Finn stood at guard and let out a loud *woof* the same time my cell buzzed, fraying my nerves even more. I'd never been so happy to see it was Ridge calling. "Hey—"

"I'm at the back door. You okay?"

I let out the breath I'd been holding as Finn led the way into the kitchen. "Yeah, just a little jumpy." I stood at the door a moment, allowing my heart to settle back into its normal rhythm. When I opened it, we were each still holding our phones to our ears. We both grinned; he slipped his phone in his jeans pocket, I slipped mine into my robe pocket.

He held a case of diapers in his other hand. "Thought I'd bring these by."

I smiled, then held the door open and motioned to the counter. "You didn't have to do that. But thank you anyway. You can just put them there. I'll take them upstairs later."

Finn nudged by him, bounding down the porch steps in hot pursuit of an opossum. Ridge unloaded the diapers then leaned against the counter. "I didn't see any lights on in the front...got a little worried."

"I'm fine. Okay, I was a little jumpy." A slight smile played on my lips.

He followed me back into the sunroom and raised an eyebrow when he saw the Glock in the drawer. "A little jumpy?"

"I haven't been here completely by myself in a *long* time. Yeah, I guess I was a little jumpy." I closed the drawer.

"Where are the kids?"

"With Doretha. She had something at church she wanted to take them to."

"Even Ivy?"

I nodded. "Yes, and they won't be home until after ten. She's going to be one cranky baby in the morning."

He smiled and the light of the fire sparkled in his eyes. "Maybe I should go and let you get back to enjoying your alone time."

The thought of him leaving scared me; the thought of him staying scared me even more. "It's okay. I was just looking over some notes about Trish and the whole crazy mess."

"You're not supposed to be doing that after hours."

I shrugged and couldn't stop the smile. "You want a beer? There's two left from the other night."

"Sure." He took off his coat and draped it across the back of the chair. When I returned from the kitchen, he was sitting on the couch reading over my handwritten spreadsheet. "How is Ed Stinger connected to Trish or Ivy?"

"He's not really. I mean, other than the possible poaching. But if he didn't suspect Trish was poaching, then there is no real connection to him." I handed him the bottle then sat down beside him. I poured myself another glass of wine. "He does seem to have an unusual interest in Trish's death."

After sipping his beer, Ridge slowly nodded. "But—and I thought I'd never defend Ed Stinger—he is running for sheriff. He has to make a good show of it. If there were a sudden rash of car break-ins, he would probably be all over that too. Anything to make it look like I'm not doing my job."

I took a slow sip of wine, wondering how to word what I was about to say. The wine wasn't helping. I cleared my throat. "I don't think you'll have to worry about Ed."

The Guinness bottle stopped mid-route to his mouth, hanging there, suspended in air. He cut his eyes toward me then took a swig of his beer. After swallowing, he asked, "Why don't I have to worry about Ed? What did you do?"

"He came by the office this morning. I just gave him an ultimatum, that's all."

He took another long sip of his beer then turned on the sofa to face me. "What kind of ultimatum? Please don't tell me it could be misconstrued as blackmail."

My eyes widened. "Blackmail? If anyone could be accused of blackmail, it would be him."

He pursed his lips and drummed his fingers on the bottle. "Let's start over. Why do I no longer have to worry about Ed Stinger?"

"He brought me a new campaign ad. He wanted me to run a picture of a still shot he had made from the video. He had some cheesy tagline to go with it. Something like, 'If you can't trust this morally corrupt man with your wife, can you trust him with your life?' And I refused to run the ad."

Ridge fell quiet. He slowly worked his thumb over the label on the bottle. "I appreciate you not running it. But he'll just find another way to get his message out."

I softly shook my head. "I don't think so. I told him if he did everyone would know about his unwelcome advances and what kind of sleaze ball does that with a sweet sickly wife at home."

He jerked his gaze up at me. "You didn't."

I slowly nodded. "Is that really blackmail? I mean, since he did it first?"

He let out a full-blown laugh that settled into a chuckle.

"It's going to cost me money, you know, so the least you can do is run a full-page ad in its place." I lightly nudged him with my elbow.

He grinned. "What about his other ads? The ones for Stinger Realty?"

I gnawed on my lip a moment then confessed to that too. "I

don't think I have to worry about those. I told him if he tried to cancel, he wouldn't like the stories I would tell."

He tipped his beer at me. "Now *that's* extortion. Blackmail, extortion...all in one day. You ever work for the Mob?"

We both laughed and my heart was so full, I couldn't stand it. There was no anger between us, no hurt. No past.

Still chuckling, he wrapped his arm around my shoulder and pulled me to him. "God...Ava...I love you." He kissed my hair and everything in the world at that moment vanished.

Was he joking? Was he just kidding around or did he mean it in the way I wanted him to? At least I thought that's the way I wanted him to mean it. I wanted him to love me the way I had loved him all these years.

"You know I've always loved you, Grayson," I whispered, but it was loud enough for him to hear.

I turned my face up to his and accepted the tenderness of his lips. So many years...so many tears. I had known I loved him the first day Tommy introduced us. His voice, so deep and soft. His eyes, those crystal blue eyes, so clear you could see down to his soul. And it was such a beautiful soul. So caring and thoughtful, almost mystical in nature.

Back then, when he was Tommy's partner, I didn't want to love him, but I had no choice. It just happened. I couldn't hide my heart from him any more than I could hide the bruises inflicted by Tommy's hands.

"Oh, Ava...you *don't* know how much I love you."

I moved closer to him, growing hungry for more of him, for all of him. He brushed the stray hair from my eyes and framed my face with his hands, kissing my cheeks, my eyelids, my lips. I wanted him now more than I did ten years ago in that motel room.

That day, on fire, he had held me against the motel room wall with his strong hands supporting my weight, his mouth on my breasts, the hunger in both of us a living breathing entity.

But that was then. In this moment, there was no one else in the shadow. No one to cast shame or guilt. I climbed onto his lap, more than ready to take what he offered. What was mine. What had been mine all along. He gently pushed the robe from my shoulders and took in the sight, my body bared before him, my soul open to him. I felt no shame in the less-than-flat stomach or the thirty-five-year-old breasts. Reaching down, I grabbed the hem of his shirt and pulled it over his head. The heat of flesh on flesh as our bare skin touched ignited a passion I'd never known. When I could stand it no longer, when the thought of having him, wholly and completely, pushed aside any guilt of days gone by, I unfastened his belt and opened his jeans.

Afterward, I couldn't stop the tears that flowed freely; I didn't want to stop them. I wanted them to wash away all the past pain of loving him and to start anew.

He gently kissed away each tear and whispered, "I do love you, Ava. So, so much."

We moved to the rug in front of the fireplace and lay in each other's arms, my head resting on his bare chest. He lightly traced lines and circles on my arm with his fingertip. For the first time in years, total contentment washed over me. I was relaxed. And I was loved.

"Thank you for never giving up." I entwined my fingers with his.

He gently kissed me. "You never give up on something worth waiting for."

My lips formed a gentle smile. "But ten years?"

He turned his head to share a grin. "You were pushing it."

I snuggled closer, breathing in the scent of him, feeling the rhythm of his heart. We laughed, we giggled, we shared. We talked about the past.

"If I'd known he was hitting you, I'd have killed him myself," he said, the harsh words feathered in softness.

"We both stayed with him too long."

He rolled over, propping up on his elbow. The glow in his eyes was as warm and hypnotizing as the flames in the fireplace. "The only reason I stayed on as his partner as long as I did was to see you when we came here for lunch."

"The only grown man I know that still likes peanut butter and jelly."

He laughed. "Still do."

In my mind, I counted the years he and Tommy were partners before Tommy was killed. Three? "You had a crush on me all that time? Why didn't you let me know?"

He lightly ran his finger along my lips. "It wasn't proper. But if I'd known what was going on behind closed doors..."

I rolled over on my side, facing him. "You would have what?"

A gentle smile toyed at his lips. "I don't know. Saved you?"

A loud laugh bubbled up and escaped before I could stop it. "Save me? I didn't need you to save me. I just needed you to love me. I would have saved myself when I'd had enough."

"I did love you. I was just slow about telling you."

We slowly kissed and all the bad memories flittered up the chimney like ash.

After a while, we sat up, leaning against the sofa. I pulled my robe on and went into the kitchen for the last beer. When I returned, Ridge had put his jeans back on and was kneeling by the fire.

I handed him the beer then refilled my wineglass. "So how are we going to do this? Our jobs aren't going to make it easy."

Laughing, he unscrewed the cap off the bottle. "Nothing has ever been easy with us. You should know that by now."

Sipping the wine, I shrugged. "True. But maybe we should keep a low profile until after the election."

He stood and nodded. "Probably wouldn't hurt."

Just as I lifted my glass for another drink, Ridge yelled my name and lunged at me, taking me down in one swoop as a gunshot shattered the window. The wineglass erupted into a shower of tiny glass shards. Another shot rang out, followed by another. From outside, Finn barked ferociously. Ridge pushed up on his hands and knees and shoved me toward the sofa. "Get behind it!" He scrambled to the side table and grabbed the Glock. He racked the slide then dug his phone from his pocket.

My heart beat so loud all I could catch was "Shots fired. Need all on duty and K9."

He frantically pulled on his shirt, never laying the gun down. "Do you have clothes in the laundry room?"

I nodded.

"I want you to crawl, army style, and get them. Do not stand up. Where's the switch to the flood lights?"

"Beside the back door."

"Is there a window in the laundry room?"

I shook my head.

"Good. Then stay there. They won't be able to see in. And stay down. Go." He pushed me into action, semi-crawling beside me. Another shot pinged off the coffee table, exploding the empty bottle of Guinness.

I screamed out, terror pulsing through every pore of my body.

"Go! Go! Go!" He was shouting, pushing me toward the safety of the laundry room.

"Don't leave me! Please don't go out there."

We were in the kitchen now, just feet away from the laundry room, feet away from the back door.

He held my panic-stricken face in his hands and kissed me quickly. "I'm not going to lose you again. Now go."

I crawled into the laundry room while he flipped on the flood lights. I could hear Finn outside, in a frenzy, barking and howling into the darkness. I pulled on a pair of dirty jeans and one of Cole's sweatshirts. I slipped on the old sneakers used for mowing then crouched in the corner. The back door opened then the beam of the flood lights painted the floor of the kitchen. I started shaking, violently, the fear spreading through my body like a fast-growing cancer.

CHAPTER 24

My yard looked like Trish's had the day I found her body. Patrol cars, unmarked cars, even personal cars of off-duty deputies filled the driveway. Ridge had called the State Highway Patrol and asked for assistance in patrolling Jackson County as the entire sheriff's department was in my yard and in my house securing the scene. The fire chief came along with three first responders and set up command lights that illuminated my backyard and the river beyond.

I sat on the steps of the back porch, huddled in Cole's oversized sweatshirt, still shivering in the cold. Finn sat beside me, restless, not understanding the flurry of activity.

Ridge stood a few feet away with a group of deputies, some in their uniforms, some dressed like they had been enjoying a quiet night at home.

One of the canine handlers, Jeff Maness, stood with them, his partner, a Belgian Malinois named Ruger, at his side with his ears at alert.

Ridge pointed into the woods. "The shots came from across the river. There were at least four shots fired and they were using a green laser scope."

I jerked my head up, out of the fog. So that's how he knew. That's how he knew the shot was coming before it shattered the window. I wondered if it too had been centered between my eyes. A slow anger churned inside me. Whoever was responsible for this had now violated the two things I cherished most: the safety of my children and the sanctuary of my own home.

Another K9 handler, this one from a neighboring county, arrived with his German shepherd and joined Ridge.

The fire chief, Larry Roland, hustled up to the group with a rolled map in his hands. "This shows all access roads along the river."

They gathered around Ridge's SUV and spread the paper out on the hood. Larry Roland ran his finger along the map. "If the shots came from across the river, they would've had to access it from the back side."

"Unless there's a shallow point nearby." Steve Sullivan was dressed in loose athletic pants and a sweatshirt, obviously on his own time. He looked at me and for the first time, I didn't see contempt. "Do you know if there's a low spot nearby?"

I joined them at the SUV and looked over the map. "It's no more than knee-high for a few hundred feet along the property line."

Ridge tapped the map with his finger, indicating two dirt roads on the other side of the river. "Jeff, you take Ruger and come in from the east. Frank, you take your dog and come in from the west. You can use these access roads here. Steve—round up two guys to go with them. I don't want them out there alone."

"How do you know the shots came from across the river?" someone asked.

"Could they not have come from the backyard?" asked another.

Ridge shook his head. "Too high powered. Whatever the hell they're using could take down an elephant. If they'd been standing that close, they'd have taken out a wall."

"Could it have been random? Someone spotlighting deer?" Steve Sullivan clicked on his own Maglite.

"Not when Ava's the one in the sights. This isn't the first time she's been shot at lately. Same green laser was used."

My heart slid slowly into my knees, lodging there, nearly causing them to buckle. I leaned against the SUV as the reality of his words hit home.

Someone was trying to kill me. Whether it was related somehow to Trish and ginseng, or to Ivy, or to an article I hadn't even written yet didn't matter. My life was in jeopardy.

The deputies scattered, each following a plan of action directed to them by Ridge. He stared at the map and made notes to the side. After a long moment, he glanced over at me. He reached out for me then pulled me to him. "We're going to get them. Whoever it is. I promise."

Another set of headlights turned in and then a minute later, Cole and Emma barreled up the driveway, screaming, "Mom!"

Oh God. I forgot to call Doretha. I ran to them, hoping to calm the terror I knew was coursing through their minds. "I'm okay! I'm okay, guys."

Emma lunged, wrapping her arms so tight around me I fought for breath. Near hysterical, she sobbed into my chest.

Cole was no less frantic. "What happened? We passed a K9 unit."

I grabbed his hand and pulled him closer. "Someone shot into the sunroom. Grayson was here when it happened."

Doretha came running up. "Are...you...okay?" She forced the words out between deep gasping breaths.

"I'm fine. Just a little shaken up. Where's Ivy?"

Doretha pointed toward the van. After finally catching her breath, she said, "I didn't want to get her out until I knew what was going on."

Ridge joined us and Emma moved from me to him, wrapping her arms tight around his waist. "Ava, why don't you take the kids and stay with Doretha a day or two?"

Doretha patted my hand in that reassuring way of hers. "Of course. I insist."

The offer was reassuring, but the thought of being run out of my own home made me want to puke. I didn't want the kids to be uprooted whether it was for a day or a week. And I was the target, not them. "I don't want to put anyone else in danger. Not you, or all the kids."

"Hogwash. The Sheriff's right. You're staying with me. *All* of you."

That was the first time Doretha had ever agreed with Ridge. "We'll put a patrol car at the house, just in case," he said.

I didn't like it but would have to accept defeat on this one. "Just for tonight."

Cole watched all the police activity with adult concern. He'd stepped up to fill an imagined role way before his time when his father died. He was still just a kid, trying to play a grown-up role. "Where was the K9 unit going?" He turned to Ridge.

Ridge looked at me, silently asking permission to talk openly in front of my children.

Cole was one thing. Talking about someone trying to kill me in front of Emma was off limits. "Emma, how about waiting in the van with Ivy? I don't want all the lights to scare her."

"She was asleep."

"Well then, she'll be scared if she wakes up."

Doretha put her arm around Emma's shoulder and gave her a squeeze. "Come on. I'll walk back with you."

When they were out of earshot, Ridge talked truthfully to Cole. "Whoever was shooting was across the river. The K9 units were heading to different access roads to come in from different directions."

Cole studied the map still spread on the hood of the Expedition. "There's a spot about half a mile from here that's pretty shallow where they could have crossed."

Ridge took another look. "I didn't see any access roads on the map that were that close."

"It's not a road. It's just a path..." He cut his eyes toward me, hesitating before speaking more.

Ridge wasn't letting him off so easy. "Like a hiking path?"

Cole swallowed hard. "Sort of. It's kinda like a...camp."

The mother in me lowered my brows. "What kind of *camp*, Cole?"

He didn't say anything for a long moment, looking back and forth between me and Ridge. After probably weighing what was going to keep him out of the most trouble, he spoke up. "It's just a camp where we go and hang out."

"Who is *we*?" both Ridge and I asked at the same time.

"Me, Brady, Josh, some of the other guys from school."

Ridge rubbed his chin then yelled for Sullivan. When he joined us, Ridge gave him the update. "Get Maness back here. We're going about a half mile up the road." Ridge whistled and waved a group of men over, including Larry Roland, the fire chief. "We're going to need a command light set up at a makeshift camp a little way up the road."

"Can we get a truck in there?" Roland asked.

Ridge looked at Cole for the answer. "Can we?" His voice wasn't harsh, but it was no longer father-friendly.

"If it's a four-wheel drive."

I left them a moment to put Finn in the laundry room. When I returned, they had one of the lights loaded on the fire department's brush truck. I walked back to Doretha's van. She was in the driver's seat and rolled the window down.

I didn't want my kids displaced but there would be no rest tonight at home. "Why don't you go ahead and take Emma and Ivy back to your house. Cole and I'll be along once we finish here."

Although dark in the interior of the car, Emma's eye shone with apprehension. "Why can't we stay until you're through?"

"It's already late, Emma. I don't know how long we'll be here." High levels of adrenaline still pumped through my veins though fatigue nipped at my mind.

"What about clothes? Can I get some clean clothes for school?"

Ivy needed clothes too. And probably diapers.

Doretha squeezed my hand. "Emma and I'll go in and pack up

a few things for her and Ivy. When y'all get through here, you and Cole do the same."

"What about Finn? We can't leave him." Emma searched for any excuse she could use to stay, to not be the kid for once.

Doretha's mouth puckered then opened in a slight grin. She nodded toward me. "You bring Finn. I don't have room in the van." She leaned out the window and gave me a kiss.

When I went back, Cole was in the front passenger seat of Ridge's SUV. I opened the back door to climb in.

"What are you doing?" Cole asked.

"I'm going with you."

"Don't you think you should stay here? Just in case."

"Just in case what? Just in case there's something at this camp you don't want your mother to see?"

He sighed heavily and lay his head against the headrest.

Ridge slid into the driver's seat then turned and looked at me sitting behind Cole. "Why don't you stay here with Emma and Ivy."

"They're getting some stuff together to take to Doretha's then she's going to take them on back to her house."

He looked at me a long moment, realizing he would have to arrest me to keep me from going. "We'll deal with the whole *secret camp* thing later. Right now we're looking for evidence that someone was there tonight. Understood?"

I did not have the heart or brainpower right now to deal with what we might find. The thought of my son being involved in something he shouldn't had pushed its way to the forefront of my thoughts. The second attempt on my life had taken a backseat.

It seemed we had barely gotten on the road when Cole pointed to a slight clearing in the trees and underbrush. I couldn't count the number of times I'd driven right past and never noticed it. "Right here on the other side of the rock. You'll have to stop and let me move the tree limb."

Ridge pulled to the side without saying anything. Cole got out, then illuminated by the headlights, rolled a fallen branch to the side like he was opening a gate. It was a good-sized limb but rolled easily. Its sole purpose was to keep people out. When this was over, this son of mine had some serious explaining to do.

Cole climbed back into the SUV. "There's an oak tree with a piece of blue tape on it right up here. You'll need to hang a sharp right."

Ridge cut his eyes at him but didn't say anything. He inched along the narrow path while branches grabbed at the sides of the Expedition with hungry fingers. A few minutes in, he asked, "How much farther? I don't want to drive right up on it in case there're fresh tire tracks."

"Not far. We're almost there."

Ridge stopped the truck and turned off the engine. He took two flashlights from the console box and handed one each to Cole and me. He pulled his own Maglite from the side door. "We'll walk the rest of the way."

We followed what Cole referred to as a path deep into the woods. I would refer to it as a highly disguised trail of teenage trouble. As we drew closer, the sound of the river grew stronger. I held the flashlight with one hand and with the other, pushed branches out of the way. Their prickly fingers snagged at my hair while the underbrush scraped against my legs. After a few minutes of hiking, we came to a clearing.

I waved the flashlight over the area, catching the gleam of metal chairs arranged in a circle around a fire pit.

Larry Roland, the fire chief, assembled the command light and moments later, Cole's private party palace was lit up like Time Square. I slowly scanned the area, taking in every inch of my son's hangout, a son I wondered if I truly knew.

Empty beer bottles and cans were stacked neatly into a waist-high pyramid. A makeshift "bookcase" crafted from what looked like wood from a pallet was partially covered by a sheet of painter's plastic. Even through the dingy dirt-spattered plastic, I could make out the glossy covers of *Playboy* and *Penthouse*. A mattress I wouldn't let Finn sleep on was off to the side, away from the party at the fire pit. Three bras, one red lace, one beige, and one zebra print hung on a limb over the mattress. Discarded condom wrappers were strewn about. As my heart sank, it met the bile rising from my stomach. I turned away before I threw up.

Ridge saw the hurt overtaking me and started to reach out but stopped when Jeff Maness arrived with Ruger, the Belgian Malinois.

"Please don't tell me it's just a teenage boy thing. I raised him better." I wanted to rewind the clock, to go back fifteen years and start over.

"I'll talk to him," Ridge said quietly.

Ruger whined and pawed at the ground, then barked loud enough I jumped. He stuck his nose to the ground then circled around the fire pit, with Maness allowing enough lead for the dog to do his job. Ruger barked again then headed down a narrow path leading toward the river.

Ridge stood in the center of the camp, slowly turning to take it all in. "When's the last time you were here, Cole?"

"After the football game Friday game. That's the last time I was here but I don't know about the other guys."

"Do any of them ever come here alone?"

Cole shook his head. "Not that I know of. There's usually at least three or four of us."

Ridge nodded slowly. "I want a list of the guys', and *girls'*, names that come here. Every single one that you know of who has ever been here."

"Yes sir." His voice was small, scared. I didn't know if I wanted to love him or kill him.

All I knew at that moment was it would be hard for me to ever let him out of my sight again. "Where are you getting the beer? And do not lie to me, Cole."

He sighed heavily, knowing he was in deep shit. "Josh's older brother. But it's not like we're out driving or anything."

I raised an eyebrow and glared at him. Did he really expect me to be happy about that fact? I supposed in the grand scheme of things I should be, but right now it didn't matter much.

"Hey chief, there's fresh shoe prints over here," one of the deputies said. He was near the path Maness and Ruger had disappeared down. "These are so fresh you can read the size imprint. Size thirteen, and that ain't no little boy's shoe either. "

Ridge went over to take a look. He knelt beside the deputy and shone his Maglite at the spot. "Get a cast. See what we can come up with."

He came back over to where Cole and I stood. "Know which one of your friends wears a size thirteen?"

Cole shrugged slightly. "Could be any of them. Most of them are football players. They're pretty big guys."

A radio crackled, followed by a muffled voice. The deputy at the footprints spoke into radio at his shoulder. "Maness and Frank met up on the other side of the river, near the bank. They're directly behind the house."

"Did the dogs pick up anything?"

"Led them right to a coat. Maness is processing it."

Ridge took a deep breath then let it out slowly. "Tell him to meet us back at the house."

CHAPTER 25

Even with the command lights still lighting up the backyard and a small army of people milling around my home, the house seemed empty. Broken and violated. Cold air flowed in the sunroom from the shattered window. Shards of the broken wineglass and beer bottle sparkled in the carpet like glitter.

Knowing someone was outside the window, watching our every move, even if they had been on the other side of the river, sent ice trickling down my spine. If Ridge hadn't come over...I would have never seen any laser light. The kids would have found me, like we had found Trish.

"Ava..." Ridge said softly from behind me. He was close enough I felt his presence. He stepped closer, putting his arm around my waist and pulling me to him. "I'll have the window fixed tomorrow. We can put plastic up tonight."

Like the plastic covering my son's library of porn. "There's a roll out in the shed. I bought it for the flower garden last year. I guess Cole used part of it for other things." My stomach churned and I seriously wanted to kill him.

I wondered if one of the bras hanging over that filthy mattress belonged to one of *his* conquests. Or maybe she hadn't been a conquest at all. Maybe she had been more than willing. Like I had been a few hours ago.

"Where's Cole?" I asked.

"Upstairs packing a bag. Maybe you should do the same."

"All the times he was with Brady...to think he was just up the road doing..." I took a deep breath. "Were there drugs there too?"

"Hey." Ridge turned me around to face him. "No, there were no drugs. If they were smoking pot or something else, we'd have found some type of paraphernalia. I'm not downplaying what was out there, but he *is* fifteen. I hid my *Penthouse* in a duffel bag under my bed."

"But that mattress, and those bras...they were like trophies."

Ridge gently kissed my forehead. "I'll have a talk with him later."

"Hey Chief—" Sullivan said, poking his head into the sun room. Surprisingly, Ridge didn't rush to break contact. Instead, he simply turned around. "Maness and Frank are back. You might want to come see this."

We headed outside where Maness was loading Ruger into the cage in the car. A jacket was spread on the hood. Ridge went to his Expedition and pulled a pair of gloves from a kit in the back. I stared at the jacket on the hood, a knot hanging in my throat. It was a yellow-gold leather jacket with white sleeves and a black panther embroidered on the right chest. It was an expensive jacket. I had bought Cole one just like it at the beginning of the school year when he made the football team. Cole's name was embroidered on his in black letters, on the left chest, across from the threatening panther.

Ridge snapped the gloves on then ran his fingers across the name stitched on the left side. He stared at it for a long time before turning away. "Damn." It was all he said. No shock, just resignation.

When he moved away, I saw the black letters, the word *Coach* as plain as day. I grabbed Ridge's arm, shaking my head. "It can't be Brent. He—"

"What? Brought flowers to her studio?" Ridge pulled me aside, away from other ears. "He may have brought the flowers out of remorse. Maybe there was something going on between them and she ended it, sending him into psychotic rage."

"But what about me? Why try to kill me too? I've never done anything to him."

He shrugged. "Maybe because you were her friend and he was worried she had told you something?"

Of course. It made sense now. The upset at home. Brady telling me his parents might get a divorce. Brady's bruises and scratches. It all pointed straight to Brent.

Was he Ivy's father too?

I sat at Doretha's small kitchen table sipping a cup of herbal tea. The kids were long ago in bed but I knew sleep would be slow to come to me. Doretha was at the stove fixing her own cup of chamomile. She was in her bedroom scuffs and tattered pink bathrobe with a high lace collar. I had given her that bathrobe the Christmas before Tommy and I got married. She told me once she couldn't part with it because it reminded her of me, and how much I despised lace but knew she liked it.

She set the tea kettle off the hot burner then joined me at the table. The rooster clock above the table said four a.m.

She reached over and patted my arm. "Been another long day for you, hasn't it, Baby Doll?"

I scrubbed my face with my hands, hoping to wake up enough to think clearly. "Cole and his friends have a party camp in the woods near the house. We found beer bottles, girlie magazines, and a filthy, nasty, germ-infested mattress where they do God knows what."

She cocked a graying eyebrow at me. "Oh, I think you know damn well what they do on it. Probably same thing you and Mr. Grayson Ridge was doing earlier."

I started to fire back at her, but truth was, she was right. And I was tired of denying how I felt about Grayson Ridge. "How'd you know?"

She smiled warmly while absently stirring her tea. "Mommas always know."

"He loves me, Doretha. He always has. And I've always loved him. I just didn't want to admit it."

"You had an affair with him, Sweetie—"

"No." I held my finger up to stop her. "We *almost* had an affair. We never went through with it."

She tapped the side of her head then her heart with her finger. "But you did here and here."

I got up and poured hot water from the kettle into my cup then dropped another tea bag in. When I sat back down she was dipping the chamomile bag up and down in the water in her own cup.

"I know Tommy wasn't good to you, Ava. He wasn't a nice man. And yet, you tried to make it work. You stayed with him for whatever reason. The kids, maybe? And here comes Grayson Ridge, tall, and charming, and my God, is that man ever good-looking...and he was your escape. But he didn't save you—"

I held a finger up. "He didn't need to save me. I was perfectly capable of saving myself. Fate just had other plans."

Doretha slowly nodded then set the spoon she stirred her tea with on a napkin. "You were still in a cheap motel room with a man other than your husband. I can't forgive him for that."

"I was in the motel room with him. And you don't hate me."

"You're family. I have to love you."

We giggled as I stared down into my tea, wondering if tea leaves really could predict one's future. My eyes dampened. "He loves me, Doretha. I know he does."

She reached across the table and stroked my face. "He probably does. We're going to get through it, Baby Doll. We always do."

Footsteps padded up the steps leading from the playroom where Doretha had set up bunks for the kids. Cole poked his head through the open doorway. "I can't sleep. Can I come up?"

My anger with him still burned but my exhaustion quelled the flames. "Sure."

Doretha got up and lightly touched the tea kettle to check its warmth then pulled down another mug from the cabinet. After adding a little sugar and squirt of lemon juice, she sat the cup on the table and motioned for him to sit. "I'm going to bed. You two keep each other company."

He looked like hell. His eyes were bloodshot and swollen, his hair a mess from tossing and turning. He mindlessly blew into his tea. He wouldn't look at me. "I'm sorry you had to see all that." His voice was soft, a hesitant whisper. "The magazines...Dylan's brother works at one of those convenience stores. He gave him some that they were throwing out."

I didn't say anything. I sipped my tea and let him get it off his chest.

"I drank a couple beers. But I never got drunk." He looked at me to gauge my reaction, as if the fact he was never inebriated would excuse him. I wasn't letting him off that easy, so I remained stone faced.

I finally took a deep breath and pushed a lock of hair from my eyes. "Cole...I'm not happy about any of it. But I also know you're not four years old anymore. I know you don't believe it now, but teenagers don't always make good decisions. That's what scares me the most. The faith that I had in you making good choices has kinda been blown out of the water, you know?"

He slowly nodded. Those strong angular cheeks I used to smother with sloppy wet kisses when they were pink and chubby were now flushed with shame. "I never used the mattress either."

I let that one sink in a moment before responding. I took a long sip of tea. "Those bras...did the girls they belong to leave them willingly?"

"Yeah. It's a game they play. If they..." His lips twisted as he contemplated what to say. "If they go all the way...they get to add their bra to the tree of fame."

I pulled a deep breath in through my nose, not wanting him to see the disgust I was feeling. I wanted the dialogue to continue and was afraid if he thought I was judging him, he would shut down.

"Mom, I swear...I've never...I've never even been anywhere near the mattress."

I propped my chin in my hand and stared at my son. "Why not?"

"Why not what?"

"Why haven't you been *anywhere near* the mattress? I mean, if the girls are willing..."

He drank his tea. After a moment, he said in a soft voice, "I'm scared to. I mean, I've kissed a girl and you know...copped a feel, maybe—"

"Maybe? You don't know if you did or not?" I allowed a slight smile to break the tension. He was trying so hard to be open, I didn't want to shame him with coldness.

His mouth parted into a huge smile. "No, I mean...yeah. I have. But I've never done, you know...it."

I reached across the table and pretended to straighten his hair. An excuse just to touch him. "When the time's right, you won't be scared. You'll be nervous, but not scared. Remember that."

He stared into his cup, clearly searching still for words that weren't coming easily. "I'm glad Ridge was there with you tonight. I saw the way he touched you at the camp."

I watched him for a long moment then got up and poured us both more tea. I didn't know that I was ready for this conversation, especially with one of my kids. Ridge had always been a presence in our lives, but this was different.

"It's okay, Mom. You deserve to be happy. And I know he makes you happy. You just never would admit it."

Oh, this son of mine was wise beyond his years. I handed him his cup then rejoined him at the table. "I'm glad he was there tonight too. It scares me to think what would have happened if he hadn't been."

"Do you still have the gun in the side table?"

I nodded. "It's been a while since I've shot it though. Probably couldn't hit the broad side of a barn. But yes, I have it with me."

"Good. I mean, in your line of work...it might not be a bad idea for you to carry it all the time."

I laughed. "My line of work? The majority of the articles I write and publish are feel-good stories, human interest. There's not a whole lot of danger involved in that."

"Well, you've sure pissed someone off enough for them to want to kill you." He lifted his mug, pointed it in my direction in a mock salute.

"Yeah..." I took a slow sip of tea. I couldn't argue with his logic on that one. I pushed a few thoughts around in my head on how to broach the subject of Brent O'Reilly. Cole had been upstairs packing his bag when Ridge examined the coat with *Coach* embroidered on it. I understood now how Ridge felt discussing Trish's murder with me. I didn't want Cole to know everything I now knew about Brent, but I wanted to know everything he knew.

"How're Brady and his dad getting along?"

He shrugged. "I don't think they're talking anymore."

"How are they at practice? That must be awkward." I felt underhanded, like I was interrogating my own son without his knowledge. Which, of course, was exactly what I was doing. It was really no different than demanding answers about the party camp, I reasoned.

"They don't speak at practice either. But that's not that bad because on the field, Coach O'Reilly's the coach, not the dad, you know?"

"Is Brent a good guy?"

Cole drank his tea and shrugged. "He's always seemed okay to me. But Brady says he's a real dickhead. Um...I mean—"

I waved him off, not happy about his language but accepting my son wasn't ten years old anymore.

"He says Coach and his mom fight a lot."

"Has it ever turned physical?" I wondered if he remembered his own father punching me in the face or slamming me against a wall. I hoped not.

"You mean like between Brady and Coach or his mom?"

I shrugged slightly. It was a difficult topic to talk about, let alone try and understand. I didn't want to make my question sound more foreboding than necessary.

"I think him and his dad have gone at it a couple times. Brady's never said anything about Coach hitting his mom. Like Dad used to hit you."

My tea mug stopped in midair as I was about to take another sip. I slowly sat it back down and forced myself to look into the eyes of my son. "Cole—"

"I'm not sorry he's dead, Mom. I know that's probably mean to say, but he was a mean person."

I reached out and took his hand and gave it a gentle squeeze. My eyes watered at the knowledge he'd had; even in his little child's mind he knew his own father wasn't a good person. It's hard for any kid to accept their parents aren't perfect; it's harder when they realize just how screwed up they really are.

"I'm glad he's gone." He continued to unburden himself of things unsaid. "And it just burns me up to go over to Grandma's and she thinks he was a god or something. Pictures all over the place like a shrine. Sometimes I just want to ask if she even knows what a mean sonofabitch he really was."

"Oh, Cole...no, you can't ever say that to her. Let her live with the fantasy. Has Emma ever said anything about your dad?" She wasn't even two when he was killed. She still thought of him as a hero. It was hard to know what, if anything, she remembered.

He shook his head slowly. "She never talks about him to me. She's never even asked."

For so many years, we had walked around carrying words we wanted to say but never did. We raised silent questions, hoping to never really know the answers. Grayson Ridge wasn't the only one who had been living in limbo these last few years. We all were. We tiptoed around the ugly truth because it was so much easier than dealing with it. The grief we carried wasn't for Tommy; it was for ourselves.

CHAPTER 26

The next morning was pure chaos, but in a good way. Helping Doretha get breakfast for the horde of kids in her house was as loud as a daycare center and as busy as a school cafeteria.

Cole and I had talked until five a.m., and here it was at seven and I was scrambling eggs. Surprisingly, Ivy was happy though it had been after midnight when Doretha finally got her down. Cole was the only one not up, and I had given him a pass for the day. I had told Emma she didn't have to go to school either if she didn't want to. After the events of last night, I felt they may need some time to rest and regroup. Emma, however, would have nothing to with missing a day of school. Missing a day with Mason.

Like an assembly line, I handed over plates filled with eggs while Doretha added a piece of jelly toast and slice of bacon to each. Emma carried them into the dining room two at a time, perfecting her future summer waitressing job. I sipped on a fresh cup of coffee while I oversaw the process, instructing Emma to pour the milk or orange juice once the plates were set.

Ivy tugged on the leg of my borrowed pajama bottoms then reached up with her chubby little arms. I lifted her and propped her on my hip. She turned her face to me and puckered her lips, wanting a kiss.

She was such a beautiful baby. The blond hair that fell in waves, the hypnotic green eyes. Slightly upturned little nose. We rubbed noses, giggling and kissing. But I kept going back to those green eyes.

Green eyes were rare. Trish's eyes had been the color of warm chestnuts, her hair auburn. I remembered she had told me her hair had been blond, like Ivy's, when she was a child but turned darker over the years.

The longer I studied Ivy, the more I saw a resemblance I didn't want to see. I remembered one thing that had struck me so much with Brady O'Reilly—his emerald-colored eyes. Could Brent be this child's father too?

She had all but leapt out of my arms into his at Minnie's Cafe. He played it off, but thinking back on it now, I was certain Ivy knew him. The flowers he brought to the studio after Trish's death. He seemed almost embarrassed that I'd walked up on him while he was there. I had told him I would be running notices in the paper about Ivy's father.

But was a little embarrassment worth an attempt on my life?

"Earth to Ava." Doretha waved her hand in front of my face. "You still with us?" She laughed as she took Ivy from me and carried her into the dining room. Emma pulled the highchair up the table, holding it steady while Doretha dropped Ivy onto the plastic-covered seat.

"Are you going to take me to school or is Doretha?" Emma asked, looking from me to Doretha.

"I will. I have an errand I need to run this morning," I said.

Doretha looked at me and raised her brows.

"I need to run by Trish's and pick up some of Ivy's stuff. All of her winter clothes, her coat, toys......they're all still there."

"And don't forget her stroller," Emma reminded me. "She gets heavy after a while."

I smiled. "And her stroller. Just for you. Go on and brush your teeth. I don't want to get tied up in the car rider line."

Once Emma was out of the room, Doretha asked, "You sure it's safe for you to go back to Trish's? Especially alone."

"It'll be fine. I won't be there long." The truth was it wasn't Ivy's clothes or a coat, or even a stroller, I was going after. If he was her father, there had to be something in that house linking Brent

O'Reilly to Ivy. Especially if Trish was ready to expose her own truth. A truth that may have gotten her killed.

After a quick sip of coffee, I hurriedly pulled on the dirty jeans and Cole's sweatshirt from the night before, combed my fingers through my hair, then brushed my teeth with Emma's toothbrush. In the Tahoe, she shoved her overstuffed bookbag into the front floorboard, proud she would arrive at school in the front seat and not have to crawl out from the back like a child. She talked about everything and nothing on the short ride and I couldn't repeat a word of what she had said.

The drop-off line inched along in front of the commons area shared by the middle and high school. I wasn't fond of the idea of my twelve-year-old sharing space with seniors but I couldn't afford private school, so we dealt with it. She climbed out of the car, giving me a modified wave so she wouldn't look like the child she was in front of her peers. The car in front of me hadn't pulled away yet so I was forced to sit there a minute. I watched Emma move along the walkway with her bookbag slung over her shoulder, looking so confident and empowered. A smile slowly crept over my lips. I continued watching her for a moment when, to my surprise, Brady joined her near the front door. She turned and pointed to the Tahoe and Brady and I exchanged tiny waves. I wondered when Ridge was going to question Brent.

The car behind me honked, jolting me out of my thoughts. I pulled away, anxious to get to Trish's.

I stopped at Sweet Treats on Main and grabbed a large mocha, unsure of how cold it would be in Trish's trailer. A few minutes later, I was sitting in her driveway, afraid to go in. The crime scene tape had been removed when Sullivan finished processing the trailer. Trish's jackass parents were waiting on a cleaning crew to clear the trailer of her belongings. Images of blood and the pulp that was once her face glued me to my seat. The stench of death aggravated my nose, although it was just a memory. I sat in the driveway and drank my mocha, trying to work up the nerve. Maybe Doretha was right. Maybe this wasn't such a good idea.

But Ivy did need her warm clothes and a thicker coat. And I was certain she'd be thrilled to have a few familiar toys. And, I would swear on Trish's grave, there was something in that house identifying Ivy's father, whether it was Brent O'Reilly or not. I'd leave it up to Ridge to find out if Brent was the one using me for target practice. But *I* was going to find out if he was, in fact, Ivy's father.

I slipped the Glock in the hand pocket of the sweatshirt, just in case, and hoped the spare key was still in the same place. I climbed the steps of the front stoop and looked under the ceramic flower pot. The key was there, buried underneath a pot of dead flowers. The whole property seemed dead. Even the air smelled like dying leaves. I held my breath as I unlocked the door and stepped inside.

The air inside was stagnant, feeling thick and foul. Bloody shoe prints, mine and Cole's, had dulled and soaked into the carpet. I moved slowly toward the back bedroom, fearing the hallway where I had found Trish's body. Most women I knew kept their most treasured items in their bedroom. It was their private space. Whether cherished or important, items tucked away in jewelry boxes or hidden inside a birthday card carried the most meaning.

I stepped over the blood spots now staining the linoleum and made my way to the hallway. I stood at where her feet had been and saw in my mind the ugliness of death.

I forced myself to peel my eyes away from the reminder and went into Trish's bedroom. A layer of thin black powder covered nearly every surface of the room where fingerprints had been lifted. The room was small and crowded; the four walls seemed intimidating somehow, as if they wanted you to know they held secrets, but would never give them up.

The queen-sized bed had been tossed and the sheets lay in a wad at the foot. A few dresser drawers were partially open, an indication Sullivan and his team had searched for something. A large jewelry armoire stood in the far corner. The stain-glass doors were open, exposing a necklace carousel on top and rows of drawers underneath. On the side wall was a large closet with sliding doors. One door was open, revealing clothes on hangers and colorful boxes stacked on the floor and on the overhead shelf.

Working left to right around the room, I started at the dresser and rummaged through the drawers. If she was going to keep letters, papers, anything important, she would probably keep it in the top drawer for easier access. I didn't find anything other than clothing so moved on to the lower drawers. Bras and panties, socks, t-shirts...nothing out of the ordinary. I moved on to the closet and scanned the labels on the boxes. Bank statements dating back five years, car title and insurance, back issues of *Art Institute* magazine, cards, and Ivy. I immediately pulled down the one labeled Ivy and carried it over to the bed.

Inside, I found her birth certificate and her immunization record. I found her first pacifier and first pair of shoes, a tiny little pair of white sandals with pink bows. I found a tattered burp cloth, pink with white lace. My eyes stung with tears as I looked over Ivy's past. A pink and green notepad with Trish's playful script written on it indicating Ivy's milestones. First smile: June 7th. First laugh: July 9th. Rolled over: August 21st...the dates went on and on, documenting Ivy's life. The partially burned candle in the shape of a number 1. Near the bottom, I found a small blue jewelry box that held a tiny pearl bracelet. Staggered between the pearls were tiny pink blocks spelling out her name. Pinned to the silky inside top of the box was a small gift tag that read: To Ivy, from B.

My breath hitched in my throat as adrenaline rushed through my veins. I leapt up and grabbed the box labeled "Cards" and carried it back to the bed. I looked through each card, whether to Trish or to Ivy, and read who it was from. I set aside a Valentine's Day card and a Mother's Day card, both signed by "B." There was a First Birthday Card for Ivy, a silly Christmas card with Santa for her first Christmas, an Easter bunny for her first Easter. They, too, were all signed "B."

There was no doubt in my mind "B" was Brent O'Reilly. But what I couldn't figure out was what happened. What had driven him to kill Trish in such a violent rage? And why come after me?

Because I'd told him I'd run notices in the paper, looking for Ivy's father? If he'd kept his identity secret all this time, a legal notice wasn't going to expose the truth.

And why the flowers at her shop? Remorse?

Or maybe that wasn't it at all. Maybe Trish was going to end it with him and he couldn't bear that thought. Maybe she had given him an ultimatum like I had given Ed Stinger. Maybe she had demanded an unreasonable amount of child support.

Closing the boxes, I set them aside. I would take them with me when I collected her clothes and other things. It wasn't much, but it was something to give Ivy later, something years from now she could look back on and say she had belonged to someone.

I went to the jewelry armoire and opened each drawer, searching for more proof of Brent O'Reilly's existence in Trish's life. A few rings, bracelets, but nothing that jumped out at me. Anyone could have given her any one of the items or she could have bought them for herself. I then popped out the velvet-lined ring holder. And there it was. A check made out to Trish Givens in the amount of ten thousand dollars. Signed by Megan O'Reilly. Megan? The check was drawn from an individual account—Megan's—with Brent's name nowhere on it. The check was dated two months ago.

I hurriedly dug my phone from my pocket and called Ridge. His voice reflected a sleepless night.

"I think I found a key piece of evidence," I said, excited.

"Where are you?"

"At Trish's. I had to get some things for Ivy and I was looking through—"

"Wait a minute...*Ava*...why are you at Trish's? I thought I told you to stay at Doretha's." He wasn't sharing my excitement.

"Ivy needed her coat. They're calling for snow this weekend. But listen to what I found—a check for ten thousand dollars made out to Trish and signed by Megan O'Reilly. Dated two months ago."

He was so silent, for a moment I thought my phone had dropped the call. I pulled it away from my ear to make sure we were still connected. "Ridge?"

"Where'd you find a check?"

"Underneath the ring holder in her jewelry stand. Don't blame Sullivan, most men don't know to look there. They don't know it pops out."

I could imagine him raking his fingers through his hair, eyes closed. "And it's signed by *Megan*, not Brent?"

"Yes."

"Okay, just get what you need of Ivy's and go back to Doretha's. I'll talk to you in a little bit."

"Hey, Ridge—"

"I love you more."

My face opened into a huge smile. "Not possible." I slid the phone back into my pocket then gathered the two boxes.

I caught the slight sound of a car engine. It didn't fade away like perhaps the car was driving by. Instead, it altogether stopped. The bedroom window was on the back side of the house, facing the backyard rather than the front, so I couldn't see who it was. Probably the cleaning crew Trish's parents had hired. Or maybe the landlord coming to check on the strange vehicle in the driveway?

Before I got into the hallway, the front door opened. "Hello," I called, my voice wavering slightly with tingling nerves. Whomever had come in didn't respond so I called again. "*Hello?*"

I rounded the corner of the hallway and kitchen. For a moment, everything went black. A blow to the side of my head knocked me against the wall, sending a shower of yellow stars in front of my eyes. I stumbled to regain my footing. Another blow knocked me to my knees. Ivy's keepsake boxes scattered across the floor. I looked up to see my assailant, shielding my face with my arm. Towering over me with the butt of his rifle poised to deliver another blow was Brady. Not Brent. Not Greg Hastings. Not Ed Stinger. Brady—this child I had welcomed into my own home. This child who had eaten at my table, befriended my son.

I scrambled to get away, the back of my jeans sticking to Trish's dried blood. The look in Brady's eyes wasn't the look of a confused teenager, it was that of a cold-blooded killer.

"You just had to take her in, didn't you?" He snarled between gritted teeth. "You couldn't just let her go to an orphanage, could you?"

I didn't understand. Did the "B" stand for Brady instead of Brent?

He took a step closer and I moved backwards, never taking my eyes off of him. "Are you Ivy's father?"

He guffawed and shook his head. The sound of his laughter sent chills racing up my spine. "She only liked married men. Like my dad, you know, the upstanding citizen that he is."

My heart throbbed in my ears. A stream of blood rolled along my jawline. "I don't understand. How could you come to my house and play with her—play with that child—after you killed her mother? How, Brady?"

He rubbed the toe of his boot against a swatch of dried blood on the floor, oblivious to the life and death around him.

"It was easy, Ms. Logan. Mom said she was making us all look like fools. Mom said she paraded that baby around town like the brat was something to be proud of."

I choked back a gush of tears, refusing to cry, refusing to give him the satisfaction of seeing my fear. "She's just a baby, Brady. She's innocent in all this."

He laughed again and I wanted to vomit. "But her mother was a whore. Kinda like you, huh?"

My lungs stopped working. They, along with my heart, slammed shut and for a moment I thought death couldn't be as painful.

Brady pointed the barrel of the gun at my neck, teasingly moving my hair with the cold metal. "Yeah. I saw what you did with the sheriff. Bet Cole'd be shocked to know his mom likes to suck one."

I wanted to lash out, to do to him what he did to Trish. But I knew better. I willed my heart to beat and my tongue to hold the vile I wanted to spew. "Why me, Brady? What did I—"

"You said yourself you were going to run some notices in the paper looking for her father. Do you know how embarrassing that would have been for my mom?" His emerald green eyes—eyes just like Ivy's—glowed in a demonic light.

"They were legal notices. That's all."

"Well, we don't need that kind of publicity. Football scores, yeah, those are cool."

"Your dad would have never even been named. We'd be looking for the father, not naming him."

He shrugged. "Whatever. It still doesn't change the fact that whore was going to break up my family with her bastard child. That's what mom called her—a bastard child."

Bile churned in my throat but I forced it down. Megan had reached out and touched Ivy at the football game. She had remarked about how horrible her mother's death must have been. "Your mother told you that?"

He shook his head and took a deep breath in the process, like he was bored. "Nah. I overheard her and my dad screaming about it. They were always fighting about something."

"Your dad—those scratches on your neck, the bruises on your hands, were they from your dad?" Maybe I was trying to justify his anger, trying to make sense of the violence. He looked at his hand then rubbed his neck, reminding himself of the marks that were there a few days ago. "My dad ain't got it in him. These scratches— they're from the whore. She put up a pretty good fight. Dad was with her that Friday night. We didn't have a game. I followed him. When he left, I protected my family."

He smiled and the blood coursing through my veins froze. I'd never seen so much hatred in anyone's eyes. "How about you? You going to put up a fight?"

I inched backwards, hoping I could make it to the bedroom where the door might slow him down enough I could escape through the window.

Just as he raised the butt of the rifle to connect with another blow, I turned and dove for the bedroom then frantically kicked at the door. I leapt up and locked it then ran for the window. Every second mattered as I knew the door wouldn't hold, let alone the lock. The moment I jerked aside the blinds, the door shattered. He was on me before I knew it. Pounding his fists into my face, my stomach, my back as I fought him off, I screamed out and fought back with everything in me. I fought for Cole and Emma, and for Ivy.

I scratched at his face like a wildcat. I bit his shoulder, ripping through his shirt with my teeth, tearing into his flesh.

"You bitch!" He drew back to pummel my face but I drove my knee deep into his groin. He bent, clutching himself, giving me time to kick away and escape the bedroom, but the reprieve didn't last long.

He grabbed me from behind in the kitchen and slammed me hard onto the floor. Brick-hard kicks to my side and kidneys took my breath. On my stomach, I tried to pull away from the beating, but he was too strong. I rolled over to face him, to know what was coming. He drove the rifle butt downward, but I rolled out of the way as the end of the gun crashed into the floor.

The gun in the pocket of my sweatshirt fell out and skittered across the floor. I scrambled for it just as Brady brought his own rifle up and took aim. I grabbed the Glock and just as I pulled the trigger, Ridge screamed my name.

Brady fell on top of me, his eyes shadowed with death. I screamed hysterically, trying to push away from the weight of his body. Ridge was over us, pulling Brady's body off of me. He was screaming into the radio attached to his shoulder.

I dropped the gun and kicked away, scrambling backwards, pressing my back into a corner cabinet. Hysterical, my entire body shook violently.

I had shot him. I had killed this child. But the boy that lay dead in the floor wasn't a child, he was a monster. The child had died long ago.

CHAPTER 27

An EMT I didn't recognize dabbed a cloth to the side of my head where the skin was split. Numb to the pain, I wondered if it hurt. I wondered if I should cry. I had no tears left for physical pain. I had taken beatings before at Tommy's hands, so I knew the pain of broken skin, the tenderness of a bruise, yet I couldn't cry. The shock wouldn't let me.

From inside the back of the ambulance, I watched Ridge brief Steve Sullivan and a small cluster of other deputies. His jeans and shirt were dark with the dampness of blood. I wondered if the dampness was the same as when you were caught in the rain. The temperature was dropping and it was too cold to be in wet clothes. Dingy clouds overhead dropped clusters of snowflakes like wayward confetti. Ridge's black hair was spattered with white. Ivy's coat? Did I ever get Ivy's coat? Did she have a pair of mittens? Three little kittens lost their—

"You're going to need a couple of staples to close this up," the EMT said, still working on the wounds to my head. Her name tag read *Hannah*. White engraved letters on a black nametag. Tiny particles of gray dust had settled in some of the corners of the letters.

I looked away and saw Bosher Garrett, the medical examiner, coming out of the trailer. He stopped to speak to Ridge before leaving. Two transport techs maneuvered a stretcher up the steps, the body bag resting on the stainless steel, shiny and new. I knew my heart was heavy; I just couldn't feel it.

I had fed him. I had given him sanctuary.

Ridge lightly clapped Sullivan on the shoulder then walked over to the ambulance. Hannah was wiping the blood from my hands with a disposable cloth and alcohol.

Ridge took the cloth and bottle from her. "Mind giving us a minute?"

She smiled then disappeared into the small gathering of first responders milling around the yard.

Ridge wet the cloth with the alcohol then gently rubbed at the blood on my hands.

"How'd you know?" I asked, my voice so shallow I barely heard it.

"When we questioned Brent this morning, he said Brady had borrowed the coat last night when he went out. And Blackwell from the Ranger's Office called and said they had surveillance video of a truck in a separate parking lot at Porter's Peak the day you were shot at. Tags came back registered to Brady."

I slowly nodded, accepting the pain the tiny movement sent running through my head. "But how did you know he was here?"

"I went to pull him out of class to talk to him and saw he was absent. I didn't know if he'd be here or not, but I didn't like the idea of you being here by yourself anyway."

"He called her a whore." I watched him wash my hands, so tenderly and caring. So lovingly. "He called Ivy *that bastard child.*" My heart tightened, squeezing the breath out of me. I choked back a flood of tears as my hands, the hands he was holding, the hands that a short while ago had killed a boy, shook uncontrollably.

Suddenly, the sound of tires crunching gravel and squealing brakes blasted through the low chatter. Megan O'Reilly was out of their Beemer, screaming, running to the house. Both Ridge and Sullivan ran to intercept her, with Sullivan reaching her first. He grabbed her around the waist and turned her away just as the transport techs brought Brady's body out.

The whole scene looked like a horrific photograph, dulled by a surreal fog. They moved in exaggerated movements in slow motion. She was screaming, I could see her mouth forming the word "No!" but the sound was muted, a faint distant hum, like the sound of a refrigerator in the middle of the night.

Then Brent was there and more deputies fought to restrain him as his son's body was wheeled by. He collapsed to the ground, on his knees, begging God, begging anyone to let it not be true. He crawled after the stretcher, pawing at the ground with his fists, the dead grass covered in a light dusting of snow.

Megan pulled away from Sullivan and lunged at Brent, pounding him with her hands. "You bastard! You bastard! You did this!"

Sullivan grabbed her and pulled her away while Ridge consoled Brent. How did you comfort someone who had just lost their child? Whether that child was a monster or not.

Ridge hung the last drape over the windows then stood back to admire his handiwork. "What do you think? Want them open or closed?"

The glass was so clear it sparkled. I stared through it into the woods, beyond the bank of the river where not long ago, Brady stood, raised his rifle, and tried to kill me.

That was a few weeks ago. Today Emma was stretched out in front of the fireplace watching videos on her tablet while Ivy played dress-up, pretending to be a princess. I couldn't help but smile when she waddled in her plastic high heels over to Cole to help her with her dress. He grumbled, but obliged, then went back to watching a college football game on the television.

Not a day had passed that I didn't worry about him. He pretended everything was okay in the way teenage boys did. He was starting to open up to Ridge some, confessing the guilt he felt in bringing Brady into our lives. It was the only thing Ridge would tell me, choosing to not betray Cole's trust.

Ridge had won the election by a landslide for his second term and Ed Stinger and his videotape slunk off underneath the rock he had crawled out from under.

Life went on, but it would never be the same. "You can close them. It'll help keep the cold air out." I tucked my hands into the sleeves of my sweatshirt.

Ridge frowned slightly but pulled the drapes across the windows then joined me on the sofa. I leaned my head against his shoulder; he leaned over and kissed me softly on the lips.

"You okay?"

I nodded, but I wasn't. Brady's death had been ruled self-defense, but it didn't lessen the pain for me or his parents. In that moment, the moment I pulled the trigger, I knew it was kill or be killed, but it didn't make it any easier.

He was buried with little fanfare, a simple private service held at the gravesite. No dozens of distraught teenagers crying over a lost schoolmate like with most kids' deaths. Cole didn't go. Ivy squealed for Cole to help her with the plastic tiara, slamming it in his hand. "Look, little girl," he said as he adjusted it on her head. "You're interrupting my game. Go bug Emma."

Ridge tilted his head in their direction. "Sounds like they're getting along well."

I rolled my eyes then went back to picking through the stuff I was able to salvage from Ivy's keepsake boxes. I had everything spread on the coffee table, sorting through what had been damaged in the fracas. The little green and pink notepad where Trish had recorded Ivy's milestones was speckled with blood. I didn't want to toss it because the dates were written in Trish's playful script. It would be the only notes written from her mother Ivy would ever have. Blood specks or not.

Judging by her bank account, Trish had begun poaching to support herself and Ivy when her art couldn't pay the bills. I couldn't find fault with her for that. I'd been a single mom most of my adult life. You did what you had to do.

But she wasn't a whore. The uncashed check proved that. Her

mistake was loving a man who wasn't free to love her back. She was no more a whore than Ivy was a bastard child. Ivy was a beautiful, beautiful little girl loved by many.

Snow fluttered against the office window and clung to the glass. The wood stove was cranking out the heat so the ice particles didn't cling long before melting. It was Wednesday, and although the office was officially closed for Thanksgiving, I was there wrapping up November's invoicing. Nola was off on a cruise to some tropical island; Ridge and the kids, including Ivy, were on a mission to find the perfect Christmas tree. Cole and Emma didn't want me to go— they wanted to surprise me. I hoped Ridge would be able to tell them "no" if the need arose.

I queued the invoices to print then went into the kitchen to refill my coffee. I had just added the creamer when the bell above the front door jingled. My nerves weren't where they used to be, but they were getting better. Still, my heart quickened its pace as I carried my coffee back to the front. As I turned the corner, I stopped as if I'd walked straight into a brick wall. Brent O'Reilly stood by the stove warming his hands.

"Hey," he said quietly. "I was riding by and saw your car here. I hope you don't mind."

I swallowed hard, my nerves still on edge. He didn't appear to be a threat. But neither had his son. "I was just finishing up."

He nodded and looked down at his outstretched hands over the stove. Neither of us said anything for a long moment, then he spoke and his voice was faint, like he was talking more to himself than to someone else. "I loved her," he said. "I was going to marry her."

I leaned against the wall, taking small sips of the coffee. I held the cup with both hands to keep them from shaking so badly.

"She was...she was so kindhearted. She had a gentle soul, a true artist's soul as I've heard it referred to. And she was so alive— you know what I mean? She never worried if her makeup was perfect, hell, she hardly ever wore it. And her laugh. Oh man, when she laughed, you knew it was real. She was real." He wiped tears from his cheek with the back of his hand and sniffled. "She didn't deserve to die like she did."

No one deserved to die like Trish had. Not even Brady. "I'm sorry it all ended the way it did, Brent. I truly am. If I could take back those last few minutes, I would."

He nodded quickly and wiped his face again. "But you can't. No one can."

I tried to imagine his pain, to understand the devastation and feeling of loss. But he hadn't been the one to see a cold-blooded killer in the body of a sixteen-year-old boy. Or looked in the cold abyss of eyes no longer human. I had. He continued to warm his hands over the stove although I was sure they were no longer cold. "I resigned from the school. Probably for the best."

"What are you going to do?"

He looked up, gazing around the office, anywhere but at me. "I don't know. I have a sister in Florida. She wants me to come down there. Megan wants a divorce, so there's nothing holding me here."

My breath hitched. What about Ivy?

As if reading my mind, he spoke about his daughter. "I was in the delivery room when Ivy was born. That's why Trish went to Asheville to have her—no one knew us there. We could be just...like any other new parents. She was this little bundle of..." he chuckled, "...chubby little rolls. Pink skin covered in peach fuzz. Blond wispy hair. And her little nose—it wasn't round like a lot of babies'. It was upturned, just a little, like Trish's. She has a birthmark on her left knee." Tears rolled down his cheeks and he didn't move to wipe them away. "Did you know Megan tried to pay her off? Gave her ten thousand dollars to go away. Trish showed me the check."

"Do you think Megan knew Brady was the one who killed her?"

He shrugged. "I don't know. I've looked back at every moment since Trish died, looking for something that would tell me she did...but I just don't know."

I gazed out the window at the snow falling heavier now. I

wondered if Ridge and the kids had found the perfect tree yet and what surprise it held. Tomorrow we'd sit down to dinner as a family, together, and later decorate the tree. With Brent's daughter hanging an ornament in memory of her mother. "Brent...about Ivy—"

"I'll sign whatever papers you need."

I inhaled and exhaled, slow and steady, not wanting to sound presumptuous. I wanted Ivy but didn't want to discount his loss.

He turned and looked at me with eyes that radiated calm. "Maybe one day when she's older you can tell her what happened."

I nodded. "I want to adopt her."

"I won't stand in your way. Just do me a favor and let her know how much she was loved. Will you?"

"*Is* loved. Despite everything that's happened, that won't ever change."

He smiled warmly, nodding slowly. "*Is* loved."

The baby that belonged to no one would never be without a home.

LYNN CHANDLER
WILLIS

Lynn Chandler Willis has worked in the corporate world, the television industry, and owned a small-town newspaper (much like Ava Logan). She's lived in North Carolina her entire life and couldn't imagine living anywhere else. Her novel, a Shamus Award finalist, *Wink of an Eye*, won the SMP/PWA Best 1st PI Novel competition, making her the first woman in a decade to win the national contest. Her debut novel, *The Rising*, won the Grace Award for Excellence in Faith-based Fiction.

**The Ava Logan Mystery Series
by Lynn Chandler Willis**

TELL ME NO LIES (#1)

Henery Press Mystery Books

And finally, before you go...
Here are a few other mysteries
you might enjoy:

CIRCLE OF INFLUENCE
Annette Dashofy

A Zoe Chambers Mystery (#1)

Zoe Chambers, paramedic and deputy coroner in rural Pennsylvania's tight-knit Vance Township, has been privy to a number of local secrets over the years, some of them her own. But secrets become explosive when a dead body is found in the Township Board President's abandoned car.

As a January blizzard rages, Zoe and Police Chief Pete Adams launch a desperate search for the killer, even if it means uncovering secrets that could not only destroy Zoe and Pete, but also those closest to them.

Available at booksellers nationwide and online

Visit www.henerypress.com for details

PUMPKINS IN PARADISE
Kathi Daley

A Tj Jensen Mystery (#1)

Between volunteering for the annual pumpkin festival and coaching her girls to the state soccer finals, high school teacher Tj Jensen finds her good friend Zachary Collins dead in his favorite chair.

When the handsome new deputy closes the case without so much as a "why" or "how," Tj turns her attention from chili cook-offs and pumpkin carving to complex puzzles, prophetic riddles, and a decades-old secret she seems destined to unravel.

Available at booksellers nationwide and online

Visit www.henerypress.com for details

PILLOW STALK

Diane Vallere

A Madison Night Mystery (#1)

Interior Decorator Madison Night might look like a throwback to the sixties, but as business owner and landlord, she proves that independent women can have it all. But when a killer targets women dressed in her signature style—estate sale vintage to play up her resemblance to fave actress Doris Day—what makes her unique might make her dead.

The local detective connects the new crime to a twenty-year old cold case, and Madison's long-trusted contractor emerges as the leading suspect. As the body count piles up, Madison uncovers a Soviet spy, a campaign to destroy all Doris Day movies, and six minutes of film that will change her life forever.

Available at booksellers nationwide and online

Visit www.henerypress.com for details

CPSIA information can be obtained
at www.ICGtesting.com
Printed in the USA
LVOW13s1431200117
521663LV00008B/502/P